The Murder Mile

Lesley McEvoy

ZAFFRE

First published in the UK in 2019 by Bloodhound Books
This edition published in 2021 by
ZAFFRE
An imprint of Bonnier Books UK
4th Floor, Victoria House, Bloomsbury Square,
London WC1B 4DA
Owned by Bonnier Books
Sveavägen 56, Stockholm, Sweden

A CIP catalogue record for this book is
available from the British Library.

ISBN: 978-1-83877-597-1

Also available as an ebook

1 3 5 7 9 10 8 6 4 2

Typeset by IDSUK (Data Connection) Ltd
Printed and bound in Great Britain by Clays Ltd, Elcograf S.p.A.

Zaffre is an imprint of Bonnier Books UK
www.bonnierbooks.co.uk

*For Joseph Alexander McEvoy, my father, who always told me
I could achieve anything I set my mind to in life.
And for my boys, Adam & Kyle.*

Chapter One

3 August – Kingsberry Farm, Fordley

I sat up suddenly, not knowing what had woken me. I squinted at the red glow of the digital clock – 6.32 a.m. I tried to slow my breathing, then jumped when the telephone rang again.

'Hello?'

'Jo, it's me.' Callum's soft Scottish tones pushed through the fog of half-sleep. 'Sorry to call so early.' He paused, not sounding the least bit sorry. I could feel what was coming, even before he said it. 'We've found another body.'

My stomach churned – the fallout from a brutal death, something all too familiar to everyone involved in the events of recent weeks.

I swung my feet onto the floor and rubbed my eyes into focus. 'Same killer?'

I heard him sigh and could imagine how he looked: tired and weary after weeks of long days and even longer nights trying to track down the man the press had dubbed the 'Towpath Killer'.

'I'm not sure. That's why I want you to come and take a look. Do you mind?'

A million reasons why I minded raced through my head, but I was trying not to sound unhelpful.

'What about Taylor-Caine? She's not exactly going to be pleased to have me trampling all over the case, is she?'

He let out a deep breath. 'Just as well it's not her decision then, isn't it? This is *my* investigation and I want you involved.' I pictured him running his fingers through his silver hair – a habit he had when he was losing his patience. 'I don't give a rat's arse what Taylor-Caine thinks. I've got bigger things to worry about than office politics.'

I knew he was referring to Chief Superintendent Mike Hoyle. Lizzie Taylor-Caine had been his appointment as the resident criminal profiler of West Yorkshire Police's intelligence unit and he wouldn't hear any criticism of her, whether to justify the role, or for other reasons that were muttered about in the police canteen, I was never quite sure. What I *did* know was that my involvement would seriously piss him off.

I stared out at the grey light above the trees in the far distance. The miserable weather seemed to reflect the way my day was already shaping up.

'OK. Is this official?'

His hesitation spoke volumes. 'Er, no. A favour to me.'

'So office politics *are* a consideration then?'

'Oh, for God's sake, Jo! Will you come out or not?'

I took a deep breath. 'Yes, I'll come. I can be at the station in half an hour.'

'No, not the station. I need you to come to the scene. I want you to see her in situ.'

My stomach dropped. I'd worked from crime scene photographs on the Linda Baker case and they had been bad enough.

'I don't know, Cal. It's a long time since I've been to a fresh crime scene.'

2

'You'll be fine.' He sounded certain. 'But I need you to see it before the place turns into a circus. That's why I called as soon as I knew what we were dealing with. It's in Shipley. Do you know the canal?'

'Yes . . .' I still wasn't sure I wanted to do this.

'Well, behind the petrol station where the canal goes under the bridge. Get that far and you'll see the activity. I'll meet you there.'

Another canal site. Another muddy towpath – and another mutilated young girl.

Chapter Two

3 August – Shipley

As I neared the canal, blue flashing lights announced the activity that surrounded an unexpected death.

Callum was leaning against the bonnet of a patrol car, the collar of his waterproof jacket turned up against the drizzling rain, his long legs stretched out in front of him as if he had all the time in the world. But his relaxed posture concealed what I knew he was feeling. His expression and the tense line of his jaw spoke volumes – this was one event he really didn't need right now.

The officers guarding the outer cordon handed us our paper scene-of-crime suits, gloves, masks and overshoes before signing us in to the scene log and escorting us through the inner cordon to the sad white tent on the canal towpath.

We stood together, looking down at the semi-naked body of the girl at our feet.

The Home Office pathologist straightened up from examining the body while Callum made the introductions.

'Dr Tom Llewellyn, this is Jo McCready, the forensic profiler. She's agreed to take a look.'

The doctor smiled. 'Didn't think DCIs got out of bed this early. Not tempted to just send your DS out in the rain, Callum?'

'Not for this one, Tom.' He glanced down at the body. 'What can you tell us?'

The pathologist slipped his glasses into his case, turning to the business at hand. 'I think she's been dead for a few hours, but you know I won't be drawn on time of death, especially at an outdoor scene. Difficult to be accurate until we get her to the mortuary. But I can tell you she wasn't killed here. This is probably just the deposition site. She's been bound, hand and foot, with what looks to be electrical cord. Again, I can get more information on those after a proper examination.' He fished his car keys from his pocket. 'Take your pick of potentially fatal wounds. Probably the stab wound to the chest or the throat. We'll know for sure after the post-mortem.'

Callum nodded slowly. 'OK. Thanks, doctor.'

We watched as the older man left, walking carefully over the stepping plates put down to preserve potential evidence. I wasn't in a hurry to turn round and face the object of our discussion. I waited, watching the exit to the tent, listening to the sounds of activity from the forensic team outside and waiting for Callum to say something. When he didn't, I slowly turned around to find him watching me in that way he had, the way that made me feel there were only the two of us in a crowded place.

Was it really only eighteen months since I had been called in to advise on our first case together? I felt as though we'd known each other forever.

I pushed the images of last Christmas away. A bad decision on my part that had complicated everything. It was difficult enough being in such close proximity to Callum without remembering the warm feel of the chest underneath that shirt.

'Meant to say – thanks for coming, Jo. Really appreciate it.'

I took the time to consider him. He was being polite. He didn't know how to behave around me, no more than I did with him right now.

I could tell that he wanted to get on, but he was obviously trying to take things slowly for my benefit.

'Where do you want to start?' he asked.

I looked down at the body. I guessed the girl was in her late teens, with long brown hair. She was slim and, for some reason, I decided she had been pretty. Though it was difficult to know that now. I forced myself to look at the bloody mass where her face should have been. Her features were all but gone, mutilated in a frenzied attack. What was left was swollen and discoloured and in the muggy August weather, the flies were already starting to gather.

The girl's white blouse had been ripped open down the front, exposing her breasts and the lower half of her body was completely naked except for white ankle socks with frilly edges; her shoes were missing. The killer had tied her arms behind her back with, as Dr Llewellyn had said, what looked like electrical flex. The ankles were crossed and tied the same way. I crouched down and looked up at Callum.

'Can I touch her?'

He nodded. 'Now SOCO have finished, she'll be touched by dozens of hands between here and the morgue.'

I gently took the edge of her blouse between finger and thumb and drew it away from the body. Callum squatted down beside me.

I pointed with a rubber-clad index finger. 'Can you see her bra?'

The remains of a white bra could be seen where the straps went across her shoulders. It was trapped beneath the body. 'And here.' I pointed. 'These light cuts – scratches, almost. I think that's where he cut her bra away. But her hands were already tied, so he couldn't remove it completely.'

'And he couldn't untie her to remove it because she was still alive when he cut it away?'

'Possibly.' I nodded, beginning to construct things in my mind, trying to see what the killer had seen, to think the way he did. 'That, and the fact that the cuts bled means they may have been inflicted before or just after death, but the post-mortem will tell you that.'

The body was on the path, curled into a foetal position with her back towards the water. There were brambles at the edge of the path and I pointed to them.

'Do they come away from the wall if you lift them?'

Sweeping his arm under the brambles, Callum pushed them away. I squatted down and peered underneath. There was at least three feet of space from the edge of the path to the retaining wall of the canal bank.

In my mind, I constructed the events that had brought this young girl here. I tried to picture the scene in the dark, as it had been when the killer was standing where we now stood.

I straightened up. 'I need to go outside.'

His face was suddenly concerned. 'You OK? You're not going to throw up or anything?'

I shook my head, still trying to piece things together. 'I need to see the scene from outside. Get the bigger picture.'

Callum led the way into the fresh air, which was a blessed relief after the claustrophobic confines of a hot plastic tent that smelled of death.

I climbed the grassy bank and looked down on the path and its pitiful white cover. It ran alongside the canal which, a few hundred yards to the left, went beneath a metal footbridge and wound its way along the outskirts of the town. At night, a haven for drug addicts and prostitutes; by day, the province of anglers and dog walkers. To the right on the opposite side of the canal was the petrol station on the main road. The killer could have come by car or along the towpath.

I could sense Callum beside me. He wasn't renowned for his patience, so I felt compelled to say something just to fill the silence for him. 'Do we know who she is?'

He shook his head. 'Not yet. Doesn't look like a prostitute, though it's difficult to tell these days. She was found about three hours before I called you.'

'Who found her?'

'A guy walking his dog. He checks out; walks along here most mornings before his early shift at the bakery.' He frowned, his mood darkening. 'No doubt Taylor-Caine will have this one down as a robbery with extras.'

I walked along the grassy bank, stopping at the metal foot-bridge as I considered the textbook analysis their resident pro-filer was fond of making. I turned to face him. 'I don't suppose the remaining clothes have been found?'

He shook his head, nodding towards the canal bank where police divers were setting out their gear. 'They'll have a quick shufti, but I'll bet my pension they don't find anything in there. Especially if Llewellyn is right and she was killed somewhere else and brought here.'

'She was.'

'You sound sure.'

I nodded, breathing in the warm air, trying to get the smell of the tent out of my nose. 'The canal-side is a mud bath.' I stared at the path, constructing the night as the killer would have seen it. 'Imagine it's pitch black, just some lights from the petrol station. Not enough to really see by, and you're carrying the dead weight of your victim. It was hammering down last night – I know because it kept me awake.'

'Should've called me.' He was grinning that wonderful, lopsided grin of his. I pretended not to have heard.

'You'd soon discover it's too slippery to scramble down the track from the road, especially carrying your victim, so you'd have to get down here a different way.'

'From the bridge, maybe?'

I nodded, still staring down at the sad little tent. 'Perhaps.'

I could sense his frustration. I wanted to offer him something more positive, but I wasn't about to speculate just to make him feel better. 'Look at it this way,' I offered. 'If we are dealing with the same killer, Taylor-Caine's theory for Linda Baker falls apart. She can't assume it's a hate murder against a girlfriend or lover. That doesn't hang together when you start to get multiples.'

'True,' he said, straightening his shoulders and looking back down the path to where the body was being moved on a stretcher up to the coroner's ambulance. 'But are we dealing with the same killer?' He turned to me. 'What do you think, Jo?'

'Have you got Linda Baker's photos?'

'They're in my car.'

I knew they would be. In the four weeks since Linda's body had been found on a towpath on the outskirts of Fordley, he had carried the crime scene photos everywhere.

He'd picked Linda's case up because he just happened to be the on-call senior investigating officer the weekend the call had come in – it should never have been his case. But now the Towpath Killer was fast becoming an obsession with him.

He put a large hand on my shoulder to move me aside as a police photographer loaded down with equipment pushed past us on the narrow track, then looked at me and frowned. 'Are you all right?'

'I don't know,' I said honestly, staring at the small tent.

He took my briefcase from me. 'I'll carry that. Watch your step.'

I felt his warm hand disconcertingly on the small of my back, as he half guided, half pushed me up the slippery banking.

'So what was so interesting about the bushes back there?' he asked.

'Nothing, except that the killer could have hidden the body under them if he'd wanted to. She's only small. He could have rolled her against the wall without much effort and it would at least have partially concealed the body.'

I felt Callum shrug. 'Perhaps he was disturbed, or didn't have time.'

'Or perhaps he didn't care.'

As we neared my car, there was a frenzy of activity. A reporter was jabbing a microphone into the face of the man striding purposefully towards us. I heard Callum groan as we both recognised Chief Superintendent Hoyle.

A former officer in the military police, Hoyle still had an unmistakeable bearing, not just in the ramrod straightness of his back, but also in attitude. To me, he always looked as though he had a nasty smell permanently under his nose.

'Sir, you know Dr McCready?' It seemed to be Callum's day for making introductions.

Hoyle looked me up and down as though I was on ceremonial parade. 'Yes, we have met.'

I almost extended my hand, but when he made no move to reciprocate, I decided not to bother. 'Didn't know this was your territory, doctor.' His thin smile didn't reach his eyes.

'I'm freelance these days,' I replied, mirroring his same smile. 'I don't have a territory.'

He clasped his hands behind his back and rocked slightly on his heels, looking even more like a sergeant major. 'Thought you were the local celebrity nowadays? Writing books, appearing on television. Wouldn't have thought you needed to grub around crime scenes any more.'

'I'm still a working psychologist, on call if I'm needed.'

His smile became even tighter. 'Well, "working" implies getting paid and there's nothing in the budget for external consultants. We have our own profiler in the intelligence unit now.'

Callum stepped forward before I could open my mouth. 'I will be taking input from Lizzie too, sir, but there's no harm in having a second opinion and Jo has worked with the team in the past.'

Hoyle wasn't convinced. 'Lizzie won't become familiar with the team if she isn't given the opportunity.' He stepped out of the way as a CSI struggled past with armloads of equipment.

'No offence, doctor, but having a resident criminologist is a trial initiative that we must fully support.'

A shout from his sergeant made Hoyle turn. The press pack was gathering, with at least a dozen photographers and journalists being held back by a few harassed-looking officers.

'Seems the media want a word, sir.' Callum tried to suppress a grin. 'You're becoming a local celebrity yourself these days.'

Hoyle turned on his heel and strode away without a word.

'Arsehole,' Callum muttered under his breath, as he put his arm under mine to lead me to his car.

Chapter Three

3 August – Shipley

Ten minutes later we were sitting in the car park of the nearest McDonald's sipping coffee from cardboard cups. Callum's head was nearly touching mine as we leaned over the photographs and it occurred to me that, to passers-by, we probably looked like lovers. I would have preferred to be inside with a table safely between us. But I could only imagine how horrified the public would be if they caught sight of these images.

One photograph had been taken from a police helicopter and showed the area from above. The path followed the route of a disused railway line, not far from where the Fordley canal cut its path along the edges of the town. The M62 motorway joining Leeds and Fordley ran along the top of the picture.

Linda had been found on a footpath three miles from the current scene. I looked first at the glossy, eight-by-ten photographs taken by CSI while the body was in situ.

It showed the blonde eighteen-year-old student, lying on her side, partially hidden beneath a hedge along the towpath. Her polo shirt had been ripped open and her bra pushed up, exposing her breasts. Her jogging bottoms and underwear were pulled down to her knees but there had been no sign of sexual intercourse.

Stab wounds from a knife that had never been recovered had brutalised her face and upper body and while one training shoe had been found further along the towpath, the other shoe – and her rucksack – had never been found. There was no evidence that the killer had tried to bind her wrists or ankles, but I could see the similarities between Linda's murder and the victim we had just examined on the towpath .

'Bad as they are,' Cal said quietly, as though reading my mind, 'photographs don't smell.'

In the post-mortem photographs, Linda's body looked like a marble statue. Perfect, still and cold, marred only by the gaping rips across her clean white skin. With the blood cleaned away and the wounds washed, it was easier to see what the killer had done to her. I flicked the page to look at the post-mortem report. In addition to the obvious wounds, there had been less noticeable bruising along her jawline and right cheekbone.

'So,' he broke the silence, 'what do you think? Are we dealing with the same killer?'

The mintiness of his breath mingled with his cologne and I shifted uncomfortably in my seat, staring at the pathology report, rather than looking at him.

'Yes, I'm certain. If it's the same weapon, that'll clinch it.'

He took a long breath. 'Right. All I have to do now is convince Hoyle that we're dealing with a serial killer.'

I closed the folder and stared out of the passenger window at all the people doing normal, everyday things. 'Technically, he's not a serial killer until he's done three.'

'Nitpicker.' Callum sounded exasperated, but I could hear the humour in his voice.

'The problem you have,' I continued, 'is convincing them of the motivation. And that will determine the kind of suspects

16

you focus your attention on during the search. Get that wrong and you could be looking in completely the wrong direction.'

'Hoyle's pet profiler has already got us tracing every one of Linda's past boyfriends and male acquaintances at Fordley College. So help me out here, Jo, what am I looking for?'

I sighed, trying to order my thoughts into a logical pattern. 'Well, there are differences, but they're far outweighed by the similarities.'

'Go on.'

'Linda was a "blitz" attack. It wasn't as well planned and he took a much greater risk.'

'Because she was killed at the scene?'

'Right. He killed her on the footpath. It's a popular spot and we know there were people about just before the attack and not long after. To have struck on a warm summer's night, in the open air, involved taking one hell of a chance, but he was so aroused he was willing to take the risk. The bruised jaw suggests he punched her in the face to disable her, before beginning the more vicious attack.'

'Meaning what exactly?'

'He didn't know his victim. At least, not in the social sense, otherwise he could have engaged her in conversation to lure her off the path. He's immature, not sophisticated enough to do this with more polish. His attack was hurried, no time to bind his victim. Plus, he didn't come equipped with anything other than the murder weapon, so I don't think he intended to act it out that night.'

'Go on.'

I shrugged. 'She was in the wrong place at the wrong time. When I first looked at this one, I suspected he might be out there on the prowl, fantasising, probably even watching courting couples along the towpath. He was in a high state of arousal, carrying a knife, and stumbled across Linda taking a shortcut home.'

'So a blitz attack on an opportune victim?'

'Right. And although there's no sign of sexual drive behind it, it's definitely sexually motivated. He was a voyeur up to this point. That's why I told you to check reports of flashers or peeping toms in the area. I suspected then that he was escalating from more minor offences because the fantasies weren't doing it for him, so he moved up a gear.'

'And similarities?'

'In both cases, clothing from the lower part of the body is missing, along with some personal belongings.'

'You think he's taking trophies?'

I nodded. 'Also, there's no sign of the murder weapon. I think he's using the same weapon and taking it away with him.'

'Because of forensics?'

'Possibly. More likely he regards the knife as a treasured possession, so he doesn't dispose of it or leave it at the scene.'

I glanced at the photographs as I continued. 'Sexual predators refine their technique and increase their skill with each new encounter. They learn and improve. He wanted more power over this victim and he needed more time for that; time to bind her and control her so he could heighten his pleasure and savour the moment. He's into sadistic control. Remember the bra? He wanted to cut it away while she was alive, bound and helpless. He wants to see his victims' reaction. With Linda, he killed her too fast – had to because it was a public place. I call the initial encounter "Crime Scene A", which is rarely ideal and not how he imagined it in his fantasies. So this time he moves the second victim to a prepared place – "Crime Scene B". Somewhere he's left things ready, where he can have more time with her. He kills her there then dumps her body by the canal.'

'Both sites run parallel to major roads. Think he gets to the deposition site by car?'

I shook my head. 'These are not just dumping sites for him. I think this is his territory. He knows the area and the canal footpaths give him an easy way to move around the edges of town unnoticed. He feels safe enough to leave the bodies in relatively open ground, knowing he can still get away unnoticed. No, he's confident in these surroundings. When you find him, he'll have a strong connection to this area, or to the canal.'

He nodded, looking down at the photographs in my lap. 'Anything else?'

'He'll have wanted relationships, but probably lacked the social skills to get a girl. If that's the case, his sexual fantasies will have had to sustain him. Along the way, he probably developed fetishes. Often these offenders become so preoccupied with these things that the fantasy is the driving force – the woman becomes less important. Eventually she's just a dehumanised object for their pleasure.'

I finally looked up. He was studying me carefully, but I had no idea what he was thinking.

'That's why he obliterates their faces,' I added. 'He doesn't hate them, he just doesn't want to look at them. They're not human to him and he doesn't want to interact with them as people, just wants to use them to act out the fantasy.'

'And you think he was working his way up to this latest one? That Linda was a practice run?'

'Not even as well prepared as a practice run. He stumbled on his first victim. Although it wasn't perfect and not how he imagined it, it did give him a taste for domination and killing – and the confidence to go through with it. After all, he got away with that one and he hadn't even planned it properly.'

'So he plans the next one more carefully? Chooses his victim, kidnaps her, acts out his fantasy, kills her, then dumps the body in the area he knows best?'

'Yes.'

'So, he'll continue to escalate. If we don't catch him . . . he'll kill again?'

I nodded. Grim though the idea was, he was right. 'Look for someone in his late teens or early twenties. A loner. Sexually immature with few, if any, previous girlfriends. Probably lives with a parent, or alone. His inability to express himself would make it difficult to hold down an office job, so my guess is he's a manual worker or labourer. From the way he subdues his victims and moves the bodies, I'd say he's in good shape, maybe into sport or the gym. Or his job keeps him fit. He's local, knows the area and operates a lot of the time on foot. He may have come to your attention in the past for lesser sex crimes. If you get a suspect who fits all that, when you get to where he lives I think you'll find lots of deviant pornography and maybe the murder weapon. But chances are he'll carry that with him, so warn officers to approach any suspect with caution.'

'Well, that's not much to go on, is it?'

I shot him an amazed look, but he was laughing at me.

'Joke!' He held his hands up in mock surrender. 'Don't suppose you've got his name and address?' He grinned. 'Beats Taylor-Caine's textbook bollocks.'

My profile wasn't vastly at odds with her appraisal, but we did differ in key areas. Linda had died as a result of eighteen stab wounds to the face and upper body. In Taylor-Caine's opinion, such savagery indicated a rage, which made this a personal killing. I disagreed at the time and said so, which went down like a lead balloon with her and Hoyle. This killing only made me more certain that I was right.

'I'll need your profile writing up,' Callum said.

'OK. But how can you use it if I'm not supposed to be contributing?'

He scooped the files off my knee and I flinched as his hand touched mine.

'You're not contributing *officially*. But Hoyle saw you this morning; even he can't think I won't use what you give me.'

He rested his arm across the back of my seat, leaning even closer. 'And when the post-mortem proves the connection between the two killings, he's going to *have* to look at your profile.'

I nodded. 'Any chance of a lift back to my car?'

He grinned. 'You think I'm going to make you walk?'

Chapter Four

3 August – Shipley

Two police officers stood guard at the scene in Shipley, keeping the press away from the police divers and the small rubber dingy bobbing alongside the canal bank.

Callum pulled his car alongside mine then followed me to it. 'Any chance of a drink later?'

'Suppose so.' I was distracted as I tried to get into my Roadster before the press spotted me. I loved it, but it was definitely not a practical car.

'Don't sound so bloody enthusiastic.'

'Sorry. It's just that I'm in for a heavy day. Jen's held the fort for ages so there'll be loads waiting when I get in. Not sure I can be bothered going out. I'll just want to flake out in front of the fire with a glass of something chilled.'

'Sounds good to me.' His eyes didn't leave mine. 'How about I come round to the farm, say eight? Takeaway and wine?'

I spotted a photographer's telescopic lens aimed in our direction.

'I'm not sure that's a good idea, Cal.'

His expression lost its softness and his tone wasn't playful any more. 'Oh, come on, Jo. Can't a mate see you for a drink to celebrate your birthday?'

The photographer was making his way towards us now.

I nodded towards the canal. 'I think we'd better move. Bandits at twelve o'clock.'

Callum looked in the direction of the press and nodded, sighing as he pulled his car door closed.

By the time the press reached the path, I was already pulling onto the ring road into rush hour traffic. The clock on the dashboard read 8 a.m. as I called Jen's mobile.

'Hi, Jen. You on your way in?'

'Yep,' came her ever-cheerful reply. 'Just fighting traffic. Should be at the office in ten minutes. I'll get the kettle on. I take it you haven't had breakfast?'

'No. I left the house at sparrow's fart this morning. Callum called me out; they've found another body.'

'Oh, God.'

'He wanted me at the scene before the circus came to town.'

'Before Lizzie Taylor-Caine found out, you mean.' She huffed down the phone. 'Why does she have to be such a bitch?'

'Perhaps,' I said, distractedly manoeuvring through traffic, 'she feels threatened. She *is* new to the job.'

'Crap at what she does, you mean.'

'She lacks hands-on experience, that's all.' I could hear myself trying to sound generous. 'It's academic, anyway. It's not official. Callum just wanted me to take a look and tell him what I thought.'

'Well, rather you than me.'

I smiled. How could I ever manage without her? Jen had been the admin manager of the clinical psychology department at Fordley Hospital when I was a junior psychologist. Ten years my senior, she decided I needed looking after and took me under her wing.

'Anything I need to know?' I asked.

'Did you call your mother? She rang twice yesterday.' She paused and, when I didn't reply, added, 'Callum called yesterday too.'

Another silence passed between us and I knew I was supposed to come up with a reason why I hadn't returned their calls.

I groaned inwardly. 'I don't know what all the fuss is about, Jen. Why can't people just let it pass?'

'You can't expect people who care about you to ignore the fact that it's your birthday tomorrow.'

'Why not?' I said irritably. '*I* never have a problem ignoring it.'

I heard her sigh, and I could picture her pursing her lips in that way she did when she was getting annoyed with me.

'I take it you haven't heard from Alex?'

My stomach felt hollow as I thought about my son. Twenty-two and just out of university, he was backpacking around India while he decided what to do with the rest of his life. When he left, I'd given him strict instructions to call once a week in order to keep images of his murdered and mutilated body from invading my dreams. It had been almost two weeks since his last call . . .

'What's that got to do with it?'

'Just thought you might be getting grumpy as it's tomorrow and he hasn't called.'

'For the last time, Jen, birthdays are not, and never have been, important to me. Even when Alex *was* here. I'm never sure exactly what I'm supposed to be celebrating. Getting one year older? Whoopie doo! Anyway, I spoke to Callum this morning.'

'And?'

'He's coming up to the farm tonight.'

'Is he, now?' I could hear the undisguised pleasure in her voice.

'Only because he wants the profile writing up.' I was trying to play it down, but Jen could see right through me. This woman who knew me better than my mother.

'He doesn't need to visit the farm for that,' she observed smugly. 'Even a technophobe like you can use email.'

'OK, he's bringing wine – so?'

'So, I think it will do you the world of good.' I could hear the grin in her voice. 'You've been on your own long enough.'

'Stop matchmaking, Jen,' I warned. 'He's coming over for a takeaway, not to plan a wedding.' It was time for a quick change of topic. 'Look, it's going to take me too long to get in to the office. I'm going to work from home.'

'Some calls came in overnight.' I could almost see her pushing her reading glasses further up the bridge of her nose as she peered at the call list. 'Senior Clinical Psychologist at Westwood Park, Dr Lister. Apparently they've tried hypnosis to regress a patient back to a point of trauma, but her abreaction is so severe they can't get past it. Thought you might be able to help?'

I knew why they would want to avoid an abreaction – the intense psychological response from a patient who didn't just go back to retrieve the memory of an event but actually 'relived' it on every level. The horror of experiencing a suppressed trauma all over again could delay a patient's recovery by months, or even years.

'But before you go dashing over there,' Jen continued, 'don't forget you've got those revisions to do for Marissa. Don't miss this deadline.'

Marissa was my publisher, for whom I was writing a book about my experiences working with some of the most depraved offenders in the UK's criminal justice system.

'I was intending to do those first thing, before a corpse got in the way.'

The irritation in my tone surprised even me. I was strung out, tired and more than a little rattled by being so close to Callum all morning, not to mention having to see a dead body before breakfast. Every nerve ending was raw and as tight as piano wire, singing at the slightest touch.

'Well, you'll have no distractions at the farm, so you should be able to catch up. I'll hold the fort.'

For the thousandth time I silently acknowledged how blessed I was to have Jen organising my life.

'But before you get too immersed, call your mother.' I couldn't miss the judgemental tone in her voice as she hung up.

Jen was one of the few people who was fond of Mamma – the eccentric Italian wife of my Irish-born father – despite knowing how difficult she could be. My father had died six months ago, leaving me alone to struggle with a mother we had always tackled as a team.

I made a mental note to call Mamma later. I didn't have the energy or the headspace for her yet.

Chapter Five

3 August, 9 a.m. – Fordley

I waited as traffic lights held me at red. The rain was easing off and, through the drizzle, I looked around at people in cars waiting to start their day. They probably assumed I was just the same, worrying about sales targets or reports for the boss. But my working days had always been filled with far darker things: damaged minds and horrific crimes.

He's out there somewhere, I thought. A man who showered, ate breakfast and slept somewhere every night. Probably younger than my forty-six years, probably unmarried and probably white, or so the statistics would suggest. After that he could be anybody. You could pass him in the street, sit opposite him on the train or at the next table in a restaurant, and never guess that his hobby was killing and mutilating young women.

Callum had always been driven, but he seemed to be pushing himself and the team even harder than usual on this one. Perhaps partly because Hoyle had told him he might be replaced as the SIO – senior investigating officer.

Images of last Christmas ran involuntarily through my head. Yuletide nostalgia and too much champagne had meant my defences had evaporated and I gave in to what I'd secretly wanted since the day we'd met. I woke up beside him the next morning with a dry mouth, a bad hangover and a head full of regrets.

Since then, the illusion that I could lead a solitary life had been challenged by DCI Ferguson on a regular basis. I had made huge efforts to hold him at arm's length, emotionally and literally, ever since, and I knew it hurt him. He assumed he'd done something wrong, but didn't know what.

In fact, he'd actually done everything right. That's what made it all so difficult. And now he was coming over with a takeaway and wine . . . tonight. I groaned audibly as I thought of the complications I was creating for myself.

Did I want it or not? Damned if I knew.

The weather was relentless as I drove to my farmhouse, located outside the village of Kingsberry. The countryside here was little changed since the Domesday Book. Sweeping moorland was broken by craggy outcrops of millstone grit, a dark sandstone that formed the Pennines, running the length of the country like a gnarly backbone. The name of the stone had become associated with the very character of the people – said to have 'Yorkshire Grit' – a resilient spirit as tough as the millstones fashioned from it.

The landscape was in turn beautiful and desolate, depending on the weather. Summer months transformed the rugged upland grasses – daubing them with bright purple splashes of heather. In winter, the fells became bleak and desolate, scenes that fuelled the imagination of writers and poets alike. Little wonder the area became the setting for *Wuthering Heights*.

I'd moved here when I became Head of Forensic Psychology at Westwood Park. It was close enough to commute and far enough away to be a tranquil refuge when I got back from the horrors that filled my working day.

I swung around the gravel turning circle in front of the house. As I opened the porch door, five stone of bounding Boxer dog catapulted past me, before he skidded to a halt then trotted back.

'Hello, Harvey.'

I rubbed his velvety ears as he pressed his wet nose against mine in a nuzzling kiss. Then he was off, crashing through the hedge and into our meadow.

My friend, George Theakston, owned the farm a mile down the lane. After that there was no one between us and Kingsberry village, which was four miles away.

My mother worried it was too secluded. I loved it for the very same reason.

Harvey galloped back to the house, wet and dripping. He stood on the tiled floor of the porch and shook himself, looking pleased with the mess as I rubbed him down with an old towel.

The kitchen was one of my favourite places. Constantly warm from the Aga, it felt as though the house was giving me a welcoming hug as I came through the door. I dropped my briefcase onto the farmhouse table and lifted the lid on the Aga, putting the heavy-bottomed kettle onto the hotplate. By the time Harvey settled down, there was a large teapot freshly brewing on the counter.

I kicked a ball for Harvey down the glass corridor that connected the main house to the barn conversion that was now my office – after the kitchen, probably the place I spent most time.

A minute later Harvey settled himself on the Chinese rug in front of the desk. As he snored contentedly, I spent the next hour writing up my profile for Callum and then turned to Marissa's edits.

31

My eyes were gritty, reminding me of my early morning start.

I stared at the screen but wasn't seeing what was there. I was thinking about Callum – debating whether to chicken out and cancel our cosy evening in.

I jumped when the phone rang.

'Is that Dr McCready?'

'Yes,' I answered automatically. 'Who's this?'

'John,' came the blunt reply. 'I'm sorry to call, but I'm desperate . . .'

I felt a twist of discomfort at the implications of a stranger having my private number.

'How did you get this number?'

'That doesn't matter.'

I closed my eyes and concentrated on the non-visual signals I was getting down the phone. For some reason, this call was trouble. I could feel it.

'Listen to me!' His tone was aggressive. 'I need you to see Matty. She's in Westwood Park. I can't do any more for her. I had to leave her.'

'Matty?'

'Well, Martha. My girlfriend. Her doctor admitted her. He thinks she'll top herself . . .'

His words tumbled out, disjointed and fragmented like a person on the edge of panic. But the verbal cues I was getting told me that John was a man who rarely panicked – someone who was used to being very much in control.

'Did my secretary give you this number?'

'Yes.' He was lying. There was no way Jen would ever give out my private number.

'You shouldn't have called here . . .'

'For God's sake!' he shouted. 'It doesn't matter. What matters is that you see her!'

'Calm down, John.' It wasn't worth pushing the point. I automatically reached for a pen. 'What's the problem? What does her GP say?'

His breath exploded down the phone. 'He's useless! She's been seeing him for months. In the end, he knew she was psycho.' There was a pause as he gathered himself. 'It's the nightmares. They scare me to death. She turns into another person.' The last word was quiet, breathed rather than spoken. 'Just like, you know . . . possessed. You've *got* to see her. The Devil lives inside her, I swear to God. Sometimes I can see him, looking at me through her eyes, and her voice changes.'

I felt irritation turning to anger. 'I need to know why you think *I* should deal with this?'

'One night I woke up and she was looking down at me, but it wasn't her – it was him. I could see him in her eyes. Murderous eyes. I didn't sleep for two nights. Daren't sleep in case she killed me, stabbed me – like the others.'

'Which others?' The hair along my arms was standing on end as I scribbled his words onto my pad.

I stared at the phone as the line went dead and 'John' left my life as explosively as he had entered it.

Chapter Six

3 August – Westwood Park Hospital

I drove through the imposing stone gateway of Westwood Park Psychiatric Hospital. The sprawling collection of red-brick Edwardian buildings had been a dominating feature of the landscape ever since it was built at the beginning of the twentieth century.

The squat, two-storey buildings rose out of the manicured lawns as if growing out of the surrounding landscape, flanked by flower beds that attempted to bring a splash of colour to what would otherwise have been a bleak setting. Huge oak trees from the woods surrounding the hospital crouched malevolently over the sloping grey-slate roofs, now slicked black by the hammering rain.

Originally called Fordley Lunatic Asylum, it had been built here deliberately, in the middle of nowhere, to isolate it from the surrounding rural villages – which only served to heighten the suspicion about what went on in such places. The name itself conjuring up terrifying images of bedlam and cruelty.

Since then, the greenbelt had been slowly eroded by urban sprawl and Westwood Park now occupied an area of parkland bordered by houses and a large secondary school. By the Second World War, the name had been changed. But for locals, it was still a place of myth and misunderstanding. Contrary to popular belief, the criminally insane were not housed here. There was a secure unit for those deemed a danger to themselves or others, and there were patients who would probably never be released into the community but they needed medical treatment, not prison. It was a fine distinction that many in the local community struggled with.

I passed the gatehouse, which no longer had a gatekeeper or a security barrier – both reassuring features in my time. The light was taking on the dim glow of a dull day as I drove past the cricket pitch and swung into the visitor's car park.

I walked up the broad stone steps and into the foyer as the receptionist slid back the glass partition and smiled helpfully.

'I'm here to see Dr Lister.'

'Have you an appointment?'

'Not exactly. He called my office and requested my help. There wasn't time to phone ahead,' I lied. 'Thought I'd call in passing.'

I didn't explain that 'John' had seriously pissed me off, and I wasn't about to waste time dealing with the endless bureaucracy involved in arranging see his girlfriend. I'd help Lister with his patient request and then use that as leverage to bypass any formalities in order to see Martha.

I hadn't called because I risked being told 'No', a word I'd never been fond of. Better to proceed until apprehended.

The receptionist's helpful smile melted like snow under a heat lamp.

'Well, I'm not sure he'll see you,' she said, with the tone of someone used to saying 'no' and being unpopular for it.

'Could you call him and ask?' I said, trying to hide my irritation. 'Tell him it's Dr McCready. I'm sure he'll see me.'

The glass partition slid shut – her way of dismissing me into the waiting room while she made the call. Resisting the temptation to glare at her through the glass, I turned and rested my back against the counter.

The waiting room was like the million others I'd spent half my professional life in, painted institutional magnolia, with rows of uncomfortable blue upholstered chairs, rigidly fixed together and bolted to the floor to prevent patients or visitors hurling them as weapons.

I turned as the partition opened behind me.

'Dr Lister will see you.' Her smile had vanished permanently, replaced by the look of a woman sucking a lemon. 'Go to the end of the corridor and up the stairs. His office is third on the left.'

'Thank you.'

I walked through familiar corridors and reflected on the way things had changed since my day. I would never have allowed the public to walk through the building alone. Staff being attacked and even killed on hospital premises had increased in recent years so if anything, precautions should have been tighter, not slacker. My opinion of Dr Lister's administration was slipping already.

At the top of the stairs the vinyl flooring gave way to carpet, announcing to the senses that this was the territory of the administrators and not the patients. The clacking of my heels was muted by the soft beige carpet and, as I approached the third door on the left, a tall thin man emerged and turned to greet me.

'Dr Lister?'

His smile was tired as he shook my hand with a weak grip before dropping his arm, as though the effort was too much for him. The white lab coat that hung loosely from his shoulders looked as though he'd borrowed it from a bigger person or lost a lot of weight. The whole image made him look ten years older than he probably was.

'Sorry you had to wait,' he said. 'I'm afraid I wasn't expecting you.'

It was obvious he couldn't remember our appointment. I decided to be generous.

'I should have called ahead, but it was a spur of the moment decision,' I lied, feeling far too animated against this backdrop of depleted energy.

He hesitated in the doorway and then stepped aside, gesturing for me to go in to what had once been my office.

The dark wood coffee table and matching desk hadn't changed. The leather chair that I had bought out of my meagre office budget was still there, though more scuffed than when I'd last seen it. The beige walls were lined with bookcases full of medical journals that spilled at crazy angles and ended in untidy piles on the floor. I tried not to stare in case the disgust showed in my eyes. I wasn't the tidiest person in the world, but there were limits.

As I took a seat opposite him, the atmosphere settled around me like a damp blanket. It was a room suffering from neglect, a dumping ground for journals and papers and the surrogate office of many people, not the loved and protected space of a single individual. It made me feel depressed all of a sudden.

He slumped in his chair, distractedly patting his pockets as he spoke.

'I've read your books,' he said, as he fished a crumpled pack of cigarettes from his lab coat pocket and held it out to me. I shook my head. Smoking was one vice I had managed to avoid. Oblivious to the 'No smoking' sign, he lit the cigarette with brown-stained fingers and took a long drag, considerate enough to blow the smoke away from me.

'I saw you at a conference last year, speaking on current life regression, so obviously I thought of you when we had problems with Martha. I understand you used to work here?'

I was still stuck on the punchline. *Martha!*

'Yes, years ago. That's the patient with the severe abreaction – Martha?'

He nodded, pulling a file from a lopsided stack on an overcrowded in tray.

'Martha Scott . . .'

Aggressive John's girlfriend and the severe abreaction were one and the same.

He scanned the page as he spoke. 'Originally attended as a day patient. Twenty-two, although she has a mental age of a ten-year-old. During treatment, it became clear she had suicidal thoughts, but her boyfriend seemed to be a stabilising influence. As she lived with him, we felt there was no need to admit her.'

I began making notes. 'Did the boyfriend attend any appointments?'

'No. He spoke to the doctors on the telephone and took an active interest in her care.' He frowned through the cigarette smoke. 'I always felt it was strange.'

'What was?'

'That they were a couple. I mean, she was probably pretty before her illness, but her mental age was not at all congruent with his. I couldn't imagine he could hold a conversation with her or have much social interaction. They'd almost be like parent and child.'

'Do you have his name?'

I could feel the anticipation as I waited for his answer. He flicked back to the original green admission form.

'John Smith.'

John Smith! It was so clichéd it was almost funny. I looked at him, waiting for some reaction. Nothing.

Stubbing out his cigarette with one hand, he passed the file to me with the other.

'Then, a couple of days ago, she turned up here. She was distraught, said the boyfriend had left her because he couldn't cope. Her violent episodes were beginning to frighten him and he had to take more and more time off work to make sure she didn't attempt suicide. He brought her here and just left. Didn't even come in with her.'

'What can you tell me about this abreaction?'

He sighed, running fingers through his thinning hair. 'She attended some sessions to learn relaxation techniques. She said her boyfriend had learned the techniques from her so he could support her at home. Light stages of self-induced hypnosis to help her relax at night, or when she felt panicky. She was a very good hypnotic subject and went under very easily, especially if it was facilitated by the boyfriend.'

I was reassessing my opinion of the 'aggressive' John. He obviously cared, but her condition had become too much for him. Not uncommon when loved ones became carers.

His smile was apologetic. 'I'm sure you're aware that hypnosis is not something we use a lot, but it was something Martha felt comfortable with. She requested it, to try to recover a memory from her past.' He referred back to the notes. 'Abused by her father from the age of seven until she left home at fifteen. She went to Manchester, earning her living as a prostitute. The man she rented a bedsit from became her pimp, raping and beating her regularly, introducing her to heroin.'

He recited the horrific litany of abuse and life on the streets with the jaded tone of someone who heard such stories regularly. As someone who heard the unbearable on a daily basis, it occurred to me that I was probably guilty of the same emotional detachment in case reviews.

'She was tormented by memories of a period when she believed she'd committed serious crimes. She was having nightmares and believed they were flashbacks to real events.'

'What kind of nightmares?'

'She thought she had committed murder . . . more than once.'

I raised my eyes to look at him, my pen poised in mid-air.

'How?' I dreaded the answer, though I knew what it was going to be.

'She thought she had stabbed other prostitutes.'

'Any evidence she might have?'

He looked at me steadily.

'As you know, Dr McCready, claims like this are made on a daily basis here. We have people confessing to every crime imaginable and some not yet dreamed up. If it's to be believed, we have a cast of characters here from Lord Lucan to Count Dracula. I even have a patient in the secure unit who assures me that at the next full moon he'll turn into a werewolf before my very eyes. He refuses to eat anything but raw meat and laps water from a bowl. In Martha's case, until we can establish a little more, I'm hardly going to alert the police to the possibility of multiple murders, area unknown, victims unknown and time period unspecified. If and when we can fill any of those gaps, then of course I will refer it on to the relevant authorities.'

I knew how unprofessional I must have looked, asking for evidence when we both knew that outrageous claims were the norm here. But I justified it to myself. After all, I'd heard about these 'dreamed up' stabbings before.

Daren't sleep in case she killed me, just like the others.

'And you want me to see if I can get past the abreaction?' I asked.

He regarded me steadily for a moment, as though debating whether or not to go further. Finally he sighed, looking weary again. 'You are, without doubt, the expert in this field.' He flicked ash onto my once pristine carpet. 'Your work with current life regression to treat trauma in patients is well documented, and well respected.'

'Thank you.' I meant it.

'So naturally, with you living here in Fordley, you were the first person I thought of. I know it was a liberty, calling you out of the blue. You must be very busy . . .'

He was hedging around a subject I was by now familiar with. I decided to put him out of his misery.

'But there is no budget for calling in external specialists? It has been mentioned to me already today.'

'Sorry?'

'Never mind. I'm happy to help out free of charge.' I looked at him with sympathy. 'I do remember what it's like, you know. Trying to manage on a budget.'

He managed a smile as he gave me the case file and smoked another cigarette while I read through it. Finally, he got up from the desk.

'If you're happy to start today, I'll take you to meet Martha.'

Chapter Seven

3 August – Westwood Park Hospital

Carpet gave way again to hard vinyl and my heels clattered loudly behind Dr Lister's sensible rubber-soled shoes. Posters on the walls reminded staff and visitors that certain items were prohibited: weapons, alcohol, glass bottles.

It was the smell that hooked my memories, leading me back by the olfactory senses to an era when I'd get in the car after my shift and open all the windows even on the coldest nights, to blow away the institutional stench of carbolic, urine and sweat that no amount of disinfectant could cover up or wash away.

Dr Lister used a swipe card, opening metal doors that led ever deeper into the maze. As we neared the end of the block, I became aware of the feeling here: not a positive energy, but rather something to be careful of.

The patients' rooms were not locked here. These patients were a danger to themselves but to no one else. I knew from experience that there were no doors on the showers or the toilets. Nowhere a patient could lock themselves away from sight or help, but that meant no privacy either.

Martha was sitting on the edge of the bed with her back to the door, her stiff, off-white hospital gown almost swamping her slight frame. I stayed by the door as Lister walked quietly around the bed and squatted down beside Martha so he could look up into her downturned face.

'I've brought someone to see you, Martha,' he said, in a gentle tone that, for some reason, surprised me.

He gestured with his right hand for me to come closer, like a nature warden beckoning me to approach some timid animal.

'This is Dr McCready. She's here to help you remember.'

I hunkered down beside the bed, getting my first look at Martha. She had the complexion of someone who'd abused substances. The white skin across her sharp cheekbones was papery thin, almost translucent.

'Hello, Martha,' I said, quietly.

She was nervously plucking at some unseen thread on her hospital gown.

I glanced at Lister. 'OK to leave us for a while?'

'I'll be just outside if you need anything.'

I waited until he left the room, the door softly closing behind him.

Behind me was a high-backed hospital chair. I moved it closer to the edge of the bed, controlling and owning the space. I sat silently watching her, waiting for her to speak.

A bright red strip of metal ran around the room at waist height – the panic button that I felt sure I wouldn't need. Muted noises ebbed from the ward outside as nurses began the routine of settling patients down for the evening. The rumble of the drugs trolley made Martha look up. Her eyes met mine and I held her gaze, still waiting, allowing my sensory acuity to notice the rise and fall of her chest as I calibrated her breathing rate. She was nervous but not afraid. She took a shaky breath, still watching me from beneath her long brown fringe.

'I know you,' she said, quietly. 'Don't I know you?' She had a heavy local accent. 'I've seen you . . . Could I have seen pictures of you?'

'Possibly.' I couldn't help smiling at her childlike way. 'I've been on local TV.'

She put her hands behind her on the bed, palms down, and tilted her head back in thought. 'It's Matty.'

'Sorry?'

'I don't like Martha. I like Matty better.'

'OK, Matty.' I watched her for a moment and she managed a slight smile. 'I watch lots of TV.' It wasn't true, but the law of reciprocation was a social interaction we were programmed to respond to from birth: give some information to receive some.

'Do you watch TV, Matty?'

'Sometimes,' she said, quietly, almost a whisper I had to strain to hear. She was still looking down. 'I let John pick.'

'Your boyfriend?'

She looked up. 'Do you know him?'

'Sort of,' I hedged. 'We've spoken about you.' I waited, looking for an emotion I could label. Love? Fear? Hate? Her reaction wasn't clear and I warned myself not to second-guess it.

She continued to pluck at her gown, studying her fingers with intense concentration.

'He's left me . . .' Her words trailed off and a large tear splashed onto the gown.

'Only for a while, until you get better.'

She shook her head and another tear fell, turning the starched linen gown grey.

'He's gone back home for good.'

'Where's home?'

'London.'

'Did you meet him in London?'

She looked up, her tear-stained cheeks red and drawn in as she pursed her lips, trying not to cry. 'No. Manchester.'

'You lived in Manchester?'

She looked at me steadily, as though trying to decide whether I could handle her story.

'I was . . . I worked. Y-you know?' She looked embarrassed.

'Yes,' I said, gently. 'Dr Lister told me all about it. Did John help you in your work?'

'He wasn't my pimp or nothing.' She was suddenly animated, her eyes darting around my face, her tone stronger as she defended him.

'I know. He cares about you.'

She nodded vigorously. 'He met me one night down Canal Street, in a bar.' I nodded, not wanting to disturb this sudden flow with questions. 'He was nice to me. We met for business, but he weren't like the others. He just talked to me.' She suddenly smiled sheepishly and I got a fleeting glimpse of the pretty girl she once was.

'So how did you come to be in Fordley?'

'He didn't like drugs, didn't want me on heroin. Said it affected my brain, so he sorted Gerry out and we had to move away.'

'Gerry?'

'He was my minder.'

'John got you away from him?'

'Yeah. Gerry paid me with a fix sometimes and John didn't like that. Said he couldn't talk to me when I was off on one. So we left. John had a job in Fordley so we came here.'

I wanted to take notes, but instinct told me she would stop talking if I began to write this down. I watched her relax. She pulled one leg underneath herself, the other dangled off the bed.

'Sounds like he cares for you a lot.'

Her eyes suddenly welled with tears and she sniffed back a sob. 'He didn't like me riding on his bike in case I came off. Wanted to keep me safe. But he wasn't bothered about me getting on it when we came here, was he? If he cared so much, how could he leave me?'

'He left you here so *I* could see you, Matty. Because he thinks if you talk to me you can get better quicker.'

Her head lifted quickly and her tear-filled eyes looked into mine. 'Really?'

I nodded. 'That's why I'm here today.'

She sniffed. 'You don't work here?'

I shook my head, offering her a thin smile. 'No. I used to, but now I only see very special patients. Like you.'

Sudden panic flashed across her face as she rubbed her nose with the sleeve of her gown. 'I can't pay you –'

'That's OK. It's taken care of.'

She smiled. 'That's John,' she sighed. 'He takes care of everything.' She seemed to relax very suddenly, to become calm. 'He paid someone to see me before. Took me down to London specially to see a lady, like you, to help.'

'That's not in your notes. Do you remember the lady's name?'

She shook her head, sniffing again.

'Did it help?'

She shrugged, turning her face away from me. She looked worried, as though she'd revealed too much.

49

I had to tread carefully. Cutting to the heart of the problem too quickly could send her mind fluttering away from me like a startled bird. I shifted so that I could see Martha's whole face in the glare of the unflattering overhead light.

'When you were in Manchester, you said John didn't like you being on drugs. You're not taking anything now, not even methadone. That's very good.'

She smiled and looked up at me, like a child being praised for a nice painting at school.

'John did it. He had to repress me 'n' everything, but it worked. He said he could and he did. I don't take nothin' no more.'

'How did he help you to stop, Martha?'

'He stroked me,' she said, simply.

Chapter Eight

3 August – Westwood Park Hospital

I'd heard almost every method of getting clean. But *stroking*? That was a new one to me. I struggled to keep my face expressionless.

'Tell me about that, Matty.'

'He would lay me on the bed and pull the covers up so I didn't shiver. When you're rattling, you get the shivers.' She paused with a half-smile. I almost held my breath to preserve the moment. 'He would kneel down beside the bed and hold my hand under the covers. Then he'd stroke my head and talk to me.'

She closed her eyes, a calmness descending on her. I was concentrating on her so intently, I jumped when the harsh overhead light went out. With an audible 'click', the room was plunged into the eerie amber glow of 'lights out' on the ward.

Martha didn't seem to notice. I watched, spellbound, as she slowly drew her legs up and, in one fluid movement that reminded me of a cat, lay on the bed. I watched the rise and fall of her chest as her breathing slowed and became rhythmical.

I eased myself out of the chair and went to kneel beside her, hesitantly touching her fingers. Her palm opened and I held her hand, gently applying a little pressure while carefully watching her eyes.

I waited for her to exhale and then began a hypnotic induction, instructing her, with each breath, to relax the muscles in her arms, her legs, her shoulders. Keeping my voice low and even, I saw the imperceptible drop of her shoulders against the pillows as the tension left her neck. Her level of relaxation was already quite deep and after five more minutes of induction, Martha was at a deep level of hypnosis.

'You can answer my questions and still remain completely relaxed.' I watched her carefully. 'If you understand, just nod your head.'

She nodded slowly, her eyes remaining closed, her breathing deep and steady.

'What did John say to you, Matty?'

'He said he was taking me back. We went back together, to my safe place . . . '

'To your safe place . . . That's right. Are you there now?' She nodded slowly.

'Describe it to me.'

She let her breath out in a gentle sigh. 'It's my bed . . . when I was little. I've got a big duvet and I can crawl inside. It's dark and safe as long as I'm on my own . . . it's safe.'

Still watching her, I reached inside my bag and pulled out the digital recorder. I didn't want the distraction of taking notes.

Her 'safe place' was going to be our escape plan in the event of my tripping the abreaction. At my instruction, she could leave whatever scene she was experiencing and go there.

I focused on her breathing, matching my instructions with each of her out-breaths. I glanced at the wall clock above the bed, slowly counting backward, instructing her to go back at each count to where we needed to be.

'And when you get to the place in time when you were afraid, I want you to nod your head.' I waited, listening to the sound of her breathing. After half a minute, she nodded.

'How old are you?'

'Twenty.'

'Where are you?'

'In Manchester.'

'What are you doing?'

'I'm . . . I'm . . .' She began to roll her head slowly from side to side. Her brow furrowed and her breathing quickened. I knew she was slipping into the trauma. This was the beginning of her abreaction.

'OK, Matty. Listen to me. I'm going to touch your forehead and, when I do, you'll go back to your safe place . . . Now.'

I stroked her forehead, mimicking the action John had used. She relaxed into the pillows immediately, her brow smoothing out. She looked like a sleeping child.

I needed a different approach.

'From your safe place, you can see over the top of your warm, snugly duvet. Can you see the scene in Manchester that used to scare you?'

She nodded slowly.

'But you're looking at it like it's on TV.'

The act of seeing herself on screen would disassociate her from the trauma, so she wouldn't relive it through her own eyes and drop into it again.

'Now, tell me what you can see.'

'I'm standing over a whore . . . she's . . .' Her eyes squeezed tighter and her jaw clenched. She was struggling with what she saw, but she wasn't going into abreaction, so I let it run.

'She's dying!'

I jumped as she screamed.

She was panting, beads of perspiration glistening on her forehead.

Her voice was eerily calm now. Almost too calm.

'I'm holding a knife so she can see it as she's dying . . .' A thin smile played at the corner of her mouth.

'Did you find her like that?'

I sensed a change. Gone was the childlike ten-year-old. Even her speech was different.

A deeper voice tore from her. '*I did it.*'

I wasn't even sure where my next question came from, but I felt I was seeing another person emerging from this gentle, damaged woman, so I asked it anyway.

'Who are you?' I could feel a thin trickle of sweat run down my neck. The room suddenly felt oppressively hot.

'*Everyone knows me . . .*'

'Who *are* you?'

'*Jack the Ripper.*'

I hadn't seen that one coming.

Somehow I had to find a handhold in her psyche to pull her back to me. If this was the cause of her fractured state, I needed to explore it. But I'd lost the road map I thought I had through Martha's mind, my route blocked by a sudden encounter with another personality.

I had to see where this would go, but that meant relinquishing control and just holding on for the ride.

I heard my words as if someone else was speaking them.

'Does Matty know you're there?'

Matty's lips curled back from her teeth in a feral snarl. '*She tries to keep me out, but she's not strong enough. At night, when she sleeps, I come and she remembers . . .*'

I swallowed, feeling the roof of my mouth go dry. 'Remembers what?'

'*Remembers when I killed them . . . the whores. They didn't catch me then and they can't catch me now. I kill through her . . .*'

'Did you try to kill John?' I could hear myself asking the questions, but I couldn't believe where this was going. I thanked God for the digital recorder.

'*She wouldn't let me. Then I got stronger than her, I almost had him. But he woke up and saw me . . . He left us here, but I can get out . . . I can leave her behind now and kill again, thanks to you . . .*'

I'd had enough. I was losing my detachment and needed to regain control. I reached out to touch her forehead and send her back to her safe place.

She shot bolt upright. The shock threw me back from the bed, my heart hammering out of my chest.

'*Jesus!*'

She turned slowly to look at me. '*You can't send me back . . . not now.*'

'Jack . . .'

I never got to finish.

Matty launched herself off the bed, seeming to defy gravity. Thrown onto the floor, I scrabbled backward, trying to create space between us.

The emergency alarm clattered as I pushed my fingers against the metal strip above my head, as though pushing it harder would make it ring louder.

The door crashed open, sending up a puff of plaster dust as it bounced off the wall, and my line of vision was blocked by a

55

flurry of green as ward staff piled into the room. Legs stood over me and around me and I heard Matty's high-pitched scream as they hauled her unceremoniously back onto the bed.

I tried to push myself up, but my arms were shaking. I gave in and slumped back against the wall, willing my breathing to return to normal, my eyes closed tight, not wanting to witness Martha's restraint and sedation.

When the screaming calmed to a grunting, I slowly opened my eyes.

Dr Lister was staring down at me, his face taut with concern. 'Are you all right? What the hell happened?'

Good question. I thought. *What the hell did just happen?*

Chapter Nine

3 August – Westwood Park Hospital

I sipped the tea Lister gave me, wishing it was a brandy. His face ashen, he sat back in his leather chair and lit another cigarette with fingers that trembled slightly.

He blew a stream of blue smoke, annoyingly in my direction. 'If we'd thought Martha was a serious risk, I would have taken more precautions.'

I shook my head, feeling as though all my strings had been cut as the adrenalin ebbed out of my system.

'Not your fault. There was no reason to think she would react like that.'

'Still . . .' He inhaled deeply. 'We are liable for the safety of our visitors.'

Was he genuinely concerned for me, or more worried about a possible claim against his public liability insurance? I'd had enough and wanted to get out of his depressing, chain-smoking presence. I stood abruptly and put my cup on his desk.

'Don't worry. If there had been contraindications to a hypnotic intervention, I should have seen them, but there was nothing.' I began to shrug on my jacket.

'We thought *we'd* seen a serious abreaction, but it was nothing like this.' He stood up, looking rattled.

I made for the door, stopping with one hand on the handle.

'Martha's had abusive relationships with all the key male figures in her life. This could be her subconscious creating a strong male character to regain some control, two elements of her personality, the weak and the dominant, struggling to be integrated. We need to do more work with her to get a firm diagnosis, but that could explain "Jack".'

'Could she be capable of murder if this alter personality broke through into her conscious state?'

The thought had crossed my mind. But I really didn't think Martha, that gentle childlike persona, was capable of hurting anyone. Not even herself.

'I'll listen to the recording and transcribe the notes, then I'll come back to you.'

'I'll have her assessed in the morning,' he said. 'If she's still agitated, we can have her transferred to the secure unit. In any event, I'll arrange another visit.'

I walked out, grateful for the cool air. The night sky was clear of cloud and, in the light of the full moon, a shiver ran through me.

My mobile went into meltdown as I started the car.

There were four messages from Callum, escalating from irritated to downright pissed off.

I could feel annoyance coiling inside me. Why did relationships have to be so bloody difficult? Even as I dialled his number, I decided I was in no mood to soothe bruised egos or calm ruffled feathers. He answered on the third ring.

'Cal, it's me –'

'Where the hell have you been? Did you want me sitting in your porch with a congealed chow mein until you decided to turn up?'

'Oh, for God's sake, stop being so bloody precious!' I snapped back, not bothering to tone down how I felt. 'You're not the only one who gets called out in an emergency. And if I'm running late, just remember who screwed up my day with an unplanned callout to a corpse.'

Callum exhaled loudly. 'All right, I'm sorry. I was worried about you, OK? I called the farm and kept getting the machine. Same on the mobile. It's not like you to drop off the face of the planet. I was getting concerned.' His tone gentled. 'You OK?'

'No,' I said. 'If you must know, I had a call from some guy insisting I see his girlfriend at the psychiatric unit. I'm only just leaving now.'

'What's so unusual about that?'

'Well, for a start, he called my home number.'

'That number's not listed.'

'Exactly. He said Jen gave it to him, but he's lying. Jen would never do that.'

My eyes hurt and I could feel a headache lurking. I was running on empty.

'Look, Cal, it's complicated. There's lots I want to tell you. Even *I* can't believe what just happened, and I thought I'd seen it all. Can you still come to the farm?'

'Sure. You still want chow mein?'

I smiled. 'Yes, but preferably not congealed.'

Chapter Ten

3 August – Fordley

I drove across the moorland road leaving the rain and the street-lights behind me. Through the skeletal branches of ominous, swaying trees, I caught glimpses of the full moon and thought about Dr Lister's own resident werewolf. Something about this night made the idea of supernatural monsters almost plausible.

A shiver tickled across the back of my neck and I flicked on Radio 4 in an attempt to break up my creepy thoughts.

My son, Alex, always teased me about listening to talk radio, said it meant I was getting old. But sometimes my mind was too full for music. Now I heard the news but didn't really listen. If I'd been asked what it was about, I couldn't have said. But it was a human voice, reaching out in the dark, reminding me I lived in a real world, not one populated by werewolves and demons.

I spotted Callum's car as I turned into the farm. The security light above my porch illuminated the yard and I could make out the head of silver hair in his car as he read a file resting on his knee.

As I slammed my car door, he looked up, a smile suddenly transforming his usually serious features into that boyish look that made me smile back.

His expressions, even now, constantly surprised me. The way he frowned as he read, or his unexpected grin. There was always something new – as if I was seeing him for the first time.

He opened his driver's door and the familiar sound of the radio station drifted out. I laughed.

'What?'

'Radio 4,' I replied, enigmatically, shaking my head when he raised a questioning eyebrow. 'Never mind, but you suddenly made me feel OK about getting older.'

He shook his head, hauling a carrier bag out of the car. 'I'll never understand how your mind works, but perhaps given what you do for a living, that's no bad thing.'

I put my key in the lock. 'Stand back.'

Harvey thundered out of the house before turning back to launch at us in a tangle of velvet fur and pent-up muscle.

Callum hoisted the carrier bag out of his way. 'My God, he's like an express train. Does he ever just walk anywhere?'

'Not often.'

We worked in domestic silence in the kitchen, pouring chilled wine, setting the table and dishing up the food. Harvey padded back into the kitchen and curled up on his bed by the Aga, resting his chin on his paws.

Callum raised his glass. 'To you. Happy birthday for tomorrow.'

His gentle expression did something to my insides that I couldn't quite describe. He could always make me smile, even when I was angry with him – which was often. Jen said it was because we were so alike. Unlike Pete.

My late husband was very different. Looking back, if Pete's job hadn't kept us apart most of the time, I questioned just how long we would have lasted.

Callum's soft voice brought my attention back to him. 'Where do you go?'

'What?'

'Sometimes when I'm with you, I see you go away somewhere in your head and I know you're not with me, not really.'

'Sorry.' I took a sip of wine. 'This looks good.' I began to eat but I could feel him watching me. He reached across and put his hand on my wrist, holding it gently. His thumb absently rubbing mine.

'I was thinking about Pete, if you must know.' I watched his face, ready to judge his expression. Frustrated? Jealous?

He smiled. 'That's nice.'

'Nice?' I wasn't expecting that.

He shrugged, scooping up a forkful of noodles. 'Nice that being here with me makes you think of him. I could take it a lot of ways, but I'll take it as a compliment.' He raised his eyes to mine and they seemed an even darker blue than usual. He took a sip of wine. 'You never talk about him.'

I was tempted to become intensely focused on my plate but resisted the urge and looked back at him.

'Pete had a job we couldn't talk about. In fact, he had a whole other life we didn't talk about.' I sipped more wine, feeling myself relax as the tension of the day slipped away. 'He was a husband and father when we were together and then he went away to play soldiers. I never knew what happened in the intervals.'

'He was killed serving abroad? Special Forces I heard?'

I nodded slowly. 'It's been twenty-two years, almost to the day, since an Army captain knocked on my door to tell me the news. I'd always dreaded it. But once I understood what he did for a living, it became almost an expectation.'

'Must've been tough.'

63

'That's one word for it. I was twenty-four, with a baby, coming to terms with being a widow; fresh out of university and not knowing how I was going to keep a roof over our heads.'

In my mind I watched the movie run all over again, though now it didn't hold the pain and bitterness it once had. Just a sadness and regret for the things Alex had been deprived of with no man in his life, except his grandfather.

'When they came to the door, they were holding Pete's ID tags, the charred remains of his watch and his wedding ring. Those three things kind of summed up his life.'

'So Alex never really knew his father?'

I shook my head. 'Pete was captured by insurgents and tortured to death. They burned his body. There was nothing to send home. We don't even have a grave to visit.'

'Shit, Jo.' He sounded as though he truly meant it. 'I'm sorry.'

'It's OK. Twenty-two years is a long time. When I moved here, I started again. No photographs, no haunting memories. Time to draw a line. Alex has all the belongings the Army sent us, including Pete's commendation for bravery. I never really saw the point of being proud of the thing that took him away from us, but I'm happy for Alex to preserve the memory of his father, the hero. I suppose this house is my lasting tribute to what we shared.'

'The house?'

'I could never afford this place on my salary, let alone the conversion. But I finally dipped into the financial award the Army paid out. It felt like an insult at the time, a sum of money to compensate for a life. But that – and the life insurance Pete took out when Alex was born – was enough to pay for all the work this place needed.'

Callum looked around the kitchen. 'It *is* a fantastic place. You didn't take his name when you married?'

'What?'

'Pete's surname – different from yours and Alex's. McCready's your maiden name, isn't it?'

He'd done his homework. But I didn't mind. In fact, I felt quite flattered.

'Because of the nature of Pete's work, he said it was better if I didn't. Safer for me and Alex. In any case, it was the one on all my accreditations, so easier all round to just keep it.'

We ate in silence for a few minutes. Maybe it was the wine, but I was glad I'd told him. It felt as though the timing was finally right to share all those private things with someone. Or perhaps Callum was the only person I could have told.

He spoke first.

'Want to tell me about your eventful evening, then?'

Over the remainder of the wine, I went through John's call and my session with Martha. But, for some reason, I left out the bit about 'Jack'. Maybe because I needed time to work through what I thought had happened in that room. Or perhaps because I feared he'd think I was as mad as Martha.

'So John's girlfriend was Martha Scott?'

I nodded. 'Could you check for me? Into her story I mean?'

He pursed his lips, swilling the last dregs of wine slowly around the bottom of his glass. 'I'll see what I can do. But we're full on with the towpath killings, so I can't spend too long on it.'

I suddenly felt selfish. 'Sorry, I should have thought.'

'Don't worry about it, I'll get one of the indexers to run the names. Never know, we might get lucky.'

I began collecting up the dishes and Callum came to help. 'Might not be that easy. John Smith? Too corny to be real.'

He grinned up at me as he crouched in front of the dishwasher. 'I know it's the name given by every couple having a dirty weekend, but there are some real John Smiths out there, you know?'

'Well, I'm not convinced. There's something about all of this that bothers me.'

'Apart from the fact that John said his girlfriend wanted to murder him and that she stabbed people while possessed by the Devil? What on earth could possibly bother you about this story? Sounds like an average day at the office to me.'

By this time, we were both laughing. I flicked the tea towel at him and he ducked out of the way, catching my arm and swinging me around in a playful hug. Suddenly the laughter stopped, our faces only an inch apart. I could feel his warm breath on my face the instant before he kissed me.

Chapter Eleven

3 August – Kingsberry Farm

I drank in the feel of him. It would be so easy to deepen this kiss. To lead him by the hand to my bed. But I'd done that before, allowed a moment to turn into a night. I didn't want to fast-forward what we'd started. I wanted to learn all the little domestic things about him that I didn't know. Somehow that was important to me now.

I put a hand on his chest and eased away as gently as I could. He held me in his arms, reluctant to let go.

'I don't want to move too fast, Cal.'

He nodded, stroking my nose with his. 'I know. I can go as slow as you like, just so long as we're travelling in the same direction.'

I changed the subject before I lost all my resolve. 'I could do with more wine. Did you bring another bottle?'

'I put it in the fridge while you were towelling Harvey off. By the way, how come he didn't rip me limb from limb for taking liberties with you just now?'

We both looked across to Harvey, snoring contentedly on his bed. 'Perhaps,' Cal observed, 'he realises I'm a protector too.'

I suddenly remembered what had happened the last time we'd opened a second bottle and decided I needed a diversion.

'I wrote up the profile, by the way.' If he noticed my blatant shifting of the moment, he was too polite to show it. 'I'll go to the office and print it off for you.'

He poured two glasses. 'Hang on, I'll come with you.'

I pushed open the door into the glass corridor. The carpeted floor took away any feeling of coldness from the huge windows, its deep pile muffling the sound of our footsteps.

I looked across to the woods, but all we could see in the darkness was our own reflections.

Callum looked the most relaxed I had seen him in weeks. The usual frown lines across his forehead were gone and his shirt was unbuttoned at the collar. His silver hair flopped across his forehead in a casual way he would never have allowed at work.

He perched on the edge of my desk as I searched the computer files.

'Here we go.' I hit the print key and the LaserJet hummed to life. 'Hope this proves useful.' I suddenly realised that I hadn't asked him anything about the investigation. 'Any more on the victim?'

He ran a hand through his hair. 'We've got a name. Julie Lamont, a hairdresser from Fordley. She completed her college course three months ago and took a job at a salon in Shipley. She didn't turn in for work yesterday or the day before. I've got officers interviewing the family, so we should have a better picture by morning. But we *do* know that Julie and Linda didn't know each other outside of college – we checked. There's no link between them, until they were both murdered and dumped by the canal.'

I chewed my pen in thought. 'The canal's your link,' I said, finally. 'That's his hunting ground. That's where he served his apprenticeship. He feels able to take chances there.' As I said it, I became more convinced. I took another sip of wine. 'Concentrate your efforts around there and you won't be far away from him.'

Callum lifted a book from my bookcase and absently turned it over in his hand.

'I tried to read it once,' he said, lingering on the photograph of me on the back cover.

'I'm flattered,' I said and smiled.

'You should be. I don't read books, unless they're technical manuals.'

'This *is* a manual. For the human mind; a manual into the strategies people develop to navigate through life.'

'You make it sound simple.'

'In some ways it is. The human mind is a computer – it delivers what you programme into it. Trouble is, a lot of programming happens when you're too young to remember.'

'So it's back to the childhood stuff then,' he teased. 'Lie down and tell me about your mother and all that?'

I leaned across the desk and shut down the computer. 'You'd be surprised. As children, our parents are gods to us. If they tell us we're hopeless, or stupid, or clumsy, we don't question it. Children believe it and act out the behaviours that go with it.'

As we left the office, he slipped his arm around my waist. 'So that's what you do with your patients? Go back to the original hang-up?'

I nodded, enjoying the warmth of his body hugged so close to mine. 'Parents aren't always the villains. A bad divorce, a bereavement – they can all lead to people developing unhelpful coping strategies. They embed it in their personal history and it becomes "the story they tell about themselves". If you see yourself as a victim, an abused child or an abuser, it defines who you are and you use it to make sense of events you've gone through. Past traumas end up shaping a person's present and dictating their future, and it's usually not in a positive way if they cross my path.'

Harvey was still snoring contentedly. I perched on the edge of the table.

'I devised a technique for "uninstalling" the trauma in a person's unconscious, allowing them to reprogram past events.'

'So they forget it?'

'No, reprogramming how they perceive it. It can be like turning a key for some patients. That was what the book was about, but I never expected it to become a bestseller.'

His hard thighs straddled mine as I sat on the edge of the table. He rested his forehead against mine, his eyes intense as though he wanted to see inside my head.

'So what's the story *you* tell about yourself then, Jo? The story that builds the glass wall I can't get past?'

The intensity of the question caught me off guard. It felt uncomfortable having my own strategy turned on me.

'Touché.' I tried to smile, and failed.

'You tell the story about Pete . . .' He said it softly, but a barb shot through my stomach. How dare he use the fact that I had opened up to him tonight? 'Perhaps the strategy you use,' he went on, 'is to never allow anyone that close again, so you don't get hurt?'

'Perhaps.' I felt the warm glow we had built all night suddenly evaporating into a coldness I couldn't stop.

'What's wrong?' He lifted his head slightly, watching me with a confused frown on his face.

My mind screamed at me to say a million different things – none of which Callum would have understood. I wasn't even sure I understood them myself. I made a mental note to stay away from the booze the next time I was with him alone. If there was ever to be a next time . . .

'Nothing.' I pushed off the edge of the table, making him let me go and take a step back.

'Nothing?' He released an exasperated breath. 'You mean everything, right? Come on, Jo, what now?'

'I'm tired, that's all. It's been a long day. Think it's time we called it a night if that's OK?'

'No, it's not OK.' He ran his hand through his hair as he squared up to me. There was a row coming and I simply didn't have the energy for it. 'I thought we were getting somewhere, but the minute I touch near the heart of you, the shutters come down.'

My frustration suddenly boiled up to meet his. The rational part of me knew he was right. He *had* touched a raw nerve that I should have dealt with years ago, but it had been easier to leave it alone. He'd turned therapist on me and hit the bullseye – and I didn't like it.

'Oh, for God's sake!' I snapped, causing Harvey to stop snoring abruptly and lift his head to watch us both. 'Stop playing at therapist and stick to being a policeman.'

'OK then, I'll be a copper.' He was getting angry. 'All the evidence points to the fact that I'm trying to compete with a dead man.'

He couldn't have winded me more if he'd punched me in the stomach.

'*What?*'

'You said that when you came here, you left Pete behind. A fresh start. So, like some dumb bloke I took that as a sign we could move on from the flirting and dancing around we've been doing ever since Christmas. Which, by the way, I rated as pretty bloody marvellous.' He suddenly turned away from me, pacing in front of the Aga, his voice getting louder. 'But the minute I get to that point where we can be real people and stop shadow boxing, I get the ice maiden again.' He stopped and turned to face me, his eyes blazing. 'Know what, Jo? I don't think you are over Pete. Or that you've ever tried to stop telling that story about yourself. In fact, over the last twenty-two years of being his widow, it's become who *you* believe you are.'

I watched with my mouth open, unable to speak as he tore his coat from the hook by the door and snapped up his car keys. 'And until it stops being that way, I may as well wait another twenty-two years before I try again.'

'Callum!' I called after him, but I could already hear the car roaring to life. He hadn't even bothered to close the door. By the time I walked into the porch, I could just make out the red tail lights disappearing down the lane.

'Shit!' I exclaimed to Harvey who stood beside me, tipping his head curiously as if asking me a question I couldn't even begin to answer.

Chapter Twelve

4 August – Kingsberry Farm

I swung my legs out of bed and padded naked into the bathroom where I peered at my reflection in the mirror, noting the dark rings under my eyes.

'Stupid bitch!' I said out loud to my reflection. 'You need a good therapist.'

I spent my professional life telling clients they needed 'closure' on troubled relationships. Why couldn't I take my own advice?

I took my temper out on my clothes and stomped into the kitchen, ignoring Harvey as he padded over to me for his morning hug. My mood wasn't improved by the weather, which was damp and humid, as we walked into the meadow.

The air still held the musty scent of damp earth as we walked across the fields. Brightly coloured finches flitted in and out of the tall hedgerows beside us and a buzzard floated lazily on the thermals overhead, looking out for unwary mice below.

Harvey amused himself by chasing the scent of rabbits long since gone, as I followed aimlessly behind him, absorbed in my thoughts.

A familiar figure walked towards us across the bottom field, dressed in a waxed jacket and old corduroy trousers, the whole ensemble topped off with a tweed flat cap. He raised an arm in greeting, his other cradling a shotgun.

'Morning, George.'

He grinned, showing a huge mouthful of tombstone teeth as he rested his elbows on our adjoining fence, using his thumb to push the peak of his cap back.

'Fine day for it, lass,' he observed without humour, as he grimaced into the drizzle. 'Yon dog doesn't bother though, eh?'

I smiled despite my black mood as I watched Harvey romping around.

'No, he's fine as long as he's out.'

Harvey sniffed at George's trousers and lifted his head to accept the rough patting on his ears. 'He's good security up at the house, though,' I said. 'Best burglar alarm I could have – no one would try the house with him inside.'

George nodded. 'But let's face it, since when did we ever get burglars round here? God Almighty, most people don't even know this lane exists. Anyways, I walk by most days and check on the place for you.' His eyes twinkled with fun. 'Part of my duties, you might say.'

He continued to pat Harvey, who was enjoying all the fuss.

'Am I right in thinking it would be your birthday today?'

I looked at him in surprise. 'How did you know that?'

He smiled but it was tinged with sadness. 'Used to walk the moors with your dad, didn't I? He'd always make a fuss on your birthday. Whenever we were out, he would tell me about the surprises he had in store for you. I reckoned it would be about now.'

I nodded, intently focused on my wellingtons as we trudged back to the house.

'Miss him like hell, George.'

I was horrified to feel hot tears pricking at the corners of my eyes. George diplomatically averted his eyes, looking across the fields. A typical Yorkshireman, full of emotion but loath to ever show it.

'So do I, lass, so do I.' He patted my shoulder roughly. 'Take care.'

With a wave of his arm, he strode back out across his field, leaving me and Harvey to stare after him.

I decided work was the only thing to push the black mood away. I rang Westwood Park and arranged to see Martha as soon as she'd been assessed. I'd been thinking about her all night.

As I got into the car to drive to Fordley, I called Jen to let her know my plans.

'By the way, Jen . . .' I tried to slip the next question in diplomatically. 'Have you spoken to someone called John? He said he'd called the practice to get my home number.'

'No – and if he had, I wouldn't have given him your number. Why do you ask?' I could hear the discomfort in her tone.

'He called the farm last night.'

'What!' She was incredulous. 'I hope you don't think for a minute I'd be stupid en—'

'Of course I don't,' I cut her off. 'He said you'd given it to him, but I knew you hadn't.'

'I've worked with you long enough to stick to protocol.' She sounded upset.

'Don't worry about it.'

But even as I said it, I knew she wouldn't let it go. Jen was a perfectionist and something like this would eat away at her.

As soon as I hung up, my mobile rang again. The display said 'Private number'.

'Dr McCready,' I answered, absently.

'Mum?'

'Alex!'

It was so unexpected that I nearly stopped the car in the middle of the road. 'Where are you?'

He laughed. 'Mumbai. The most civilised place I've been in weeks. Anyway, just calling to wish you happy birthday!'

A mix of emotions rolled through me all at the same time. Relief at hearing his voice and knowing he was safe. Frustration that he hadn't stuck to the rules and called as often as he'd promised he would.

For an instant, a reprimand crossed my mind, but I bit it back before it came out of my mouth. I used my own mother as a 'how not to parent' manual. Habitual criticism was her stock in trade.

I could feel the heat of totally unexpected tears. 'Oh, thanks, baby. You don't know how much I've missed you.'

'Are you *crying?*' He sounded incredulous, and I remembered the hard-nosed reputation I'd worked so hard to develop, even with family.

I sniffed loudly, reaching for a tissue. 'No. I have a cold. But I've missed you all the same.'

I heard him sigh. 'I know. Sorry, Mum. India's phone network might be good but they haven't quite reached the out-of-the-way places I've visited lately.'

'When will I see you?'

'I'm planning on coming back before Christmas. I've got a couple of interviews lined up in London, then I can spend a few weeks with you.'

'Great. Who're the interviews with?'

'Oh, nothing special.' His tone was instantly cagey. Or did I imagine that? 'Don't want to jinx it. I'll tell you when I'm back?'

'Sure.' I tried to inject some positivity into my voice as I rubbed my nose with the tissue.

'I'll catch you up when I see you. Give my love to Nonna.'

'I will. Bye, baby.'

I was quiet when I went into the office and Jen knew me well enough not to ask. I buried myself in work for the rest of the afternoon, only realising as I was leaving that we'd hardly spoken.

She barely looked up from her computer as I shrugged on my jacket, too used to my moods to be affected by them any more.

'Callum called. He said it was urgent and could you call him as soon as you are finished.'

I stared at her, before remembering that she didn't understand how important Callum's message might be, given last night's events.

'Oh.' Was all I could manage. 'Anything else?'

'Nope.' She flicked through the notes I'd just dropped on her. I put the digital recorder down on the desk and headed for the door.

'If you can transcribe that first thing, please. I need it for Martha's assessment up at Westwood. See you in the morning.'

'Not unless you pay me double time you won't.' I stared at her, puzzled. Still chewing the end of her pencil, she said: 'It's Saturday tomorrow, stupid.'

'Oh, God!' I laughed. 'Sorry, Jen, I'm losing the plot.'

'Hmm, well I won't be in on Monday either – I booked it off for my granddaughter's birthday. Family party at mine for all the brood.' She raised her eyebrows like a parent with a hopeless child. 'I suppose you forgot that too?'

I had.

She called after me as I went down the steps to the car. 'Remember what all work and no play does. And don't forget to call Callum!'

Chapter Thirteen

4 August – Fordley

'Everything happened at once.' Callum's voice came over the Bluetooth as I drove back up to the farm. 'We got the post-mortem report back on Julie Lamont and at the same time forensics gave us a lead on the electrical flex used to tie her up. It had traces of marine oil.'

'Marine?' I echoed back. 'There's your link to the canal.'

'Could our killer own a boat?'

He had launched into the facts as soon as I'd called. No reference to last night at all. I wasn't sure whether I was relieved or upset.

I dragged my mind back to the matter in hand. 'It's possible he lives on a boat, but my original assessment still stands. You're not looking at someone high on the socio-economic ladder. I'd say it's more likely he works around boats or the boating community. A labourer maybe? That fits with his physical strength and fitness.'

'Post-mortem confirmed it's the same weapon as the one used on Linda. They also found traces of duct tape adhesive in strands of her hair and around her mouth, which suggests she'd been gagged. That's consistent with your theory that he held her for a while before killing her.'

I could imagine the dizzy exhilaration the killer would feel at finally capturing a victim and having the opportunity to act out fantasies that he'd probably played out a thousand times. That was, until the fantasy didn't help him reach climax any more and he had to take more chances, go out and look for a victim to play with for real.

Then reality would hit home. She could identify him and there was no option but to kill her.

I'd built up a psychological profile of this faceless killer, to the point where I could almost hear the pleasure in his voice as he told Julie what he was going to do with her. He would enjoy the power he had over another human being, the power of life and death. The feeling of total authority and domination he would have in his closeted fantasy world where he made all the rules. The polar opposite of his real existence, where he was a loser and a failure – both in society and in his relationships.

The fear and horror she would have experienced in those hours was unimaginable. I felt a tightening in the pit of my stomach at the thought.

'It certainly wasn't a quick death,' I said quietly, still trying to switch off the mental images that, unfortunately, came with the job.

'She was punched in the face prior to the attack, just like Linda,' Callum continued. 'He broke her cheekbone when he hit her. Interestingly, there were also traces of concrete dust in some of her wounds and on her clothing,' Callum added, obviously still reading the post-mortem report.

'Concrete?'

'Probably from the murder scene – when we eventually find it.'

I could hear the shuffling of paper as he consulted his notes.

'The pathologist thinks the killer is left-handed.' He sighed and I could imagine him raking his hands through his hair as he frowned in concentration. 'So, together with your profile, we know just about everything there is to know about this guy except his name and address.'

'Anything from the boating community?'

'Some of the boats on the canal that day have moved on, but we're tracing as many as we can. One interesting report came in from a local fisherman. He'd packed up for the day and was walking along the towpath by the boatyard just after six when he saw a young couple cuddling on the path. The timing means they must have seen Julie if that's the direction she took. The gap between the fisherman taking the same route and the courting couple is a minute or less, so either they saw something we need to know about, or Julie was lured off that path by the killer. Either way, we need to speak to them. We've put out appeals on the radio and local TV for them to come forward, but so far no luck.'

'That's unusual?'

'Maybe not.' He sighed heavily down the phone. 'I don't think they're boat owners. More likely local kids, but I just think it's strange they haven't heard the appeal. You'd have to live in a damned cave round here not to know about the murder and ... Oh, yes, you'll be seeing Hoyle on TV. He's holding a press conference to appeal for information.'

'Can't wait,' I said, sarcastically. 'How did he take the fact that you used my profile, by the way?'

Callum snorted in disgust. 'Didn't say anything, but he and Taylor-Caine were closeted away for a couple of hours after he saw it. I think they had some damage limitation to do to cover their arses, now that it looks as though your profile was more accurate than theirs. Hoyle might have to field some embarrassing questions regarding his choice of analyst on this one.'

He hesitated, as though he wanted to say something else. I caught my breath, waiting. 'I'll call you when we have something.' And with that the phone went dead.

I felt tired, strung out and miserable. I'd obviously blown it with Callum, and on top of that I was one year older and facing the weekend alone. Automatically, my fingers dialled a familiar number. It was answered on the second ring.

'Hi, Mamma, it's me.'

'Josephina! Happy birthday, bambina. *Happy birthday to you, happy birthday to you, happy birthday, dear Phina, happy birthday to you!*'

I gritted my teeth throughout the whole tuneless rendition.

'Thanks, Mamma. How are you?'

'I'm wonderful. In fact, you just caught me – I'm going bowling with the girls. If you hadn't have called I would've been so angry with you! I've been trying to get you all week.'

'I know, Mamma.'

I sighed, resigned to the fact by now that every conversation between me and my mother, regardless of original content, turned into her reprimanding me in some way.

'I've been working with the police this week on this latest towpath killing and –'

'Terrible . . . terrible,' she interrupted, in her heavily Italian accented English. 'No job for a woman, dealing with killers and rapists. Why you can't get a proper job, eh?'

'Yes, Mamma, I know. Go work in a shop or an office?'

'It's good enough for other people, but you . . . you always have to be different, just like your papa.' She sighed, perhaps realising after all that this was my birthday. 'I only worry, bambina. You know it's only that I worry about you.'

'I know, Mamma. Anyway, I heard from Alex today.'

'Sandro! Ah, when can I see him?'

'He'll be back for Christmas. He's got job interviews lined up.'

'See, sensible boy, he goes for proper jobs.'

Knowing Alex as I did, there would be nothing ordinary about his choices, but I kept the thought to myself.

'Listen, Mamma, I need to pick your brains.' Ever since she got her bus pass, she had become a walking encyclopaedia on bus routes. 'The number forty-six bus from Fordley?'

'To Shipley, yes I know it, but what do you want it for? It's against your religion to take a bus!'

I ignored the dig. 'If a person got the bus to Shipley and was heading for the salon on Ryan Street, where would the nearest stop be?'

'Well, the forty-six ends at the interchange. If you didn't mind a long walk, you could get off there then walk all through the centre of town. That would take me about half an hour, with *my* feet . . .'

I carried on quickly, before we got into a long discussion about her feet. 'And if you didn't want a long walk?'

'Well, you could walk along the towpath for about ten minutes, then cross the iron bridge over the canal and come up by the petrol station on the other side. You wouldn't do it at night though – too lonely down there. But that would bring you to the end of Ryan Street. Nice salon. You going there, Phina? You have such beautiful hair. Blonde like your papa . . . but always too busy to take care of it now. I put coconut oil on it when you were a little girl – you're too busy now for such things. Just a quick comb and then –'

'Sorry, Mamma, I have to go, but thanks. Have a good night. I'll catch up with you next week.'

As the phone went dead, I picked up my car keys – deciding to take a drive out to Shipley.

Chapter Fourteen

4 August – Shipley

At 9 p.m. on a Friday night, the streets were almost deserted. The commercial district was already empty as people hurried away to begin their weekend. There were a few cars on the petrol station forecourt as I parked my car and everyone ignored me as I plunged my hands deeper into my coat pockets, crossing the road to the short flight of stone steps that ran down to the metal footbridge.

It seemed a lot longer than twenty-four hours since Callum and I had been in the shadow of this same bridge, witnessing the results of the killer's brutal handiwork.

I stopped and looked across the water to where her body had been. A man with a little dog walked past Julie's last resting place. The poodle stopped, sniffed then cocked its leg and peed on the spot until its owner jerked the lead impatiently to move him along.

So much for dignity in death.

The light was dimming, the sky still grey with unshed rain, the atmosphere close and oppressive. By the time I stepped off the bridge and walked to the dumping site of Julie's body, the dog walker was nowhere to be seen.

A jogger padded past me, wired for sound and oblivious. Boats were moored along both sides of the canal, gently lifting and falling on the water and the soft creaking of their mooring ropes carried on a faint breeze. Most of the barges were tightly locked up – hatches padlocked, decks cleared, curtains drawn against curious passers-by.

It took another two minutes to reach the spot where the path snaked up a right-hand turn and onto the road above – opposite the Interchange where Julie would have gone for her bus.

I stood at the bottom of the path and looked around. In my mind, I pictured the young couple the fisherman had seen. Standing on the path, 'cuddling'.

Perhaps they were saying goodbye? A girl about to go for her bus, hugging her boyfriend? Wouldn't he have walked her those last few yards to see her safely on her way?

A thought was forming at the back of my mind, my profiler's database of facts and circumstances providing a possible solution to an inconsistency.

'*Look for inconsistencies,*' my teacher and mentor Professor Geoffrey Perrett used to say, '*for that is where the answers are found.*'

The teenage lovers, the fact that they had suddenly disappeared – these were inconsistencies my instinct didn't like.

Ahead of me was the boatyard, a large, sprawling graveyard packed with the skeletons of dead or dying boats, their massive, rusting hulls hauled out of the water like beached whales waiting to be dissected.

I spotted an old Dutch barge; its original iron hull had been cleaned and recently renovated. On the top deck, a new wooden structure had replaced the old wheelhouse and the back of the structure was covered by a heavy tarpaulin, fastened down by huge ropes tied on to giant metal rings set into the dock. As I turned back to retrace my steps, something on the houseboat attracted my attention. I looked back.

Nothing.

The corner of the tarpaulin lifted slightly in the warm breeze and I could see a dim light coming from deep inside the cavernous hull. Then the canvas flapped back down gently and the light was gone.

There was no one to be seen in either direction along the towpath. I glanced back at the houseboat; it glowered silently at me across the quickly darkening water.

What was it that was so wrong with this picture?

I had the unnerving but very definite feeling that I was being watched. Nothing was moving except for the corner of the tarpaulin. *What had changed?*

My skin began to crawl. The light inside the hull had gone out.

I suddenly felt totally exposed and alone. The footpath was deserted and the light was fading fast.

And just then I suddenly knew what the inconsistency was and a thousand disjointed pieces suddenly crashed together to form a complete picture.

My heart hammered as I saw it all as the killer had seen it. As he was seeing it right now!

My breath came faster as I debated my next move.

Go up the steps to the main road, to bright lights and traffic.

Then the twenty-minute walk back to my car.

Or brave the deserted towpath and get to my car ten minutes faster?

The same choice Julie Lamont had made a few days earlier – a choice that had cost her her life. I wasn't about to make the same mistake.

I turned to my right and began to climb the steep path up to the main road. Was it my quickening imagination or did I hear a sound behind me, from the towpath below?

A twig cracked and I almost cried out, but I didn't have the breath.

I willed myself not to look back as I scrambled for the top just a few feet away, certain now that the killer was behind me. Over my own laboured breathing and the pounding in my ears, I could hear the grunting of someone coming up the steps in my wake.

I practically sprinted the last few feet to the road, anticipating with every step the rough hand that would claw at my ankle and drag me backwards into the darkness below.

I fell onto the pavement at the edge of the road, nearly knocking into a jogger going past. I ran a few more steps and then risked a backward glance.

The dark silhouette of my pursuer was there for a fleeting second, then gone. Now all I could hear was heavy breathing gradually getting fainter as he disappeared back towards the dark water.

Suddenly I was surrounded by people getting on and off buses, kids hanging about by Costa Coffee, sharp, naked neon lights and noise.

I leaned back against a barrier, struggling for breath and drenched in sweat, my whole body trembling. I reached for my mobile at the same time as a white city taxi pulled up at the kerb. Without thinking, I pulled open the door and fell into the back seat.

'Ryan Street petrol station!'

The cabby turned to look at me, puzzled. 'You new in town, luv?'

I shook my head, irritated to be quizzed at a time like this. 'No, so don't make it a twenty-minute round trip – I know exactly where it is,' I said, acidly.

He turned back and looked at me in the rear-view mirror.

'I was about to say, it's stupid to take a cab when you could walk it from here.' He signalled and began to pull out into traffic. 'But as you just got back from charm school, I can see you're too exhausted to make the walk.'

I dialled a number and almost sobbed when I heard Callum's voice.

'Jo?'

'Cal . . .' My voice wouldn't come.

'Oh, sorry, I forgot about the flowers. I ordered them in advance so you'd get them on your birthday, before last night and everything. If you got home and found them then –'

'No . . . I . . .' I hardly registered what he was saying. 'I'm in Shipley, I've been down by the cana—'

I heard the explosion of his breath down the phone.

'Are you insane! Going down there alone at night?' His voice had an edge to it that I hadn't heard before.

'Cal, I . . . Oh God . . .'

There was a pause for a fraction of a second as he registered that something was badly wrong. His tone suddenly became all business.

'Where are you? I'm coming to get you.'

'My car's by the petrol station on Ryan Street. Can you come now?'

'Lock the doors and stay put. I'll be there in five minutes.' His tone softened. 'Tell me you're all right?'

'I'm fine.' But my voice didn't sound convincing, even to me. 'I know how he did it, Cal. I know where he is.'

'Tell me when I get there. Just keep the doors locked, OK?'

Chapter Fifteen

4 August – petrol station forecourt, Shipley

Callum was staring out of the partially opened passenger window of my car as he listened to what I had to say. I could see the muscles bunching in his jaw, as if he might explode at me at any moment.

The whole story poured out like a torrent I couldn't stop: how I couldn't face the weekend alone just thinking about Alex; my birthday . . . I left out the bit about me thinking of him, and how much of a mess my non-existent love life was. I told him instead that I'd decided to spend the weekend working on the towpath killings.

It was when I got to the part about seeing the light on the houseboat that he finally turned to look at me. His blue eyes were dark with anger and I could see he was having difficulty controlling his temper.

'It didn't occur to you to call me before going off half-cocked, playing bloody detective?' He turned, putting his arm across the back of my seat.

'I didn't have time.' I was still shaking inside but trying hard not to show it. 'Besides, I had nothing to tell you – just half-formed theories. My mother talking about different routes from the bus got me thinking.'

I couldn't stand the scrutiny of those dark eyes and still concentrate on what I was saying. It was my turn to face away and look out at the passing traffic.

'We needed to know where Julie met her killer. She didn't know him – I was sure of that – but I was fairly certain he knew of *her*, that he'd seen her before or knew her route and had stalked her before.' I watched my reflection in the glass. 'I knew the canal was his hunting ground and the route to the bus was the perfect connection between the two of them –'

'So you decided to go down there? Where you suspected he stalked his victims? Alone, when the place was deserted – are you *mad*?'

I turned to face him, the adrenalin still surging. My eyes flashing a warning I knew he would see. 'For God's sake, Callum,' I snapped, 'that's my job!'

'To get yourself *killed*?' he spat.

'No!' I snapped back with equal venom. 'To walk through the murder – literally. To see events unfold through the killer's eyes. To imagine his drives and impulses. To work out his motivation, why he picked these victims.'

I could see people filling their cars and looking over at us in curiosity, probably thinking we were having a lovers' tiff. The thought only irritated me more.

'I breathe the same air he does, see the things he sees and, God help me, I think the thoughts he thinks!'

Suddenly his expression softened and his hand slid down to touch my shoulder.

'Don't!' I snapped, shrugging my shoulder away from his hand. '*You* involved me,' I reminded him. '*You* took me to stand over her. *You* made me look at her faceless corpse and smell the stench of her death and asked me to get inside the killer's head.

And once that process starts, I can't switch it off. God knows there are times I wish I could.'

'Jo –'

But I wasn't in the mood to listen. Besides, I had to tell him everything and I had to do it fast. The clock was ticking – only a matter of time before he killed again.

'It's normal for me to visit the scene –'

'Jo, I just –'

'So there would have been no harm in doing that,' I persevered, ignoring his interruptions. 'Because usually the killer isn't *still there*.'

'What?'

'The boatyard,' I said, simply, as if that should explain everything. 'He's in the shell of a houseboat.'

Callum was staring at me, his face as still and hard as carved marble.

'I think that's where he took Julie. That's where he held her, tortured her and killed her before dumping her body on the towpath.'

I waited for him to say something. His jaw tightened again and he breathed out slowly, cranking the window down another inch and taking a deep breath of warm, sultry air, as if we had all the time in the world.

I was exasperated. 'Didn't you hear what I just said? I think he's still there!'

'We searched the boatyard already, and the houseboat,' he said, quietly, his tone disappointed. 'I thought when you said he was still there, that you'd seen him –'

'I did!'

He turned back to look at me. 'What? But you said –'

'I saw light coming from inside the hull. For all he knew, I was the police or maybe a journalist.'

He was listening intently now, his eyes searching my face as I spoke.

'He turned the light out when he realised I'd seen it – that's when I made a dash for it up the embankment.' My heart began to beat faster as I recalled it. 'Callum, it's him, I know it is.'

'Why would he stay so close to the scene?' he asked, wearily. 'Surely he wouldn't want to be within a mile of the place with us crawling all over it?'

'He has nowhere else to go,' I said, simply. 'With all the publicity, it would attract more suspicion if he were to disappear. He stays because people living and working along the canal or at the boatyard would notice if he didn't. Besides,' I added, quietly, 'he gets off on being so close to the fallout.'

'We went over that boatyard with a fine-tooth comb,' he said, but I could see some doubt creeping across his face.

'How fine?'

'If I call in the cavalry and you're wrong . . .'

'And if I'm right?'

I could see the possibilities and strategies running in his head. Finally, he seemed to come to a decision. He held my shoulders in his hands, looking at me squarely.

'Go to the farm, do not pass go, do not collect two hundred pounds.'

'Cal—'

'No arguments,' he said, and from his tone I knew it was useless to try. He pulled me to him and I felt his lips brush the top

94

of my hair. 'And if you give me any trouble, I'll have you locked up. So what's it to be?'

I suddenly felt weary. 'OK,' I said. 'I'll wait for you at the farm – please be careful.'

Chapter Sixteen

4 August – Kingsberry Farm

As usual, work was my distraction. My emails arrived at a crawl as I tapped a pencil against my teeth and cursed the download speed. Even though Marissa had arranged for satellite internet to be installed, it still wasn't brilliant.

I rarely visited her in London, so email and Skype were our mainstays. My technophobia was a constant source of amusement for her, for which she ribbed me endlessly. When my book had first been accepted and she'd realised what a technical Neanderthal I was, Marissa had organised everything, even going as far as sending her techie from London to the farm to set everything up and show me how to use it.

I dialled into the Fordley practice to pick up my voicemail. There was a message from Dr Lister. He sounded tired and more than a little irritated.

'*There's been a development. The changeover staff weren't aware of Martha's pending assessment, or that we were considering a move to the secure unit. So they allowed her onto the day ward. Understandable as she wasn't listed as high risk. And . . . well, it appears she absconded during a shift change.*' I heard the loud exhale and knew he was smoking. '*We don't know how it happened . . .*'

I groaned as I listened to his litany of thinly veiled excuses and bullet-dodging logic. If that had happened when I'd been director, I would have kicked his arse all around the grounds.

'*The Section 2 papers hadn't gone through, so there's little we can do. I've reported her to the police as a missing person – we can only hope she turns up.*'

Cursing his promise to call me back, I made a note to speak directly to someone at Fordley nick about it. Perhaps if I stressed that Martha was vulnerable and there was a safeguarding issue, I might get some help finding her, then I worked on some changes to the manuscript Marissa had requested until Harvey growled softly, lifting his head up from his paws.

The phone rang.

'I was beginning to think we were on a wild goose chase.' Callum was calling from his car and the reception was poor, but I could still hear the triumph in his voice. I felt relief flooding through me like a warm tide, relaxing the muscles in my neck and shoulders. It was only then that I realised how knotted with tension I'd been all night.

'To be honest, I was cursing you –'

'Thanks . . .'

'Well, be fair, it wasn't much to justify calling out the cavalry.' There was a pause and for a second I thought his signal had gone, then, 'I think we've got him, Jo.'

'Oh, thank God! Was he on the houseboat?'

'No, but the team found a space in the hull under the wheel-house. I'm on my way to yours now. I'll explain when I get there, but seeing you must have spooked him. He's done a runner but he didn't get much of a head start. We're all over the area – helicopter with heat detectors, dogs. We'll get him.'

'Do you know who he is?'

'David Woodhouse. Boatyard owner gave us his name and address. He's his electrician. I'll be there soon and I can show you what we found.'

I sat on the living room floor with Callum, his laptop between us so we could both see the video taken from the body cams of the search team.

The interior was still under construction and there were tools and debris lying about. The team moved through the main room and headed towards the stern.

'No more work was scheduled until next spring. So if you hadn't sent us back there, God knows how long this would have stayed hidden.'

Callum shifted his position and I felt his arm slide across the seat of the sofa behind me. I could smell the soft cologne he wore as he leaned closer.

'The hull is hollow with a crawl space under the whole thing that they fill with concrete for ballast.'

'Concrete?' I thought back to the post-mortem report and the concrete dust found on the body.

He nodded. 'They poured it six weeks ago and laid the suspended floor over the space. Once Woodhouse had finished the electrics, that part of the hull should have been sealed.'

Harvey nuzzled up against me and lay down by my side. I ruffled his ears as I thought it through. 'Work stopped on the boat just when Linda Baker was killed. He didn't have his little hidey-hole then, so she was a rushed job on the towpath. He knew he couldn't act this out on one of the holiday boats – too messy. Anyway, he wanted time with his next victim, to savour the moment, so that's probably when he constructed this. No one would be working on it and he could hold Julie there and go back to her every night.'

He fast-forwarded the video. The camera illuminated an iron-walled room about five-feet high that sloped down at the sides and was rounded at the stern of the barge. The suspended ceiling was held up by huge, square wooden posts sunk into the concrete floor.

'They found a digital camera,' Callum said. 'These were taken off it.'

Obscene photographs of Julie Lamont in various stages of nakedness and distress. In most of them she was alive, her eyes wide and petrified. I imagined her terror and the utter horror of realising just how she was going to die.

In all of them, she was bound with white electrical flex and gagged with wide strips of duct tape, her eyes giving a hint to the horrific scene being played out in front of her.

The last few images were so horrific I had to turn away.

'Oh my God,' I breathed, quietly. 'He's butchering her alive!'

Callum switched back to the body cam video. I could make out a pair of Reebok trainers. There was a bundle of clothing and a rucksack neatly stacked beside the trainers.

'The rest of Julie's clothes, and we think the rucksack, will turn out to be Linda Baker's.'

There was a small wooden platform against one wall, which the cameraman focused in on.

Callum breathed softly. 'Bloody unbelievable. It's like a shrine.'

There, in the centre of the short wooden table, was a serrated hunting knife. Beneath the table was a coil of electrical flex and a roll of duct tape.

Callum reached across and switched the video off.

We sat on the floor in silence.

That could have been me. A shudder ran down my spine. I remembered the sound of his grunting as he chased me up the embankment. *If he'd caught me tonight, I would have died in that torture chamber, so close to safety that I would have been able to hear the traffic outside as he cut me to pieces.*

I felt Callum's arm around my shoulder as he squeezed gently. 'Need a drink?'

I nodded numbly and felt him get up and go into the kitchen. A minute later he was back, but not with the wine I'd expected. He held the brandy glass out for me.

'Thought you might want something a bit stronger.'

I took it gratefully, suddenly looking up as I realised he didn't have a glass.

'I can't,' he said, reading my thoughts. 'I've got to get back. I have to be at the incident room. As soon as we got a name, I woke up a magistrate to get a search warrant for his bedsit in Shipley. The team are over there now. I just wanted to show you the footage. Tonight was down to you, Jo.'

I sipped the brandy, feeling the welcome burn in my throat as it worked its way down.

'How come he wasn't questioned with everyone else at the yard?'

Callum ran his hand through his hair and I tried not to notice how good he looked, even at a time like this.

'He was delivering a narrowboat to Skipton. Apparently it takes over a week to sail that far. Uniform made a note to pick him up later. Events overtook them and he got overlooked. It happens.'

He looked at me in silence for a moment, and then asked, 'How did you know?'

I took another sip of brandy. 'The cuddling couple.'

'What about them?'

'When I walked it, I realised that Julie would have been at the same spot as those lovers when the fisherman saw them. And if she had been there at the same time, she'd be alive because she'd have walked up those steps to the interchange and caught her bus. But she never made it to the bus. The fisherman didn't see her – why not? It didn't fit.'

He raised his eyebrows in a silent question.

'The lovers had to be Julie and her killer.'

Callum sat on the sofa, his thigh brushing my shoulder.

'Lovers?' he said in disbelief.

'I don't think they even spoke at all before he punched her in the face and broke her cheekbone. He held her limp body against his just as the fisherman came around the bend in the path. I timed it tonight. It takes twenty-four seconds from there to the Interchange. So he just hugged her to him and tried to look like they're a couple until the fisherman was up the steps and out of sight. After that he couldn't have moved her far. He only had a minute or so before she came round and started giving him trouble. I looked across and saw the light in the disused boat and it all fell into place.'

'Trouble is,' Callum said, softly, 'he saw you too.'

I couldn't hold his gaze, so instead I looked at the carpet and fiddled with the stem of my glass.

'Which was why I ran for it.'

Callum sighed and got up to leave.

'I'll have uniform outside the farm tonight – until we track him down, I'm not happy about you being here alone.'

'Is that *really* necessary?'

'He saw you tonight, Jo. He came after you because he couldn't risk you getting away and blowing the whistle.'

'But I did get away.'

'Precisely.' His tone was exasperated. 'That's why he'd shoved off by the time we got to the boat. He knows it's over and he's on the run. But he's going to be pissed off with *you*, isn't he?'

I stood to face him, still having to look up at him, but feeling less like a scolded child than I had when sitting on the floor at his feet.

'He doesn't know where I live, or even who I am, for that matter.'

He raked his hand through his hair and shrugged. 'I don't care what the hell he knows. People *do* know you from the TV and the press. Perhaps he did recognise you. Perhaps he *does* have transport. He might know where to find you – I don't know. But what I *do* know is that at this late stage of the game, I'm not taking any chances. So, whether you like it or not, I'm going to have a car up here tonight.'

I opened my mouth to reply, but I was already looking at his back as he walked out of the room, calling over his shoulder, 'Lock the door and pull the curtains. Don't go outside. If Harvey needs a pee, get one of the officers to take him out.'

Chapter Seventeen

5 August – Kingsberry Farm

I woke up and winced. Turning my head was agony. I slowly slid my legs off the sofa and put my feet on the floor. The crick in my neck felt like it was going to be permanent. My foot knocked over the empty brandy glass and Harvey lifted his head to watch me curiously as I sat forward and held my head.

After Callum had left, I knew there was no chance of sleep. I heard the police arrive, before the officer knocked on the door and introduced himself and I paced up and down and poured another brandy – then another. Funny how, after the first one, the others went down so easily. I must have dozed in the early hours, waiting for Callum to call with more news.

I slowly parted the living room curtains and bright sunlight jagged at the back of my eyes, sharpening the dull headache. I groaned as Harvey brushed against my leg, jumping up to rest his massive paws on the windowsill and look outside with me.

The patrol car was still there, the PC leaning against the open door. He glanced up and raised his hand in a half wave. I nodded gingerly and let the curtain fall back.

The clock on the wall said 7 a.m. It'd been a long day already.

I was loading the dishwasher and contemplating my second dose of paracetamol when the telephone rang, jagging bright red pain across my eyes. I dived for the receiver to stop the agony.

'Yes?'

'Jo, it's me.' Callum's voice banged like a drum.

Using economy of effort, 'News?' was all I could manage.

'We've got him. Early hours of this morning.' I expected him to sound happier about it, but he just sounded bone-weary.

'Why didn't you call?' I knew I sounded petulant, but decided my hangover was more than enough justification. 'It's after seven.'

'Sorry to state the obvious, but you weren't exactly my top priority. You're bloody lucky I've snatched a minute now.'

I pushed the dishwasher closed with my foot, drying my hands as I cradled the phone under my chin.

'OK, OK, sorry.' I tried to soften my tone, realising we were both too strung out to risk an argument. 'I've been worried, that's all. Are you OK?'

'Just knackered. I could do with a week's sleep and a change of clothes. CSI are processing the houseboat and we need to get samples of his DNA from the flat to tie him to the scene. Now we've got him in custody, the clock's ticking.' I imagined Callum checking his watch as he spoke. 'I've got my best tier-three trained interviewers lined up to have a crack at him as soon as his brief arrives.'

Tier 3 officers were trained in advanced techniques, looking for hidden 'tells' in interviewees – body language, speech patterns that indicated deception. I'd been part of a team of forensic psychologists called in to help design some of the training years ago.

'We should be good to go anytime now. I just took the chance to nip out and call you.'

'Thanks.' I meant it. I needed to know that he still wanted to keep talking to me. 'Need any advice on what you're looking for at the flat to evidence his state of mind?'

There was a pause, slightly too long, and then he said, hesitantly, 'No, it's fine, Jo, we've got that covered.'

I felt that sickening sensation you get when you find out your best friend had a party at the weekend and neglected to invite you.

'Oh?'

I let the silence at the other end lengthen. I'd long ago learned that there was something about the power of silence that often made people say far more than they would otherwise.

'Hoyle wants Taylor-Caine to advise.'

The knot in my stomach tightened and the bile of outrage rose in my throat, along with the words that spilled out before I could stop them.

'*Great.*'

Harvey jumped as I slammed my mug onto the table, spilling tea. I could feel the throbbing pain across my eyes intensify as my blood pressure went through the roof.

'It was *my* profile, Callum, and me on that sodding towpath last night – or have you forgotten that?'

'Jo, listen –'

But I was too far gone to listen.

'No, *you* listen.' I paced across the kitchen as my anger boiled over. '*You* roped me in on this, *despite* my saying that Taylor-Caine should be your first port of call. But *you* insisted and said Hoyle would just have to live with it. That you would let him know you used my profile in preference over hers –'

'And he does know –'

'You let me put in half my week and over twenty years of experience for free, while that inefficient lightweight sits on her arse in a nice warm office and gets a hefty salary, thank you very much.'

'It's not about money, is it, Jo?'

'Damn right it's not!' I exploded. 'It's about professional credit for bringing sexual psychopaths like Woodhouse to justice. None of which I'll get now, thanks to Hoyle and his bit on the side.'

'But everyone knows it was your profile, Jo.' He was trying to calm me down, but his gentling tone just made me even angrier. 'Everyone on the team knows it. That's what we all worked from and that's what got him.'

'So how does Hoyle square that one now?'

'It's all about justifying her on the budget, Jo. You know how it is. He just wants her to be visible. No one will say it was her profile.'

'*No*, they just won't say it was *mine*.'

'Jo –'

'Don't *ever* ask me to help unofficially again, Callum. Not *ever*.'

I slammed the phone down and winced as my head banged in sympathy. My stomach was churning and I knew it wasn't the brandy. I sounded like a spoiled child, but my professional pride was punctured. There was something else, too – Callum had called me in as a personal favour, one he knew would cost me time and effort. And after last night, nearly a hell of a lot more.

I didn't want the glory. I just wanted to know that Callum had the strength of character to support an unpopular decision when it counted. It felt as if he'd backed down when it was polit-ically expedient, leaving me out in the cold because it wouldn't be a good career move to upset the established order. That hurt. It hurt like hell.

Chapter Eighteen

5 August – Kingsberry Farm

The rest of the day dragged by, with monotonous grey weather that matched my mood.

My mother rang to see what I was doing for the weekend and I lied. I just couldn't face the play-acting I always had to do around her as she dropped unsubtle hints about my being 'unattached'. That and the fact I had a job she couldn't understand anyone wanting to do, least of all a woman, a job that meant I didn't see enough of Alex.

I pottered around the garden, making a half-hearted attempt to clear weeds from some of the paths, then finally gave up and decided to walk Harvey across the fields.

Old George was striding across the top acre by the woods, his shotgun across his arm. He waved as he saw us and leaned against the fence.

'Did you have a good birthday, lass?'

'Worked it, as usual.'

He frowned, absently patting Harvey's head. 'All work an' no play.' He tutted.

I laughed. 'Careful – you're starting to sound like Jen.'

'Wise woman, that.' He scratched his forehead. 'Heard from your Alex?'

'He called me to say happy birthday. He'll be home for Christmas, hopefully.' I threw a stick for Harvey. 'Do you ever hear anything from your boy – Simon, isn't it?' I vaguely remembered George's son coming to visit once, just after I moved into the farm. An abstract image of a fancy car and an expensive suit that looked out of place along our old dirt track.

He sighed, looking out over the fields rather than meeting my eye. 'Nay, lass. He was never one for staying in touch. I get a Christmas card – but that's about it.'

I studied his weathered profile, aching at the thought of growing apart from Alex like that. I could tell he was trying hard to give nothing away.

'You must miss him?'

His wide shoulders shrugged beneath the Barbour jacket. 'Nothin' in common, lass. Soon as he could, he left home. Nothin' here for him. I mean, he was never going to be a farmer, was he?' He turned to me and smiled. 'Moved to Durham for a while but once his mam died, he went off down London for some fancy job that I don't even understand. Reckon he must've got his mother's brains.'

I patted his arm and raised a smile. 'Well, if he got her brains, he must've inherited your looks then?'

'Aye.' He grinned at me. 'Lucky bugger, eh?' He sniffed and wiped his hand across his face – looking out towards the woods. 'I've cleared the old cottage of some muck, lass, and done a few running repairs.'

I smiled, touched as always by his consideration and happy to let him change the subject. 'Thanks, George. What do I owe you for your time?'

He snorted. 'Catch yourself on, girl. I'm not going to bother about a few days fixing up the old place.'

I watched Harvey as he bolted around the field, running off pent-up energy.

'Not sure what to do with that old building, George. Needs a new roof for a start – it'd cost a fortune – and for what? I wouldn't want to sell it.' I grinned at him. 'Don't want any neighbours apart from you.'

He looked across to the edge of the woods at the small white building that was more of a one-roomed bothy than a cottage. He pushed his cap up with his thumb.

'Could always rent it out. You know, holiday cottage, like.'

I frowned as I thought about it. 'No. Couldn't be bothered with all the hassle. Anyway, can you imagine a family with a couple of screaming kids descending on us?'

He grinned. 'On second thoughts, let's just leave the old place as it is, eh? Anyways, what would the foxes do if we rented it out?'

'Are they still in there?'

He puckered his lips. 'Not sure. There's been something in there all right. Could be foxes or the old badger maybe. Probably should put a door on it if that's OK with you? I've got an old one up at the farm.'

'OK. Do whatever you think. But don't be out of pocket, George. If you have to spend anything on it, let me know and we'll square up.'

He grinned and with a casual wave, went on his way. I knew he'd never ask me for a penny.

I lost the day in my study. Answered emails and put in a call to Westwood Park. Martha hadn't surfaced and in the absence of a Section 2 order, there was little we could do beyond reporting her as a missing person. As I got up to leave, the phone rang. It was my mother.

'Have you seen the TV?'

'No, why?' I reached for the remote.

'Go to BBC news,' she said. 'It's about this Towpath Killer.'

As the image flickered on, I could see a room set out for a police press conference. Hoyle sat at the centre of the table, beaming proudly. Beside him, the bird-like figure of Lizzie Taylor-Caine, looking professional in a dark skirt suit and white blouse, her pixie-cut blonde hair making her look more manly than she probably intended. As usual, she wore no makeup and no smile. She shuffled papers in front of her, looking at her notes as Hoyle addressed the press.

'In the early hours of this morning, a twenty-two-year-old man was arrested in connection with the towpath killings. Teams also searched several locations in Shipley. Vital evidence was recovered and forensic examinations are underway.'

There was a barrage of questions from the floor as the press demanded answers. Hoyle held up his hand to stem the flow.

'All I can say at the moment is that we are keen to question this man in relation to these events.'

The press pack bayed for more, directing questions at Taylor-Caine. Hoyle answered first.

'Psychological profiling was used in this case and I cannot emphasise enough the vital part it played. Which means that at this time we're not looking for anyone else in connection with this offence.'

He glanced across at Taylor-Caine, who still continued to look down at her notes. I wanted to think it was because she was ashamed of the bare-faced implication that the work had been hers, but somehow I couldn't imagine her having that much of a conscience.

One of the press pack shouted out, 'Isn't it true, Chief Superintendent, that there were conflicting profiles initially? And could this have hampered the enquiry?'

Hoyle cleared his throat and ran a finger along the inside of his collar in a classic gesture of discomfort.

'That is true to an extent. We had the input of an external forensic psychologist and that person's profile did differ from our own. These things do occur, but thankfully we followed the advice we felt most appropriate and it has resulted in a successful arrest.'

More questions came, but I wasn't listening. I felt sick. I stared at the TV screen in disbelief. The misdirection was so blatant. I was stunned.

My mother's voice was buzzing in my ear.

'Is it *you* he's talking about? Phina?'

'I'll call you back, Mamma,' I said and hung up the phone.

Harvey came and nuzzled my hand, resting his chin on my knee as I sat on the edge of my coffee table, watching the end of the press conference, my mind scrolling through endless possibilities.

The phone rang. It was Jen.

'The bastards!' she exploded down the phone. 'Did you just see that utter crap?'

'How much damage can it do me? I'm not officially involved in the case,' I reasoned. 'My name doesn't appear anywhere. Who's to know I was the other psychologist? It's only if I'm named that the implication is damaging.'

113

'I don't *care*,' Jen ranted in outrage. 'You did this as a favour to Callum.'

I winced at the reminder.

'Where does he get off, allowing them to even *hint* at such a thing? He should challenge that – it's not *fair*.'

'But if *we* challenge it, we're telling everyone I was the other profiler.' I tried to keep my tone calm even though I was as outraged as she was. 'We'd shoot ourselves in the foot. At the moment, we're not implicated directly. All the investigating officers know my profile was spot on. As long as it stays like that, why should we care? We should just let it lie.'

'Maybe,' she said, huffily. 'But Callum deserves a flea in his ear and you should tell him to get stuffed if he ever wants another favour!'

'I did that already.'

'Good! If they think Taylor-Caine is so bloody good, let them use her crappy profiles in future and see where that gets them! Why let her bask in the glory of all your hard work?'

I heard Jen's husband calling her from somewhere else in the house. She had obviously slipped away to call me.

'Better get back to your weekend, Jen,' I said. 'I'll see you on Tuesday.'

I sat and watched the news unfold for the rest of the day. Hourly bulletins came round, and more and more details about Woodhouse unfolded under the bright red banner of 'Breaking News'.

All the details fit my profile.

Six feet tall and weighing in at fifteen stone, Woodhouse was muscular and fit. He had a fascination for martial arts and worked out at a gym three times a week, although staff there said he was a loner. Originally from Blackburn, he'd moved to take up his job in Fordley. He didn't have a girlfriend, but the local prostitutes in Fordley were giving interviews to journalists saying they'd done business with him around payday at the boatyard. When he got a reputation for violence, they'd stopped seeing him.

I half expected Callum to call. It hurt that he didn't and I had to hear all of these details on the news like everyone else.

I wasn't sure how I felt. Used – certainly. Humiliated – definitely. Alone – absolutely.

Chapter Nineteen

6 August – Kingsberry Farm

Saturday drifted into Sunday and being cooped up in the house was doing nothing to help my mood. I finally decided to walk Harvey in companionable but grumpy silence across the moors – with my mobile phone switched off.

At four o'clock, I got back to the farm to find my answer machine in meltdown.

Three calls from my mother and two from Jen, all asking whether I had seen the Sunday papers. The office machine had one call from Marissa asking the same thing, and at least a dozen calls from journalists on newspapers across the country asking for my opinion on a story that had been run by *Fordley Express*.

I left the house without returning any of the calls and drove to the nearest newsagent in Kingsberry. Normally I would have walked to the village, but thought it best to keep a low profile until I saw the paper.

I couldn't bring myself to look at it until I was back at the farm. Nothing could have prepared me for what I saw when I finally opened it on the kitchen table.

There it was across a double-page spread – a grainy black-and-white photograph of me and Callum standing by my car, heads together, looking very conspiratorial. It had obviously been taken by the paparazzi on the canal bank on Thursday morning.

The banner headline read:

DID BOTCHED PROFILE COST JULIE HER LIFE?

Botched profile.

I stared at the article in total shock. My stomach churned and twisted in a tight, cold knot of anger and a feeling of monumental betrayal.

My name wasn't mentioned once. But references to 'A police spokesman' alleged there had been two different offender profiles – one of them by an external psychologist, who was not on the payroll and had *not* been officially invited to contribute to the investigation.

The article continued:

> One of the offender profiles was so wide of the mark that it took detectives down a completely false line of enquiry, undoubtedly meaning the offender was at large for longer. Did that fatal delay cost Julie Lamont her life at the hands of this brutal killer? This is something that a review into the way this investigation was handled needs to address. With hindsight we ask, in these most serious criminal cases, should investigators rely so heavily on a branch of science that many feel is unproven and, at worst, can cost an innocent woman her life?

It ground on and on.

I sat riveted to the spot, not wanting to read any more, but at the same time compelled to take in each painful, miserable detail, which crucified me with every inference. As I reached the end of the article, the phone rang.

'Phina, it's me.'

I groaned. 'Before you ask, Mamma, yes, I got the paper.'

'Is it true, Phina? That your profile got that little girl murdered?'

'No, it's not true!'

My mother always saw the negative side of everything. And, like most people who read the article, she would think there was no smoke without fire.

'They don't mention my name – it's not me they're talking about.'

'But your picture is there, Phina. Why would they put your picture there if they're not meaning you?'

I rubbed my temple, willing the throbbing in my brain to give me a break.

'Don't worry, I'll take care of it.'

'What can you do?' she ground on, as relentless as the article. 'It's out there now – everyone has read it!'

I could hear the panic as her voice went up an octave. 'What do I tell the girls at the bowling club?'

And there it was.

She talked to her friends about, *'My daughter the doctor'*. Never actually saying what *type* of doctor. Never having to explain my world to those with sensitive dispositions, who would be horrified to discover I worked in psychiatric hospitals and prisons with some of the country's most criminally insane.

'Tell them they should be ashamed to read a crappy tabloid like *The Express*.'

'Phina! Be serious. This means you can't work! You'll have to give it up now – and what about Jen?'

She rolled on with her endless stream of disjointed non-logic, which for years had driven my father to despair.

'I can prove my profile was right. In the meantime, I'll get a solicitor. By next Sunday, you'll have a more positive article to show the girls at the club.'

Her tone was hurt now. 'It's not about what I show the girls at the club. It's you I'm worried about. I never liked you doing this job and this just goes to show you –'

She never elaborated on what exactly it did show me, but it was one of her favourite ways of ending a conversation on what felt like a victorious note.

As I hung up, the phone rang again.

'Jo, it's me.' Jen's voice was a welcome relief. 'I hope you're going to sue?'

'You were going to be my next call.' I sighed as I imagined her family cursing me for robbing them of a normal weekend. 'I'll make it up to you.'

'Forget it,' she huffed, and I could hear the anger in her tone. 'I'm going to call Fosters tomorrow.' They were top-flight litigators in London. Marissa had put me in touch with them when we'd needed representation in a case a few years before. They had called on me occasionally since then to be an expert witness.

'They'll have that editor swinging by his balls!'

I couldn't help but laugh. Jen was usually so calm and composed. This was so unlike her.

'Shame Taylor-Caine hasn't got any,' she ranted, protectively, 'or I'd have them for earrings! What a bitch! We've got to go after her for this, Jo.'

'You're supposed to be taking the day off tomorrow, remember?'

'I can still do the family party around making a phone call. This is more important, Jo.'

'Maybe we can release our original transcript through Fosters? They'll sort it. I'm sure this'll be tomorrow's fish and chip wrappers.'

'Well . . .' she said, slowly, 'I hope Marissa thinks so. She's already called my mobile. She's worried about the book.'

Marissa had persuaded me to write my latest book after realising that, over the years, some of the most infamous murderers in the country were behind bars as a result of my profiles or testimony as an expert witness at their trials.

In the Minds of Monsters – not a title I was wholly in favour of – was due out at the end of the year and this journalistic silver bullet could end my monster's premature life.

'Has Callum called?'

'No. He probably got it in the neck from Hoyle for using me in the first place.'

Was he just keeping his head down? I wasn't sure how that thought made me feel. Disappointed, I supposed

'I thought he was different, Jen,' I said, quietly, feeling the unexpected sting of hot tears. 'Some expert profiler I am!'

'Hmm. Well, it's not your fault if he turns out to be a bastard like the rest of them,' she said, stiffly. 'But if it's any consolation, I thought he was different too.'

I put the phone down. I really couldn't bear any more of this. Before I wearily went upstairs for a bath and an early night, I switched off the office phone and my mobile. Let the journalists sweat until tomorrow.

Chapter Twenty

7 August – Kingsberry Farm

The bed was oppressively hot. I tossed and turned, trying to quieten the maddening chatter in my brain. I didn't remember falling asleep before a relentless pounding pressed at the edges of my tumbling nightmares.

I sat up suddenly, disoriented, trying to make sense of the insane commotion I could hear throughout the house.

The alarm clock said 5.30 a.m.

Harvey was barking and throwing himself against the kitchen door, which was being hammered on by frantic fists. The whole house reverberated with banging and howling.

As I crossed the kitchen, blue flashing lights from outside illuminated the room in a surreal, pulsing glow.

Harvey strained at his collar as I heaved him back and swung open the oak door.

The police officer's face told me instantly – something I had come to recognise and dread ever since my first experience of it over twenty years before.

Someone had died.

'Sorry, doctor, we tried all your listed numbers but couldn't get through.'

My throat went dry. 'Is it my mother? Alex?'

His expression altered. 'No, sorry, nothing like that. Your family are fine, doctor, absolutely fine.'

I looked behind him to his colleague sitting in the car. The window was down and radio chatter crackled through the still and humid early morning air. The blue light painted his face a garish colour.

The feeling that they were bringing me death wouldn't go away. My pulse raced.

'Then *what,* for God's sake?'

'Martha Scott.'

My brain froze momentarily as I processed what he had just said. I stepped aside as he followed me into the kitchen. Harvey growled suspiciously.

'Harvey, stand.' He took his cue and came to stand beside me. His posture defensive. His gaze never leaving the officer.

I felt shaky as I realised that my body didn't need the sudden surge of adrenalin for fight or flight.

'I don't understand. What about Martha?'

'She's dead,' he said, simply.

I automatically began to fill the kettle, flipping the lid on the Aga.

'She's a potential suicide. Is that what's happened?'

'Not unless she stabbed herself over thirty times.'

I stared at him for a moment as his words sank in. He nodded, gesturing towards the humming kettle.

'So if it's OK with you, I don't think we've got time for a brew, doctor. CID want you down at the station.'

I'd made the journey to central police headquarters in Fordley more times than I cared to count, but never in the back of a police car. It gave me a different view. A view a lot of my clientele were familiar with, and one I never wanted to get used to.

As we pulled into the high-walled courtyard at the rear of the building, my mind was busy running through all the possibilities for Martha's murder.

What were the chances of her being murdered the same way as the women in her nightmares? Slim to none. Or was she just monumentally unlucky to cross the path of a vicious killer by chance?

Then there was the haunting recording of my last interview with Martha – with 'Jack'. I still didn't know what to think about that.

Had Martha committed murder as she'd believed? I didn't think she was capable of it. If that were true, then any fragmented personality her mind may have created would also be incapable of it – that's what all the research concluded.

Or was it an elaborate faking by Martha? Unlikely. She hadn't the intellect for such a deception. Then what was I left with?

My thoughts were interrupted as the car stopped. The air was humid and sticky but at least it wasn't raining. We walked in silence around puddles and across the high-walled courtyard to the rear door of the station.

'What's wrong with using the front? Or am I a suspect now?' I was half-joking, but I couldn't muster a smile as I said it.

'Press,' he said, simply. 'Swarming around the front, hoping to doorstep an investigating officer. This is the only place they can't get access.'

It hadn't occurred to me before, but in light of the Towpath Killer, another killing just a few days later meant the press would be having a field day.

The interview room was stark and depressing. Bright strip lights illuminated the small, white-walled, windowless room that smelled faintly of sweat and stale coffee.

The PC left to get me a cup of tea. I had seen countless video recordings of police interviews and, in my time, had listened to thousands of recordings of suspect interviews. But this was the first time I had experienced it from their side of the table and I didn't like it.

There was a definite shift in the way I was being treated. The police were no doubt having to fend off unwanted scrutiny into the way the David Woodhouse case had been handled, and maybe they didn't want me making any waves over the press article in yesterday's paper.

The door opened and an officer entered the room.

'Thanks for coming down, Dr McCready. Appreciate your time.' He smiled pleasantly enough, but my guard was up now and I wasn't inclined to lower it. 'Obviously, you're here as a witness – so you can leave at any time. I'll try to make it as quick as possible.'

A knock came at the door and my tea arrived.

'Station tea is never the best,' he said, brightly. 'But at least it's warm and wet.'

He settled himself opposite me and made the introductions.

'I'm DC Hanson, one of the investigating officers on the Martha Scott case. Sorry about the formality, but we need to take a witness statement for the official record as you're a material witness to a murder inquiry.'

I simply nodded.

'We understand you were the last person to assess Martha, and that your interview with her was recorded.' He twisted a ballpoint pen between his fingers as he spoke, his eyes never leaving mine. 'Dr Lister tells us that the interview was . . . er . . . eventful and that, as a result, Martha was scheduled to be moved to the secure unit.'

'That's right.'

I knew his disarming manner was designed to build rapport, but I was keeping my distance.

He flipped open a file. 'What exactly happened?'

'She suffered a severe abreaction and attempted to attack me. She was restrained by ward staff.'

'Were you hurt?' he asked, glancing up at me from beneath a blond fringe.

'Only my pride. I was dumped on the floor – nothing serious.'

'You weren't angry about the attack?'

I looked at him with genuine surprise.

'That's like me asking if you ever get cross when someone breaks the law.'

'What caused her to attack you?'

His question was straying into dangerous waters surrounding patient confidentiality.

'I was regressing her back to events that frightened her.'

'Which were what, exactly?' he pressed on.

'She felt she had done things she'd rather not recall.'

'What things?' he pushed.

I sat back in my chair, looking at him over the top of my clasped fingers. A pose that subliminally indicated intellect and authority. I wondered if he'd been taught that in his interview technique courses.

'What you're asking me violates confidentiality. I'm not sure I can divulge that just yet.'

'Your patient is dead, doctor,' Hanson said sharply. 'And in view of the circumstances, I'm sure she won't mind if you help us out.'

'I'm sure you're aware that, until I get authorisation for the release of her records, they remain confidential.'

He sighed, looking exasperated. 'She was cared for by Dr Lister, not you. So confidentiality isn't an issue, surely?'

I sighed, mirroring his exasperation. 'Detective, I'm sure you already know this, but I'll tell you anyway. Although I was advising Lister's team, my session with Martha is still confidential, as are any transcripts or recordings. And if they're going to become evidence in a murder trial, I'm going to do this by the book. So I want the relevant releases signed first.'

Hanson sat back, looking at me curiously.

'Surely you want to help us, doctor? You have the discretion to divulge what was said in that room without the relevant paperwork.'

I sat back in my chair, mirroring his use of space.

'But I'm choosing not to, for all the reasons I've explained. As Martha has no living relative, you can apply to the NHS Trust for the release of her records. Once they've done that, you can have all my notes.'

'Doctor, this is a murder investigation,' he said, tightly. 'I can get a court order to force you to release them if I have to.'

'Yes you can. Or you can have release forms signed by Martha's GP and Westwood Park. All of which will take far less time than getting a court order.' I leaned forward in my chair. 'I've been there before, detective, I know how it works.'

He stared at me for a moment and I could see the swing from annoyance to frustration before he abruptly stood, the chair scraping back as he dropped his pen onto the notepad. Then turned on his heel and left.

I sat listening to the silence in the room, imagining the expletives as he complained to his boss that I was being a hard-arsed bitch.

I was still bitter about the way I'd been treated over the weekend, left swinging in the harsh wind of press annihilation. One word from the police press office could have cut me down in an instant but they'd left me hanging.

I was so deep in thought I almost jumped when the door swung abruptly open and DC Hanson walked in, followed by another man I didn't recognise.

'This is DS Heslopp.'

Heslopp had a large belly that hung over the waistband of his shiny black trousers. His tie was pulled down and his top shirt button was undone. He slung his jacket across the back of the chair and took the seat opposite. Hanson sat on the edge of the table, one leg swinging like a pendulum.

I looked steadily at Heslopp. 'So, we've gone up a rank. Am I supposed to be flattered or intimidated?'

Heslopp launched straight into it.

'Where were you last night, Dr McCready?'

'At home.'

'Alone?'

'I am old enough to be home alone.'

I couldn't ignore the churning in my stomach and the feeling that something nasty was coming.

'What time did you get back home?'

I didn't miss the word 'back', which implied I had been out. As interview techniques went, it was pretty blunt.

'I hadn't been out to come *back* from anywhere,' I said, pointedly. Finally my patience came to an end. 'What's this all about? I thought I was here just to make a witness statement? This is beginning to sound like I'm a suspect.'

Heslopp simply stared back at me.

'We have to follow every line of enquiry, doctor. One of your patients has been murdered. You were the last person to interview her and she tried to attack you. We wouldn't be doing our job if we didn't ask you where you were at the time she was killed.'

'I deal with violent offenders every day of my working life, Detective Sergeant Heslopp. To think that you even *consider* this a legitimate line of enquiry is ludicrous.'

He sat back in his chair and regarded me silently for a moment, before leaning forward again, assaulting me with tobacco-tainted breath.

'Are you refusing to answer the question, doctor?'

'Am I being charged with anything?'

'No. We simply want to eliminate the possibility that you could have seen Martha after she left Westwood Park and before she was murdered.'

My mind was racing.

Both men sat silently, waiting for me to say something. I decided to pull down the shutters. If I had to play the game, I'd be clinical about it.

'You had police officers stationed outside my house Friday night and into Saturday morning. I'm sure if you check, they'll tell you I didn't leave.'

'We will.'

'I walked my dog across the fields during Saturday and spoke to my neighbour, George Theakston. I worked in my office and took calls from family and my secretary telling me that the news on David Woodhouse was breaking. I watched that for most of the day and went to bed.'

'That was Saturday night?' Heslopp asked. Hanson was writing it all down.

'Yes. Then Sunday I was alone at the farm. Some office work then walked the dog. I got back around four o'clock. I had calls from various people telling me about the press article, so I went to the newsagent to get a paper –'

'Which newsagent?' Hanson asked – his pen hovered over the paper as he paused in his note-taking.

'Kingsberry main street.'

'Then what?'

'I took the paper back to the farm, read it and took a call from my secretary.'

'What time was that?'

'Around five.'

'What was the call about?'

'Suing the editor of the newspaper and possibly the West Yorkshire Police for libel!' I let the sentence hang for a moment before continuing. 'Because of their inference that my profile cost Julie Lamont her life.'

I stared pointedly at Heslopp, who had no trouble meeting my eyes. 'When we all know it was Lizzie Taylor-Caine's profile that was at fault. That's why the SIO asked *me* to produce a profile he could actually work with.'

'Isn't it true you have a relationship with that SIO, doctor, and he was just doing you a favour by bringing you into the investigation?'

'What favour would that be?' I raised my eyebrows. 'Getting me out of bed to see a mutilated corpse? Or perhaps working for free?'

'Doctor, I –'

'Or the favour of not coming to my defence when I got hung out to dry at the press conference? Maybe *Hoyle's* relationship with Taylor-Caine explains why he's covering her arse by exposing mine?'

Heslopp had finally heard enough. He sighed heavily. 'OK, doctor. Let's leave that for now and move on to Sunday night . . .'

'Yes, let's.' I was determined not to be rattled. 'After arranging with my secretary to instruct our legal team, I had an early night. I was woken at 5.30 this morning by you and . . .' I stretched my arms to encompass our surroundings '. . . here we are.'

'We couldn't reach you on any of your numbers. Perhaps because you weren't there at all?'

'No. Because I unplugged my office line and turned off my mobile – the press were ringing them off the hook and I wanted some peace. If you'd tried my home number, you would have reached me.'

He flicked through the file. 'We don't have your home number listed.'

'I know.' I smiled, tightly. 'I only give it to friends and family.'

'What about DCI Ferguson?' he said, sarcastically. 'Does *he* have it?'

'Yes. Did you think to ask him for it?'

Heslopp looked down at his notes rather than at me and I could see the muscles bunching in his jaw.

'So at approximately 3 a.m. you were in bed – alone?'

'Correct. Is that when Martha was murdered?'

'The pathologist estimates her time of death at approximately 3 a.m., yes.'

I tried to look bored by the whole thing, but my heart rate was off the scale.

'Before you ask, I couldn't have met up with Martha earlier. By my reckoning, when she absconded from Westwood, I was with DCI Ferguson in Shipley telling him about the boatyard. After that I had police stationed outside my house and they can vouch for my whereabouts.'

'But you *were* alone all day Sunday?'

'What exactly are you implying?' My tone was as tight as my nerves. 'That I arranged for Martha to abscond? Then met her on Sunday and stabbed her to death? Do you mind telling me *why* I would want to do any of that?'

'She *did* attack you.' It was Hanson who spoke.

I turned my most withering glare towards him, gratified to see him look down at his notes.

'If I murdered every sick patient who'd attacked me in my career, there would be a trail of bodies that would clog up the M62! If you are seriously considering that I might have – then arrest me. But if not, I suggest we end this farce and I'll be on my way.'

Heslopp opened his mouth to say something when the door opened and a PC stuck his head around the door. 'Boss, need a word.'

Heslopp and Hanson left the room.

Chapter Twenty-One

7 August – Fordley Police Station

I had often sat in the observation room across the corridor, advising interviewing officers on the type of questioning to use on any given suspect. I never imagined I would ever be on *this* side of the glass.

I jumped as the door opened and the constable who had brought me to the station appeared again.

'Your brief's here to see you, doctor.'

Brief? I waited for a second, expecting a duty solicitor.

I've never been so relieved in my life to see Jen walk in with a man I took to be the solicitor. I must have looked shell-shocked because Jen took charge.

'Jo.' She brushed past Hanson and Heslopp who had also come in. 'This is James Turner from Fosters. I called them as soon as I knew you'd been brought in here.'

I accepted Turner's outstretched hand. His gold cufflinks flashed as he delivered a firm handshake. The sharp, dark suit and crisp shirt oozed success; the whole image of affluence carried on a subtle waft of expensive cologne. His smile was confident and his piercing blue eyes met mine easily.

'I'm from the criminal law division based in Manchester.'

'Highest paid bloody defence lawyer in the country,' Heslopp half muttered under his breath. Hanson looked more uncomfortable by the minute.

'Only because I'm the best.' Turner grinned broadly. 'And now, if it's all the same to you, gentlemen, I'll speak to my client in private.'

He ushered Jen to a chair and pushed the door closed with the back of his heel, hefting his briefcase onto the table.

'Jen, how did you know what was happening, and to call Mr Turner?'

'James, please.' Those disarming blue eyes almost made me forget my train of thought.

'I couldn't get hold of you so I called Callum. Couldn't get him either so I called the station, thought maybe Callum had brought you down here. The duty sergeant told me you'd been brought in regarding the Martha Scott murder.'

She watched as James arranged his legal pad and Montblanc pen on the table.

'I'd just finished transcribing that spooky recording of your interview with her on Thursday. To hear she was dead and that they'd dragged you in as a material witness ... I was going to call Fosters anyway about the press conference and the Sunday papers, so it made sense to tell them about all this as well. James took my call.'

'Just lucky I was on call. I'm normally based in London, but I'm here temporarily to recruit for the new Manchester office. So I picked up the case.'

'I didn't ask for a solicitor,' I said. 'Because I didn't think I needed one. They said I was here to give a witness statement – not as a suspect.'

'You are,' James said simply.

He twisted the top off his pen and scribbled some notes onto the bright yellow legal pad.

'The duty sergeant gave me the details when I arrived and I've also had a brief chat with Handsome and Gristle out there.'

I laughed, despite everything.

'The theory they put to you in there has no foundation that I can see. Their supposition that you might have met with Martha is flawed and you're alibied by their own officers. But I don't think for one minute that's what this is about.'

He paused to take a sip of coffee. I opened my mouth, but he silenced me with a commanding wave of his hand and I glimpsed the tough persona that lurked beneath the polished charm. I bet he could be a complete bastard to face in court. Suddenly, I was more than glad he was on my side.

The heat rising from my cup felt comforting on my face. 'Then what *do* you think this is about?'

James looked at me with those piercing eyes again. 'I take it you *can* prove yours was the correct profile in the towpath killings?'

'Of course we can,' Jen bristled. 'We have an electronic trail of it being uploaded to the server in Fordley after it was written.'

'They haven't brought me in about the towpath killings,' I said. 'This is about Martha.'

'You think so?' He looked at me steadily. 'Because whoever authored the *incorrect* profile has far more motive to discredit you and distract the press away from how the police handled the Woodhouse case.'

The theory rattled around the room as we all absorbed it.

Finally, I shook my head. 'Lizzie Taylor-Caine authored the other profile and, much as I despise the woman, I can't believe for one moment that she'd play these games.'

He smiled. 'But she's certainly capable of constructing a scenario around Martha's death to rattle you. And at the same time demonstrate to the press and the public that you are definitely *not* part of the investigation team – and *not* getting any special treatment.'

Jen and I looked at each other in shocked silence.

'You can't be serious!' Jen was incredulous.

James grinned. 'Maybe I'm just cynical? Shocking, I know, but I have been accused of it before – makes for a good defence counsel.'

He sipped his coffee before continuing.

'This weekend the press got out of hand. Hoyle would have kept quiet about the two conflicting profiles, but you'd been photographed at the scene and the picture splashed all over the papers. The police are being criticised for overspending on the budget while not achieving their targets. How bad would it look if it came out that not only did they use an external psychologist over their own, but that *you* produced an accurate profile while theirs didn't? Hoyle had to do some damage limitation.'

'It might even be asked whether they could justify keeping Taylor-Caine on the payroll,' Jen murmured, almost to herself.

'So,' James continued, 'maybe they could pressure you enough into not kicking up a stink about being blamed in the media – and not handing your profile to the papers.'

'And they dragged me down here to achieve that?' I was still struggling to grasp that it could be a possibility.

'Well, it *is* reasonable for them to question you about Martha as you were one of the last people to see her alive,' James pointed out, with annoying logic. 'But no harm in freaking you out at the same time by painting you as a witness rather than an advisor for the benefit of the press. Plus, once they'd kept you here long enough over this line of questioning, Hoyle may have hoped you'd be rattled enough that you'd just agree to suppress your original profile. Which I'm sure would have come up at some point later today. That would solve Hoyle's problem.' He raised an eyebrow with the same handsome precision with which he seemed to do everything else. 'Wouldn't you agree?'

'I suppose so.' Even to myself I sounded less than convinced.

'Word on the grapevine,' he said, clipping the top back onto his pen, 'is that DCI Ferguson is in hot water for bringing you in without authorisation from Hoyle. Not to mention the fact that you were almost suicidal in putting yourself in the killer's way without police backup and Hoyle only found out about that after the fact. If this gets any messier, it'll look like left hand doesn't know what right hand is doing and Hoyle, in my estimation, will do anything to prevent the force looking so fragmented on his watch.'

I rested my chin on my fist and watched as he packed his expensive-looking briefcase.

'What grapevine do you use that can tell you what's going on around here?'

He grinned and winked at me as he hefted his case from the table.

'The kind that make us the most effective criminal law firm in the country,' he said, enigmatically. 'So I wouldn't be surprised if you don't hear from Ferguson for a while. Think he's probably being kept away from you until the press furore settles down.'

My head was pounding. I was vaguely aware of Jen clearing away cups as James left to speak to Heslopp and I sat staring at the coffee stains on the table, trying to order my thoughts.

A moment later James was back. 'OK, ladies, we can get out of here whenever you're ready.'

I looked up at him, feeling suddenly bone-weary. 'What have they said?'

'Let's just say I've made it go away for now. I've confirmed the NHS Trust should have releases for Martha's records and all your notes will be released to them through our office tomorrow.' He grinned down at me. 'Always assuming you *do* want me to look after this for you?'

'Yes, of course,' I muttered, wondering just how expensive the most expensive criminal lawyer in the country would be.

'I'll draft a statement to the media for a retraction. It's written in the same vague terms that Hoyle's statement was at the press conference, so all faces should be saved.'

'Hang on a minute,' I said, suddenly irritated. 'What if I don't *want* to let them off the hook over the Woodhouse profile?'

His strong hand was in the small of my back, confidently steering me towards the door.

'Believe me, you're not letting them off the hook. You're getting the retraction you deserve and restoring your reputation.'

'And if I want to hand my profile to the press to show how accurate it was? What then?'

'Then you would be operating out of ego, rather than common sense,' he said, irritatingly. I stopped in my tracks, forcing him to stop abruptly beside me.

'This is *not* about ego.'

'Then it's revenge. Either way, you're above all that and if you want a logical reason for *not* doing it, the Woodhouse case is sub judice. You'd be prejudicing his case by revealing details to the press before his trial. And I know that once you've had time to get some sleep and think about it, you'll decide that would be unprofessional.'

I looked at him for a moment before saying quietly, 'I'll bet you're a complete bastard in court.'

He laughed. 'Absolutely. So be thankful that right now, I'm *your* complete bastard.'

He was still smiling as we opened the door into the corridor. Jen went off to get the car and I looked down the corridor to see Hanson coming out of the observation room.

I ducked away from James' guiding arm and strode down the corridor.

'Jo!'

I could sense Hanson following me but ignored him, pushing the door open with a sweep of my arm.

Lizzie Taylor-Caine looked up, startled, her hand knocking over the coffee cup on the table. Opposite her, Hoyle jumped up to avoid the spreading pool of liquid.

I could feel James arrive at my shoulder just as Taylor-Caine rounded on me.

'So how does it feel to be on the other side of the glass?' She almost curled her lip.

Hoyle shot her an uncomfortable look. 'Lizzie, I really don't think –'

'I might have known you'd want to be here for this.' I was contemptuous.

'Writing books and appearing on TV like a celeb doesn't make you Teflon, McCready,' she spat, unable to keep the venom out of her tone.

'I think track records around here speak for themselves, don't you?' James said with irritating calmness.

Taylor-Caine was prevented from stepping towards us by Hoyle placing a hand on her shoulder.

I watched her fuming in front of me and suddenly found her amusing.

'Political manoeuvring to cover up incompetence. Class act, love. You tipped off the press about the towpath scene on Thursday, didn't you? That's how they got there so fast.'

The rising colour in her cheeks told me I was right. Hoyle shot her a look that told me they'd be having a conversation about this later.

'You were expecting to be photographed there, weren't you? But Callum spoiled all the fun by getting me out there first.' I looked at Hoyle. 'And you were pissed off because *you* wanted to justify her role in your pet project.'

He opened his mouth, then closed it. Taylor-Caine had no such restraint.

'*Screw you!*' She spat the words at me.

'You're not up to the job,' I bit back.

Heslopp barely suppressed his laughter. Hoyle looked furiously at her.

'Intellectual lightweight,' was my parting shot, as I turned on my heel and walked out.

James laughed quietly as we walked down the corridor. '"Intellectual lightweight", I like it. Might steal that to use in court sometime.'

'Be my guest,' I said through gritted teeth, not quite feeling the humour.

142

Chapter Twenty-Two

7 August – Kingsberry Farm

The clock above the Aga read 11 a.m. Jen had refused to leave me and we were on our fourth cup of tea as we sat in war council around my kitchen table.

'Now that Fosters are onto this, I think we should leave it to them.' She sounded tired.

'OK by me. I'm shattered. Feels like I haven't slept for days.'

'You probably haven't.' She squeezed my hand across the table. 'Why don't you go up and try to sleep?'

'Do you think that's the last I'll hear from Callum?'

I wanted her to be honest but dreaded the answer if she was. Why was it that now I thought it was probably over, I realised how much I didn't want it to be?

She shrugged. 'Who knows?' She squeezed my hand again. 'But if he's put off by Hoyle warning him away, then he doesn't deserve to have you.'

'Careful, Jen.' I gave her a weak smile. 'You're starting to sound like Mamma.'

'Thanks.' She grinned.

'Believe me, that's not a compliment.' I stretched. 'Look, I appreciate everything, but there's still some of your day off left. Feel bad keeping you away from family. I'll be fine if you want to get back?'

'Sure?'

'I'm sure.' I tried to stifle a yawn. 'I'm going to bed. I'll see you tomorrow at the office, OK?'

I waved her off on the drive and locked up the house. Harvey was snoring on his bed by the Aga, not having had much sleep himself with all the excitement.

The house was quiet as I settled down in bed. I stared at the shadows created by slim fingers of sunlight that sneaked around the edges of my blind to play across the ceiling.

Eventually my eyes felt gritty and I closed them.

Nightmares flickered bloody images across my mind: faceless women with gaping stab wounds, screaming and writhing, reached out to drag me down into swirling black depths of a horror I couldn't see or name.

I pulled my legs away, trying to escape their clawing hands, and suddenly sat bolt upright in bed with tangled bed sheets wrapped around my legs.

Sweat trickled down my neck and shoulders, matting my hair into a tangled mess. The room was in half darkness and the clock read 4 p.m. I pulled up the blind to watch dark, brooding clouds which, in the half-light, had the purple tinge of bruises as they scudded across a bleak skyline, announcing another thunderstorm on the way.

I was grateful for the cool water on my skin as I stepped into the shower. The events of the morning seemed a million miles away. I tried to order my thoughts, standing motionless under the powerful jets.

The house was unbearably hot and, after the cool shower, I couldn't face getting dressed. I pulled on my silk robe and went into the kitchen. I let Harvey out into the damp afternoon to do his business and then I made the obligatory mug of tea to take into the office.

The computer hummed into life behind me as I looked across the fields at the glowering thunderstorm approaching across the treetops. I entered my password – and ice ran through my body as I watched the screen in total horror.

Instead of the familiar wallpaper, an image of red fluid dripped in rivulets down the screen. Looking for all the world as though someone had just poured a can of red paint over it.

As I stared in frozen shock, black script scrolled across the dripping red background:

Jack's back . . . Jack's back . . . Jack's back . . .

The red gore gradually receded, pushed up by the appearance of a photograph, revealing itself one grainy line at a time. A harbinger of horror unfolding itself before my eyes: a pair of booted feet, pale white calves, a heavy skirt pushed up over white, bruised thighs. The picture continued its progress, saving the gruesome best for last. Torn flesh, gaping abdomen, exposed breasts slashed and barely recognisable as the body of a woman. A slender white neck, splashed with dark red blood and then her face . . . finally her face. Pale and still in death, like cold marble with wide, startled dead eyes staring at me.

The face of Martha Scott.

For an endless moment I stared in shock at the screen. Someone knew enough to send this to my personal computer and the implication of that clanged in my brain like a warning bell.

The voice of 'Jack' coming from Martha's mouth echoed from the grave to haunt me in my own home.

'. . . I can get out . . . I can leave her behind now . . .'

I struggled to comprehend what I was seeing.

If 'Jack' was just a construct of Martha's damaged mind, who had killed her? And who was sending me these images, claiming to be him?

A freezing shiver ran down my back as another, more chilling fact bubbled to the surface. There had been no one in that room except Martha and me. No one even knew about the existence of Jack except the two of us, and now Martha was dead and 'Jack' was sending me photographs of her mutilated corpse.

Unconsciously, my hand reached for the phone. I stared for a moment. Who was I going to call? 999? Jen? My mother? Everyone I knew had people they could call on in a crisis. Armies of friends. Legions of helpful acquaintances. I suddenly realised how limited my own options were. Who could I tell about this?

Automatically, my fingers began to punch out Callum's mobile number. Then I stopped. He had always been my go-to. The one person I could always trust. But he'd abandoned me – so now who?

I scanned the desk, spotting the business card I had dropped there earlier. I dialled the number, not sure how I'd even begin to explain.

'James?' I said

'Jo?'

I was still staring at the computer screen. Terrified that if I looked away, the image would disappear and no one would believe me.

'Jo, what's the matter?' His tone was concerned now. The worry in his voice shattered my numbness.

'Are you back in Manchester?'

'No, I'm still in Fordley.'

'Thank God! I need you at the farm, something's happened. Can you come? Now?'

'Are you all right?'

'I'm OK. It's – it's Martha. I can't explain over the phone, you need to see this.'

'Give me directions, I'm on my way.'

Chapter Twenty-Three

7 August – Kingsberry Farm

Twenty minutes later I opened the door to let James into my kitchen. He'd left his suit jacket hanging in the back of the car, removed his expensive silk tie and opened the top button of his collar. He looked more relaxed, but somehow just as professional as he had at Fordley police station.

His eyes conducted a quick swoop over my figure and it was only then that I realised I was still in my dressing gown. If he thought anything of it, he was too polite to say.

The sight of Harvey made him stop in his tracks, but after I made the usual introductions, Harvey finally allowed him into the house.

'Sorry, I'm not very good with dogs. They don't seem to like me.'

James skirted warily around Harvey and followed me to the office, our footsteps muffled on the thick carpet as we walked down the glass corridor. Neither of us spoke. It felt weird having a man – almost a complete stranger – with me in what seemed such an intimate way.

I indicated the computer. This was one slideshow that needed no introduction.

He sat in my chair, staring at the screen for a long moment. I sat on the corner of the desk, pulling the silk gown across my knees, and ran a hand through my hair, trying to smooth out my tangled thoughts.

'I logged on and this just appeared,' I said. 'I called you straight away.'

He nodded and looked back at the screen. 'So this wasn't an attachment? It just appeared?'

'Yes.'

'And you're sure this is Martha Scott?'

I nodded, not really wanting to look again into those dark, glassy eyes staring at me from the other side of life.

'Who's Jack?'

I slipped off the edge of the desk and walked over to the huge arched window that looked out across the darkening fields and scudding storm clouds.

I hesitated. 'You wouldn't believe me if I told you.'

'Try me.'

'Jack the Ripper.'

Chapter Twenty-Four

7 August – Kingsberry Farm

After listening to my story, James put a call in to his office, followed by another to Fordley police station. His eyes held mine with an intensity that was bordering on uncomfortable.

'We need to find out who produced that image and how they managed to send it to your computer. The police will get their computer specialists onto it.'

'Have *you* got any ideas?'

'*Me?*' He snorted back a laugh. 'I thank God every day that my profession still take notes by hand on a legal pad. What I know about technology, you could fit on the back of a stamp.'

I looked back at the image. 'At first I thought it was a crime scene photo, but it's not.'

'How do you know?'

'I've seen enough of them in my time to know the difference.'

'I'm impressed.'

'Don't be. I stared at the damn thing long enough. Believe me, it wasn't the first thing that occurred to me when I saw it.'

'What was?'

He was in professional mode now. Questioning me as my defence counsel would. I didn't mind. In fact, it was a relief to begin taking this thing apart, without the emotion that had hit the pit of my stomach when I'd first seen it.

'How could this "Jack", the creation of a damaged mind, become a physical entity that could commit a murder?'

'He can't. Jack the Ripper can't come back after over a hundred years and kill again.'

He had finally said out loud what I hadn't dared. The outrageous possibility that I had spoken to Jack the Ripper through Martha, and that, true to 'his' promise, he'd freed himself and made her his first victim.

'Then, as there was only me and Martha in that room, how does Martha's murderer know about Jack and what was said during that session?'

I could see he was processing all the possibilities. He frowned. 'Who else heard the recording or saw the transcripts?'

'Me, Jen and Martha are the only people who know what went on in that room. And if Fordley CID's performance this morning is anything to go by, I'll give you three guesses which one of us is the most likely to pique their interest.' I glanced at the clock on the wall. 'Speaking of which, they'll be here any minute. I should go put some clothes on.'

He grinned. 'Not on my account.'

Surprisingly, I felt myself begin to blush. 'Does flirting with your clients come with the fee, or do you charge extra?'

He laughed. 'Only if it doesn't work. But if they agree to come for dinner, I write it off.'

I looked back at him and couldn't help but meet his smile.

'Just how am I supposed to respond to that?'

'Agree to come to dinner?'

'The way my luck's running, I'll probably be spending the night banged up in Fordley nick.'

He shook his head. 'No, you won't.' He sounded confident.

I opened my mouth to argue but he waved away my protest, his eyes holding a different kind of intensity this time.

'Trust me, Jo.' His tone was gentle. 'You *are* a material witness, but receiving that image makes you a victim in this. I'll insist you've been put through enough. No need to drag you down to the station.' His eyes held mine just a fraction too long. 'I'll take care of everything.'

I was distracted as I heard tyres on the gravel drive. As I swung open the door, standing there was the last person I'd expected to see.

Chapter Twenty-Five

7 August – Kingsberry Farm

'Callum!'

He was leaning against the door frame, his face weary and drawn as though he hadn't slept much. I noticed he was wearing the same clothes as when I'd last seen him.

He nodded his head towards James' car and then stared pointedly at my dressing gown. 'Seems like I've come at a bad time. Got company?'

His assumption infuriated me, but I bit back the denial and decided to let him think the worst. Without a word, I gestured him inside.

As he crossed the porch, I could almost smell the testosterone firing between him and James. I couldn't decide whether it was embarrassing or flattering. I stood between the two of them, feeling like a referee at a stag-rutting.

'Callum, this is James Turner from Fosters solicitors. James, this is –'

'DCI Ferguson. We've met in court.' He extended his hand to Callum, who took it somewhat reluctantly, I thought. 'It was a while ago, maybe you don't remember?'

'I remember.' I was surprised at the venom in his voice; renowned for keeping his personal feelings to himself, it was unusual. 'Three months' work to nail a bastard that took you thirty minutes to get off.'

James sat down, shrugging his shoulders. 'If it's any consolation, he only walked because of a technicality. Nothing wrong with the policing. The lab let you down.'

Callum took the seat opposite, his blue eyes locking with James'.

'Not to worry, eh?' Callum's Scottish accent could be so deceptively soft. 'He was killed a year later. Gangland shooting. So I suppose justice was served in the end.'

I couldn't stand this any longer. 'If you don't mind, do you think we could deal with the situation at hand?'

Callum looked up. 'Sorry, Jo. I suppose I owe you an explanation?'

'Damn right,' I exclaimed, unconcerned by James' presence. 'Don't tell me you didn't know about the press conference Hoyle gave?'

'I heard about it –'

I wasn't in the mood to listen. 'He hung me out to dry and the Sunday papers had a field day with the photo they took of you and me at the scene.'

'I know, Jo, listen –'

But I wasn't about to listen, not for a minute.

'So where were you, Callum? When Hoyle paraded Taylor-Caine at the press conference and admitted there were two profiles, two and two made five! The tabloids crucified me, for God's sake!'

Callum held up his hand and, only because I needed to draw breath, I let him get a word in.

'I know how it looks, but it wasn't like that.'

'Then how was it, exactly?' My tone cauterised as it cut.

Callum sighed, raking a hand through his hair. He looked down at the table. I wasn't sure whether it was a device to help him order his thoughts, or discomfort at having to do this in front of James Turner.

'After I left you, I didn't see daylight for forty-eight hours. As soon as I got a break, Hoyle collared me. To say he roasted me would be an understatement.'

'About bringing me in to run a profile?'

'That and more. Taking you down to the scene really pissed him off and the fact that you did it for free almost made it worse! Me calling in personal favours instead of sticking to protocol.'

'So you decided to leave me in the lurch?' He opened his mouth to protest, but I cut across him. 'What's wrong, Callum? Bad career move to be associated with me, was it?'

He stood abruptly, his chair scraping across the tiled floor.

'OK!' he shouted. 'Either you listen or I may as well just walk out now.'

A tiredness flitted across his face and he suddenly looked bone-weary. When he spoke again, his voice was quiet. 'For God's sake, do you *really* believe that?'

My eyes settled on his and I fell deeper into them, as though, if I tried hard enough, I could see inside his head. Another chair scraped as James rose to his feet. Without looking at us he began to gather cups off the table and walked over to the sink, putting his back to us to take himself out of this intimate arena.

I turned and walked into the living room. I felt the warmth of Callum a fraction before his hands rested on my shoulders and he slowly turned me around. I had to look up to meet his eyes and his breath was warm on my face.

'Hoyle was totally pissed off, but there wasn't much he could do. Everyone knew that *your* profile was the one that got us the result. I could make that public knowledge – and if I'd been there, Jo, I would have. But Hoyle made sure I didn't have advance knowledge about the press conference. He made sure I didn't see daylight over the weekend. I had to go to Blackburn to coordinate things with the team there and I've been buried in the back of bloody beyond trawling through Woodhouse's life. Haven't even had a chance to change my clothes – it's a wonder Harvey can't smell me from here!'

'So they don't have phones in Blackburn then?'

'I *tried*. Your mobile was off and the office phone wasn't answered. I called the house but that must have been while you were at the station.' His eyes held mine as tightly as he grasped my hands. 'Please, Jo, give me a break! You know I would never drop you in it for career reasons, for Christ's sake.'

It was only when I let my breath out that I realised I had been holding it. Suddenly I couldn't hold his gaze any longer. I looked down at the carpet.

'This weekend I felt so alone with it all.'

He held my hands tighter. 'I know. I'm sorry.'

'Tea?' It was James, poking his head round the door.

I took the chance to pull back from Callum. 'Please.'

Callum turned back to me when James had gone.

'You know I only got the towpath killings because I was the SIO on call?' I nodded. 'Well, Hoyle took the chance to replace me over the weekend.'

'He can't do that! At the eleventh hour? When *you've* done all the work?'

Callum shrugged. 'He can and he has. His way of rapping my knuckles, not letting me get the public recognition for the collar.'

He moved to look out of the window. 'Shot himself in the foot now, though, hasn't he?'

'How do you mean?'

He turned to look at me. 'Because when the shout came in about Martha's killing, I was the SIO to pick it up.'

'And he *let* you!'

Callum shrugged. 'It's legitimately mine this time. He *could* reassign it, but he'd have to explain that to the hierarchy. In any case, I told him I'd already set some inquiries in motion about Martha's time in Manchester and the stabbings she talked to you about, so I was already involved.'

'That simple?' I sounded sceptical.

He shrugged again. 'No. But he did make a point of asking whether we were having a relationship. If we were, then he *would* have reassigned it.'

I drew a shaky breath and tried to sound unemotional.

'You obviously said we weren't?'

'Well, we're not – are we?' he said, softly.

I felt my emotions turning to ice.

'No. I don't suppose we are.'

James nudged the door open with his foot and came in juggling three mugs of tea. He was keeping one eye on Harvey, who was following him around, growling softly.

'That dog really doesn't like me,' he said.

'You'll be fine,' I said. 'He's been fed today.' The joke seemed lost on him. 'I'll go pull some clothes on.' My voice sounded brittle, even to me. 'You show Callum what he needs to see.'

Chapter Twenty-Six

7 August – Kingsberry Farm

Callum and James were staring intently at the gruesome image that continued to scroll down my screen.

'The techies will track this,' Callum said, as I entered the office. 'Though I doubt his IP address goes back to the eighteen-hundreds.'

'So how did he get my personal email address here?' I said, to no one in particular.

'You don't give this address out then?' It was James' turn to ask.

I shook my head. 'The office in Fordley, but not here.'

'Who has *this* address?'

It wasn't a very long list. 'Jen, of course. My publisher, Marissa, in London.'

'Anyone else?'

'You and Callum of course, and Alex –'

'Who's Alex?' James asked.

'My son. He's a student and he travels a lot. I have to make it easy for him to get hold of me.'

James snorted. 'So this one's in the public domain as well, then?'

I bridled at the inference that Alex would be stupid enough to give out my private details.

'Come on, Jo.' He spread his hands in a gesture of appeal. 'A student?'

'My son,' I said sharply, 'has been brought up in the knowledge that I deal with some of the most dangerous criminals in the justice system, and he isn't in the habit of giving my private contact details out to *anyone*.'

Callum shot James a conspiratorial look. 'Careful, counsellor – dangerous ground.'

I glared at Callum, who simply grinned and looked back at the computer screen.

'This isn't a police crime scene photo. Not sure we've even got those pinned up in the incident room yet.'

'So, taken by the killer then?' James asked.

'Or someone with him,' I added.

Callum shot me a look. 'Is an accomplice likely?'

I hesitated, trying to stay objective, though it wasn't easy when the killer had brought his crime right into my home. 'Too early to say. I need more information. You know the form, Callum.'

He sat back, stretching his long legs under the desk, his hands easing a knot in the nape of his neck.

'I can give you what we've got so far.'

He stood up from the desk and walked over to the arched window, staring out at the outline of the woods against a purple-blue sky.

'She was found at 3.30 this morning by a taxi driver picking up a fare from George House,' Callum said to his own reflection in the now-darkening glass. 'That's a block of council flats. He waited five minutes but when no one came, he went in. The lift was out of order, so he took the stairs.' Callum turned from the window and looked again at the image on the computer. 'Found her lying on the first-floor landing, just as she looks there. His call was logged at 3.35. We're conducting door-to-door interviews at the flats, but so far it appears everyone is deaf, dumb and blind. There's been a blanket put over the press – it's a media blackout until we know more.'

James was looking at the image again, his lips pursed thoughtfully. 'Why you?' he asked, quietly.

'What?'

'Why has the killer sent this to you? What's the connection?'

'Because I spoke to Jack. I called him out and he made Martha his first victim and sent me the image to prove it was him.'

Callum shot me an incredulous look. 'You're not serious?'

'I set him free. Martha's death is my fault and he either wants me to feel guilty or he's thanking me.'

They looked at each other with uneasy expressions. But I wasn't really directing my comments to them. I was tracking possibilities. The way I worked through the criminal mind. Processing the often illogical, impossible mental leaps murderers make to validate what they do and who they do it to.

Somewhere in the mental clutter would be the answers I needed to find out who Jack was and why he had chosen Martha, and now me, to be players in his sadistic fantasy.

Callum pulled up a chair and sat beside me, his voice quiet. The demeanour of a man speaking to a madwoman.

'Jo, Jack the Ripper lived over a hundred years ago. This is a modern-day murderer who sends email, for Christ's sake.' He raked a weary hand through his silver hair. 'And *whoever* he is, I'll sure as hell stake my pension on the fact that he's *not* Jack the Ripper.'

I turned to meet his eyes. 'He believes he is,' I said, simply. 'And if that's his reality, then that's what I have to work with, because it's only when I get inside his head that I'll be able to see what he sees, think like he thinks.'

James visibly shuddered as he gestured a thumb towards the computer.

'Who'd want to live for one second inside the head of whoever did that?'

'*I* want to,' I said. 'Otherwise he's going to keep on killing.'

My house was quiet again.

The police had taken my computer away for examination. Callum confirmed I wouldn't be questioned down at the station and James had finally taken no for an answer to his question about dinner.

Until the post-mortem report and results from the CCTV from Westwood Park were all back, there was little to be done, but the thought of sitting and waiting was driving me insane. I decided to go to my library in the office and see if I could research some of the threads that were beginning to weave into the murder.

The atmosphere wrapped around me like a comforting blanket as I went in and switched on the lamps.

The whole left wall was floor-to-ceiling shelves. The volumes covered every topic on murder, mayhem and monstrous minds. Alex had once jokingly called it the 'psycho shelf'.

If a murder had been committed since documents had been kept, I would have some reference to it. From the Borgias to the Boston Strangler, the Yorkshire Ripper to the Zodiac Killer, I had an urge to collect, read and research it. A collection of material, photographs and post-mortem reports that most people would not want to share their homes with.

The crimes and times of Jack the Ripper were something I had plenty of material on, having covered it in my first book half a decade ago. With a glass of wine and a notepad on my knee, I trawled back through the terror of the East End of London a hundred and thirty years ago. If my instincts were right, it was a truly terrifying prediction of what was to come.

Chapter Twenty-Seven

8 August – Fordley Therapy Practice

Callum raised an eyebrow as I dumped a pile of notes and reference books onto my desk. 'Christ, it would take me years to trawl through that lot. How come you can read so fast?'

'I don't move my lips.' I picked up the notes I'd made the night before. 'Do you know there are more books written about Jack the Ripper than all the American presidents combined?'

'Probably because he's more interesting.' Callum glanced at my scrawled notes. 'You should have been a doctor – your handwriting's shit.'

'You should have been a policeman with powers of observation like that.'

He sat back in his chair, stretching his long legs beneath my desk.

'So, what did this lot tell you?'

'That there are as many theories of "whodunnit" now as there were a hundred years ago. But instead of worrying about the original killings, we need to work out who's behind the new one.'

'And?'

'I don't have enough information to do a profile, do I? You haven't shared the post-mortem report, crime scene photographs, etcetera. Need me to go on?'

He ignored the dig.

'But you *will* have something.' He flicked the pile of papers with his finger. 'I know you well enough to know you won't wait to be invited.'

'Jack himself emailed me a private invitation – remember?'

Jen chose this moment to open the door and come in with two mugs of tea. I looked back at Callum as she left.

'Where am I with this?' I asked, quietly.

Callum looked at me for a long moment, before drawing a deep breath. 'You're involved up to your neck. The killer saw to that when he emailed you the snapshot of his little hobby.'

'I mean professionally?'

'You can't be involved officially. You're a material witness.'

I opened my mouth to interrupt him, but he raised his hand to cut across me.

'But you and I both know that you can't help it.' He nodded towards the pile of notes on my desk. 'It's what you do – right?'

I couldn't help smiling. 'Right.'

'He emailed you. So it could be someone you know. Maybe a patient or former patient? Let's face it, with your clientele, we have most of the country's criminally insane to go at for starters.'

The photograph of Martha, sent by Jack, flashed through my mind.

'This isn't anyone I've dealt with before,' I said, quietly.

'How can you be so sure?'

I looked up into those perceptive blue eyes, my mind still trying to piece together what had begun last night.

'I've never dealt with an MO like this before.'

'So?' He shrugged. 'Maybe he's changed his MO?'

I shook my head. 'That doesn't happen very often. In fact, hardly ever. A savvy killer might change certain aspects of his crimes to fool the police, but certain signatures always surface somewhere.'

'Signatures?'

'Any behaviour done just to satisfy his psychological need is called a "signature". Repeated patterns by the same offender become his signature.'

'And they can never change it?'

I thought for a moment. 'The Zodiac Killer in America killed for over a decade because he continually changed his MO. With hindsight, we can pinpoint certain trademarks of his today. So, yes, it's happened, but with what we know now, I think we'd pick up personal signatures a lot faster.'

I sat back in my chair and took a sip of tea. 'His choice of victim, location, some aspect of the way he kills, or what he does with the body. Posing them in some way or thinking about the way they'll be found and what effect that has on the person who discovers the body.'

Callum was studying me intently.

'I don't believe I've dealt with this killer before, Callum. But I can tell you one thing for sure . . .'

'What's that?'

'That if this is what I think it is, we'll be dealing with him again.' I hesitated a heartbeat before dropping the bombshell. 'By the thirty-first of this month, to be precise.'

He stared at me for a long moment, becoming very still.

'How come?'

'Because I think our man is a copycat of Jack the Ripper.'

He watched me before slowly shaking his head. 'I think you're letting this so-called "conversation" with "Jack" affect your judgement, Jo. At this stage we can't make that leap. This could be a one-off.'

'Tell me what you've got first,' I countered. 'If it fits with what I found last night, I'll give you the rest.'

He pulled a preliminary report from his inside pocket.

'Martha Scott, aged twenty-two. Found on the first-floor landing of George House on Manchester Road. Pathologist estimates time of death at around 2.30 to 3 a.m. Body found by a taxi driver at 3.30, who said she still felt warm, so that fits with the pathologist's estimate. Cause of death, probably multiple stab wounds. At the moment, he's unsure which was the fatal blow. But you can pretty much take your pick. Out of thirty-nine stab wounds, her left lung was penetrated five times, her right lung in two places. There was one stab wound to the heart and five to her liver. Her spleen was severed in two places and she had been stabbed in the stomach six times.'

'Type of weapon?'

'Two weapons involved. Looks like a thin, short-bladed knife inflicted most of the wounds, but a strong, longer-bladed knife was also used.'

'Anything about the killer?'

'So far, blood splatters on the walls are in an upward direction, indicating the wounds were inflicted while she was on the ground. He also thinks the killer sat over her to inflict the wounds, and the shape and direction of the blows would indicate a right-handed killer.'

I thought for a moment. 'You said cause of death was *probably* multiple stab wounds?'

He glanced back at his notes. '"Probably" because there was extensive bruising to the face and some on the neck. Plus no sign of defence wounds. Doubt she just lay down and waited for him to stab her.' He pulled out another sheet of notes. 'I asked Frank to get some info on the original Ripper murders.'

'Frank?' I asked.

'Frank Heslopp. I believe you've met.'

'Oh, the obnoxious, foul-smelling misogynist?'

'You obviously caught him on a good day!' Callum grinned. 'I asked him to look at the original murders of 1888 and tell me about the first one. I had a feeling you'd be looking at similarities, so thought I'd pre-empt you.'

'Really?' I raised an eyebrow. 'I love it when you try to outwit me, chief inspector.'

He grinned. 'If you think this killer is replicating the Victorian murders, how closely would he stick to the originals?'

'As closely as possible.'

'Well, I can tell you he hasn't. You're barking up the wrong tree, Jo.'

I smiled. 'You'd better put me straight then.'

He leaned back in a gesture of cocksure confidence. I savoured the moment and the pose. It would make my counter thrust all the more delicious when it came.

'Jack the Ripper's first victim was Polly Nichols. She was found in Buck's Row in Whitechapel at 3.40 a.m. on the thirty-first of August. She had a circular bruise on the left side of the face caused by pressure of fingers. On the left side was a circular incision, which completely severed all the tissue down to the vertebrae, almost decapitating her. Jagged wounds to the abdomen, which opened her up. Three or four similar cuts running downwards on the right side, all of which were caused by a knife that had been used violently and downwards.'

He looked across to me as he finished.

'Martha's throat wasn't cut. She wasn't killed on the same date or in a similar location; she had far more injuries than Polly – and although she was stabbed in the stomach, it wasn't ripped open in what became his classic style and gave him his name. Most of Martha's injuries were to her chest and upper body rather than lower body.'

The night before I had written out a list in two columns. On the left were details of the original Ripper murder in Whitechapel. On the right, corresponding details of Martha's murder.

I looked at my notes. 'Pick up any book on Jack the Ripper and most will cite Polly Nichols as the first victim of his series – what became known as the "canonical five". However, recent studies allow us to go back and look at other unsolved murders in the same area at the time. It's generally accepted by researchers today that it's more likely to be six. Search hard enough and some say he could have done nine or even fifteen.'

'So think of a number and double it, right? Where does that leave us then?'

'I've always agreed with other experts that it's six.' I looked across at Callum, who was watching me in anticipation. 'And if you go with the six, Polly Nichols is number two.'

172

'Then who's number one?'

I pushed the sheet of paper over to him. He glanced down at it without picking it up.

Victim:	Martha Tabram
Date:	7 August 1888
Time of death:	2.30 a.m.
Body found:	First floor landing of George Yard Buildings.
Discovered by:	Alfred Crow – licensed cab driver.
Cause of death:	Loss of blood through thirty-nine stab wounds to the trunk and upper body. Wounds inflicted while the body was prone.
Wounds:	Left lung penetrated five times; right lung twice. One stab wound to the heart; liver stabbed five times. Spleen severed in two places; six stab wounds to the stomach. Eighteen other wounds, scratches or minor flesh wounds.
Weapon:	A penknife and a long, strong-bladed knife, possibly a bayonet or dagger.
Killer:	Right-handed. Killed the victim where she was found.
Identity:	Unknown.

Callum slowly looked up from the list. 'Shit!'

'Polly Nichols was number two – and she was killed twenty-four days later.'

When he looked at me, his eyes were filled with emotion I couldn't quite read.

'So the only way we know that your theory fits, is to wait for another murder in three weeks' time? You'll be pleased to be proved right then?'

I was shocked by the slur. 'I may deal with cold-blooded psychopaths, Callum, but it doesn't make *me* one. I don't want the body count to rise any more than you do. I'd love to be wrong – but I'm not!'

'Shit!' was all he said.

Chapter Twenty-Eight

21 August – Fordley Police Station

It had been two weeks since my last meeting with Callum. In the intervening period the team had been following up dozens of actions and lines of enquiry and I'd been invited to join them at their latest briefing. As I entered the room, the team began to settle. A few familiar faces nodded in recognition as I followed Callum to the front. Callum had called me the day before to tell me that when they had applied to the Home Office for an expert on the Victorian Ripper murders, my name had been put forward. Despite being a material witness, my involvement had been approved. It was unusual, but nothing about this case was normal or straightforward – and the irony wasn't lost on anyone, least of all me.

Callum made the introductions.

'Most of you know Dr McCready. She's helped us out before. She's here to explain the connections and similarities between Martha's murder and the original Jack the Ripper killings. Jo?'

I took my cue and stood at the front, looking out at a dozen or so receptive faces. I couldn't help but notice Heslopp in the front row. He slouched with his legs stretched out in front of him, his belly straining at the buttons of his shirt. Surprisingly, he smiled at me, nodding slightly.

'This is the photo that was sent to me.' I tapped the picture of Martha taken in the stairwell. 'Presumably by the killer, who calls himself "Jack".'

I noticed everyone had a folder and a few started flicking through the paperwork, until they came to what I recognised as Jen's transcript of Martha's last hypnosis session.

'If you've read the file, then you know an alter-ego appeared, during a hypnosis session with Martha, claiming to be a reincarnation of Jack the Ripper.' I glanced over to them. 'I'm sure no one here needs an explanation as to who *he* was?'

There were polite chuckles around the room. One young officer held up his hand.

'You're talking about "Jack" as though he's a real person. Surely this was just Martha talking to you? There was no third person involved here.'

'I can't explain yet what exactly happened during that hypnotic induction. Dissociative identity disorder – DID, or split personality as most people know it – is a recognised condition, but it's extremely rare. Martha displayed what looked like DID and the "alter" personality said he was Jack. So far so good. But what completely defies explanation is that the only other person present during that session who knows about Jack was Martha herself, and she's dead. Since then, Jack's communicated with me. He claims to be "out" and to have murdered Martha.'

No one said a word. A few officers looked down at their notes, some shuffled uneasily.

'So what you're saying is that our prime suspect is an alter personality of a dead woman?' It was Heslopp.

'You and I both know that's impossible. What we have to work out is how else it could happen.'

'Martha's not the *only* person to know what was said in that room, doctor, is she?'

Everyone recognised the edge in Heslopp's tone.

'No, I was there too. But I've got a distinct advantage over you, detective.'

'Oh, and what's that?'

'I know for a fact that *I* didn't do it.'

'Who else could have known what went on in that room?' Detective Sergeant Ian Drummond asked, from the back row.

'Lister was there just after the event. He came in with the crash team but he wasn't present during the hypnosis session.'

'But you told him what happened when you went back to his office?' Ian asked, looking down at his notes.

'I told him about the abreaction, but I didn't mention Jack.'

'OK,' Callum said. 'Ian, take a closer look at Lister's movements after the hypnosis session. Where was he? What time did he go off duty? Where was he when Martha absconded? The usual drill.' Callum indicated another officer. 'Lister's got a swipe card linked to the security computer, so track that around the events we're looking at.'

'OK.'

'And let's find out if he talked to anyone else about what went on in that room,' Callum went on. 'Who else had access to the notes? Who else was on duty? Let's look back at all their track records, see if we have any backgrounds that might lead us somewhere.'

Callum turned back to me. 'Can you tell us more about the similarities between this murder and the original Jack the Ripper killings?'

'Martha's murder exactly matches that of Martha Tabram in 1888,' I said. 'You can see from the table that the time, date, location, number of wounds, use of weapon and position of the body are all identical to the original Ripper killing.'

'It says Tabram was found by a taxi driver,' Ian said. 'Just like our Martha. Is that a coincidence?'

Callum stood as he spoke. 'No. We checked the flat where the driver thought the booking had come from. The couple there didn't know anything about it. Looks like the call came from the killer to set the taxi driver up to find the body.'

I nodded. 'The victimology could never be random in this case. He set Martha up to be his first victim, just as he planned everything else. Her name, the fact that she had such a troubled past, that she came to our attention the way she did. She left Westwood in time to meet her death on the right night in the right place – all planned.'

'The boyfriend is the obvious one to look at,' Ian said.

'Or Lister,' Callum added. 'Anyone who could make sure she was out of Westwood Park and in the right place, at the right time, to fit the killer's timetable.'

'Or the doc here?' Heslopp threw the suggestion in like a grenade.

'I think that one has been covered,' I said, picking it up and throwing it back.

Callum said, tightly, 'Move it on, Frank.'

'Have to keep an open mind, boss,' Heslopp said, with a grin. 'Wouldn't do to let personal relationships get in the way, would it?'

'We heard it the first time,' Callum raised his voice, just enough. 'Everyone's being looked at and if new evidence comes to light, they'll be looked at again. In the meantime, we have enough to be getting on with.'

'What about the boyfriend then?' Ian supplied a welcome deviation. 'John Smith?'

Callum nodded towards two officers on his team. 'Beth and Shah are looking into him.'

Callum turned his attention back to me. 'So, what else can you tell us about the original Ripper murders?'

'Jack the Ripper of 1888 was the first documented serial killer. He killed six women in what came to be known as the "autumn of terror".'

I looked out at the sea of faces before me.

'Certain characteristics made his killing spree become legendary. They all took place within a one-mile radius and that became known as his "murder mile". All the murders were committed over a thirteen-week period, culminating in the almost total destruction of the body of his final victim, Mary Jane Kelly. After which he disappears without trace, never to kill again and never to be identified. That's what makes him such an enduring figure of terror. He struck anonymously and melted away as if he never existed, and a supernatural myth surrounded him that still exists today. Even his name conjures up a primeval fear of being stalked and murdered by a ghost-like figure who can never be identified or caught.'

'What about a profile of our modern "Jack"?' Callum asked.

'If I'm right, he's a copycat. He's chosen to replicate the Victorian Ripper. He's announced himself. Given us his name and set the scene for us. Martha matched the victimology so closely, there could be no missing the similarities. He's studied the original killings in detail, so he makes it as perfect as possible when he presents his victim to us. Don't fall into the trap the people of Victorian London did – believing our man is some kind of lunatic. He's highly intelligent, educated, precise and methodical with a calculating and coldly logical mind – an organised offender. If the "autumn of terror" is his template, then we know when and where he will kill.'

'We don't know that for sure,' Heslopp interrupted. 'He's done this one, but that doesn't mean he's going to do all the others. How do we know this isn't a one-off?'

'We don't,' I agreed. 'But we don't know that he *won't* try to replicate all the others, either.'

I sat on the edge of the desk as I thought out loud. 'If he's picked this series to copy, he's picked it for a reason. If he continues, he recreates the terror of the most infamous serial killer of all time. Why would he go to all this trouble and stop now?'

'OK,' Callum said. 'We prepare for the fact that he might – and we go on the assumption that it will follow the same pattern. If it does, we can't get caught with our pants down. So how does the series run, Jo?'

I handed out a sheet showing the chronology.

'The killings took place at the beginning and end of each month. In 1888, each date fell on a weekend or a Bank Holiday, which meant the original Ripper probably had a job that prevented him killing during the week. Our man is following the Victorian timetable – not picking his own. But what we *do* know, if I'm right, is that he will stick to the dates, which were: Martha on the seventh of August, Polly Nichols on the thirty-first of August, Annie Chapman on the eighth of September. The thirtieth of September he committed two murders in less than an hour, in what became known as the "double event" – Elizabeth

Stride first and Catherine Eddowes second. His final, and most brutal of all, was Mary Kelly. Murdered in her own home on the ninth of November, the only victim not to have been killed in the street. I believe he'll stick to those dates as closely as he can. He's confident enough to provide us with his MO and his timetable; all we don't know is *who* and exactly *where* he'll kill.'

'Thank God for that,' Ian muttered. 'For a minute there I thought this was going to be a tough one!'

There was a ripple of uneasy laughter around the room, and then Shah raised his hand.

'If our man is copying the original as accurately as possible, then why isn't he doing this in London? I mean, he could go to all the original sites. Why here?'

'I'm not sure yet,' I said, honestly. 'Maybe if he *was* in London, it would be too easy to catch him. All the police would have to do is stake out the scenes –'

'Or,' Heslopp said, 'someone or something has drawn him here. After all, he sent the photograph to *you*. Perhaps *you're* the reason he's here.'

Before I could answer, Callum interrupted.

'We've already thought it could be an ex-patient of Jo's, or someone she helped convict. And seeing as you mentioned it, Frank, you can be the one to look into the doctor's back catalogue of cases. Should keep you out of mischief for quite a while.'

'Cheers, boss,' Heslopp said, sarcastically.

Chapter Twenty-Nine

21 August – Fordley Police Station

Callum went to the percolator and poured two cups. He still had his back to me when he spoke.

'Listen, Jo, I'm sorry about the other day in your office.' He turned and put the steaming mug in front of me. 'What I said was out of order.'

'That's OK,' I said, quietly. 'You were thinking the same as me. Not another Ripper in Yorkshire on my watch.'

We'd both been children when the last Ripper terrorised the people of West Yorkshire. Callum's parents had moved down to Fordley from Edinburgh the year before, so, like me, he'd lived through those killings and their fallout.

I was just nine years old when the court case began, but I had vivid memories of sitting with Mamma and her friends around the TV in our warm kitchen, listening to them talk about it, remembered Dad spreading the newspaper out on the kitchen table every morning to read the latest updates.

Events from that time had a fallout into my teenage years. My parents – like most other parents in West Yorkshire after that – imposed restrictions on my social life they previously might not have. A kind of innocence and a sense of security had been polluted by Peter Sutcliffe and his crimes and teenagers were robbed of what should have been carefree social lives, as a legacy of his predatory years.

Callum sat back in his chair, looking at me over his cup.

'It leaves me cold when I think about how it was then,' Callum said. 'The suspicion that made every woman look a bit more closely at her husband or boyfriend. Can you imagine what would happen if the public think we have *another* Ripper? Here? Now? It doesn't bear thinking about.' He shook his head. 'My first thought about becoming a copper started as a kid back then.'

Reading about the trial had also been the starting point of my interest in psychology. I could trace my ambitions back to studying reports of the proceedings at Dewsbury Crown Court and later at Court Number One of the Old Bailey, the jury grappling with the question of whether Sutcliffe was insane, or just plain evil.

Mad or bad? A question that had formed the basis of my whole career ever since.

He sipped his coffee, then got to the point.

'This copycat,' Callum said. 'How do you get a profile on him? It's not his original work so how much can we learn about *him* when all the signatures are from the Victorian Ripper?'

I tipped my head back to ease the tightening muscles in my shoulders. It was a good question and he was right – it wasn't easy.

'I'll be honest,' I said. 'I've never worked a profile on a copycat killer, so the short answer is: I don't know. But it seems to me that even though he's working to another killer's formula, there are bound to be signatures of his own that'll come out.'

'What are your thoughts on him?'

'He's chosen the Victorian Ripper for a reason. If I can work out why he's picked that particular killer, that might give us something. He's obviously intelligent and computer literate, can cover his tracks using technology. Perhaps he has a technical background of some sort?'

'The techies say he routed his IP through several proxy servers in universities or companies across the globe.'

'Now you've lost me,' I confessed.

'I'm not much better,' Callum said, with a smile. 'I just repeat what the techies tell me.'

'He's chosen Yorkshire over London. As Shah says, there'll be a reason for that, so there's another individual signature. He's injected himself into the investigation, which is typical of psychopaths who think they're clever enough to hide in full view.'

'Injected himself into it?'

'By sending me the photograph. He's communicating with someone involved in the investigation and who was involved with the victim. He's opened a dialogue with me.'

Callum looked worried. 'I think Heslopp has a point, Jo, that you're somehow connected to him. I think he's chosen Fordley to get close to you. He has your personal email address. Does Lister have your personal numbers?'

I thought for a moment. 'No.'

He frowned. 'I thought he called you at the farm when Martha absconded from Westwood?'

'He didn't call the farm. He left the message at the practice in Fordley. I used remote access to dial in.'

He scanned a sheet of paper in front of him. 'The techies have installed a tracker on your computer. By the looks of it, they can see every keystroke you make. So you'd better not go on any of your usual porn sites for a while.'

'Very funny.'

He flicked the paper back onto his desk. 'We think you should have a dialogue with Jack if he contacts you again. The techies are on duty twenty-four seven, assigned to keeping an eye on you electronically. So if you get any more messages from him, you can respond.'

'OK,' I said, tentatively.

'The original plan was that one of us replied as if it was you, but apparently it's better if a psychologist designs the game plan for that kind of dialogue, to make sure we get it right. Too provocative and we tip him over the edge and make things worse. Not provocative enough and he could just melt away.'

'You need to play him, with just enough tension so he'll trip himself up?'

Callum nodded. 'And as you already know all that stuff, why bring in another psychologist to complicate things?' He looked across at me and his expression changed. 'But there are strict guidelines to this, Jo, and you've got to agree to them or all bets are off and I'll get someone else in.'

I immediately thought of Taylor-Caine and my blood ran cold. 'Agreed.'

He nodded. 'OK. I'll get technical support to set everything up on your phone, just in case he calls. That OK?'

I nodded, still wondering whether I wanted to do this, but knowing, at the same time, that I certainly didn't want anyone else to do it. I owed it to Martha. She had chosen me to open up the silence of her death. I felt I owed it to her to finish the conversation.

Chapter Thirty

25 August – Kingsberry Farm

Time seemed to drag, until a few days later when Callum called to say he'd received more information from the pathologist. I invited him to the farm so that we could take a look together.

Once I'd made us both a brew, Callum took the photographs from Martha's post-mortem report and spread them out on my kitchen table.

'This is a herringbone pattern in blood on the edge of some of the deeper wounds.' He explained. 'Pathologist thinks it's probably an imprint from the knife handle, which bit into the lips of the wound.'

I straightened up from looking at the gruesome image and took a sip of tea – the intimate details of violent death were something I had never quite become used to. Part of me thought that if I ever did, it was probably time to quit.

'There's something else,' Callum said. 'Final results from the post-mortem show that cause of death was strangulation.'

'The same MO as the Victorian Ripper. He strangled his victims first. No struggling, no screams, and *then* he mutilated them. Jack didn't rip to kill. He killed so he could rip.'

Callum leaned back in his chair. 'What's the difference?'

'In outcome, as far as the victim and the investigators are concerned, there is no difference. The victim is dead and the body is mutilated. But in the mind of the murderer, there's a *huge* difference. It's the order in which he does things, the chosen behaviours that give us clues to his drives.'

'But our man is a copycat. These are not necessarily *his* drives.'

'True, but it's that very fact that makes me think they're *his* drives too.'

'Not sure I follow.'

'Not sure I do, yet,' I confessed. 'But to quote Sherlock Holmes, "Singularity is almost invariably a clue".'

We both jumped as the large bell above the Aga rang, shattering the stillness of my cosy kitchen.

'What the hell?' Callum almost spilled his tea.

'Sorry.' I headed for the office to catch the call before it stopped. 'I had the bell put in here so if the office phone rang, I could hear it anywhere in the house.'

By the time I pushed the door open to the office, Callum was already behind me. Harvey was hot on his heels, wondering what all the fuss was about.

I grabbed the phone. 'Hello?'

'Doctor.' The voice was eerie. Synthesised. Robotic.

I froze, knowing it was him, but my mouth opened and, for a second, nothing came out.

'Who's this?'

'Please don't disappoint me, not when I've waited so long to speak with you again.'

Callum gestured for me to keep him talking.

Think! I had to get this right. This might be the only chance we'd get.

I sat on the edge of my mahogany desk, looking down at the carpet to avoid being distracted by Callum. I pressed the speaker button so he could listen in.

'Have we spoken before?'

'You know we've spoken.' The metallic voice was cold with disappointment. 'You know we've met. Playing games with me is a very dangerous thing to do.'

'When did we meet?' My clinician's tone was calm. I was pleased to hear it.

'When you set me free,' he grated, chillingly. 'I have you to thank. It feels good to be back together, doesn't it?'

'Together? I don't understand.' I played for time.

'Doctor,' he chided, like a parent to a child, 'don't waste our precious moments like this. If you're giving the police time to trace this, don't insult me. They won't. Any more than they could follow my computer trail.'

His tone, if it hadn't been electronic, would definitely have been oily.

'I like to keep our intimate moments private.' He laughed softly, the sound making my stomach turn over.

'You're saying we met through Martha?'

'When your mind entered hers, it brushed against mine.' His whisper was intimate. 'I know you, doctor. I know all there is to know about you.'

'Why are you here, Jack?'

'Because it's time,' he said, simply. 'You opened the door and freed me.'

'Why me, Jack?'

'It had to be you. You were the only one who could open Martha's mind and let me out.'

'You're not a figment of Martha's mind, Jack.' I let my tone harden, to show him know I wasn't playing the game. 'A phantom can't kill.'

'I was a phantom in 1888 and I'm a phantom now. But the pleasure this time is having you to share these most intimate things with. That makes you very special.'

'What exactly do you want, Jack?'

The voice laughed softly, like the laughter that echoes through haunted houses in horror films.

'Polly put the kettle on,' he began to sing. *'Polly put the kettle on, Polly put the kettle on, we'll all have tea . . .'*

'Jack?' The line was dead 'Jack?'

'He's gone.' Callum took the phone from me.

We stared at each other in silence, neither of us knowing quite what to say, then we both nearly jumped out of our skins when Callum's mobile shrieked through the ghostly silence of my office.

He fished the device from his pocket, still looking into my eyes as he took the call.

'Yes, I know,' Callum said into the handset. 'I was here when he called.'

I half listened as he talked to the techies, who must have been privy to every chilling word.

I walked to the huge arched window and looked out across the fields. Afternoon sunlight caressed the treetops, silhouetting their spreading limbs against a dark turquoise sky.

'OK.' I heard Callum in the background. 'So no trace, then?'

Harvey came to stand beside me and pushed his wet nose into my hand. I absently stroked his silky ears, my mind replaying Jack's call.

He was like no other killer I had ever dealt with before.

He was beginning to unnerve me.

Chapter Thirty-One

28 August

The media had agreed to a two-week blackout on coverage of Martha's murder. At least that gave me some peace. After the last brush with the press, I was in no rush for them to discover the killer had sent me photos of his handiwork.

I was driving back to the farm when Callum called.

'I've got some info from Manchester. We found some prostitutes who knew Martha before she met the boyfriend. None of them ever saw him, though, so no ID. After she got involved with him, they said she dropped off the scene and they never saw her again. Can't question the pimp she had either, because he died of a drug overdose last year. Also, Martha isn't her real name. It's Susie Scott.'

Something jarred in my mind. I negotiated a roundabout as I tried to think.

'So when did she become Martha?'

'No way of knowing. She didn't do it officially, just assumed the name.'

'She didn't like the name, though.' That was the bit that I found strange.

'What do you mean?'

'She asked me to call her Matty. *She* didn't choose the name, Cal, it was chosen for her. She didn't like it, but she went along with it.'

'So you think the boyfriend made her adopt the name?'

'And why would he choose Martha? An old Victorian name for his twenty-something girlfriend – unless it fitted his purpose?'

'To have the same name as the Ripper's first victim,' he concluded for us both.

'I ran Susie Scott through the Police National Computer. She had several arrests for soliciting and, interestingly, one for wounding with a knife.'

'What were the details of that?'

'Gerry Ward, her pimp, was the "victim". Apparently, he didn't take kindly to her new boyfriend and they had a domestic. She took a kitchen knife and stabbed him in the arm. It wasn't a serious wound and he was discharged from hospital the same day. She was arrested, but once he'd calmed down, he refused to press charges. He had a history of violence towards her and she claimed self-defence, so it didn't come to anything. After that she moved to Fordley. We've no idea where they were living. Could be that the boyfriend rented using a different name. All transactions were paid in cash and all were signed by Martha. As far as we can see, the boyfriend never showed his face to landlords or signed any paperwork – he spoke to them over the phone.'

'Anything else?'

'Yes. The pathologist called about the murder weapon.' He paused for effect. 'You sitting down?'

'I'm driving, so it's to be hoped so.'

'He says it matches the shape and description of a Victorian amputation knife, used in operating theatres in the early to mid-nineteenth century. He sent details of where we can see one that matches.'

'Where?'

'The Old Operating Theatre Museum in London. And get this, it's on the site of what used to be St Thomas's Hospital from Jack's time. I'm going down there tomorrow – fancy a trip?'

Anything was better than sitting around waiting for Jack to call again.

Chapter Thirty-Two

29 August – London

The curator of the Old Operating Theatre and Herb Garret Museum ushered us up the tortuous winding staircase and into the galleried operating theatre, discreetly cleared of visitors for our private visit.

'God,' I panted when I could finally get my breath, 'I hope patients didn't have to make that climb?'

'No.' The curator smiled. 'The women's ward was adjacent to the herb garret in the church and they were brought straight in here from the ward. Students would come in via a separate entrance – over what is now the fire escape.'

He stroked the basic wooden operating table almost lovingly.

'Putting the operating theatre up here meant they could take advantage of the huge skylight to maximise light during operations. It also offered a degree of soundproofing, which was necessary for obvious reasons.'

'No anaesthetic?' I ventured a guess.

'Not until after 1847. But the surgeons were very skilled at making the process as fast and efficient as possible to minimise shock to the patient. A leg, for example, could be amputated in as little as twenty-six seconds.'

'Which brings us to why we're here,' Callum said.

'Ah yes, your amputation knife.'

We followed the curator through a small doorway into a corridor. The wood-panelled walls were lined with posters and sepia photographs of what the hospital looked like back then. A wooden display case with a sloping glass lid stood against one wall; inside were an array of cutting tools, saws and blades.

The curator carefully set the lid back and lifted out a curved blade.

'A broad-backed amputation knife with checked and grooved ivory handle,' he said. 'From the information you sent through, this matches the pattern on the handle almost exactly. I'd say this is what you're looking for.'

He handed it to Callum, who turned it over in his hand. It still looked like it could do the business, over a hundred years on.

'Where would someone get hold of a knife like this today?' Callum asked.

The curator pursed his lips. 'Not on the open market. All the ones still in existence are owned by museums. Maybe a few in private collections. Examples could turn up in people's attics, I suppose, but if the injury you mentioned was inflicted by a well-preserved piece with no chips on the blade, then you're looking for a museum-quality piece. Yours, if it's out there, is very rare. It's a Laundy blade.'

'Laundy?'

'Yes, they were instrument makers with a workshop on St Thomas's Street, opposite Guy's Hospital, from 1783 to 1843 They used the herringbone pattern on the ivory handle as their trademark. The initials of the workshop can be partially seen on the print you sent me.'

Callum fished the photograph of the bloodstained herring-bone pattern found on the body out of his pocket and put it on the edge of the display case. The curator traced the faint imprint of the letter 'L' at the edge, then lined it up with the 'L' on the ivory handle of the knife. It matched.

'Their knives are rarely seen outside museums today and only two private collectors in Europe have Laundy blades that we're aware of.'

'Could we have their details?'

'Of course. I'll get the printout before you leave.'

Almost as an afterthought, the curator went to another case and produced a silk-lined green leather box.

'They come as a set.' He ran his finger along the empty inden-tation reserved for a much smaller blade. 'Any collection that has a case as well as both knives would be worth a fortune.'

'You said Laundy stopped making these in 1843?'

'That's right.'

I looked at Callum. 'That's forty-five years before Jack the Ripper's killings.'

The curator's eyebrows shot up. 'Jack the Ripper? Is *he* what this is about?' He chuckled. 'Won't the trail have gone cold by now?'

Callum shot me a look and I could have bitten my tongue off. Still, it was out now.

'Could Jack the Ripper have used a knife like this, even though they stopped making them forty-five years before?'

The curator pushed his glasses further up his nose. 'Oh yes, these blades would still have been around then. Surgeons in those days could get very attached to an instrument. Often had their own collections, much like any other craftsman.'

He took the knife from Callum and replaced it in its box.

'Once Laundy stopped making them, Maw and Sons took over as suppliers to most of the prestigious surgeons in London. They sharpened and serviced instruments and took on a lot of Laundy's old stock. So, yes, Jack probably could have used a knife like this.' He grinned. 'Who knows? Maybe even this very one!'

As we left, I couldn't quite shake the images of what might have gone on in that Victorian operating theatre.

'Did you see the space in that box for the sister blade?' I asked.

Callum nodded. 'A smaller knife, like the one used to inflict the other wounds on Martha.'

'What do you think?'

'We'll check the private collectors and see if any Laundy blades are missing. Also check that no museum pieces have gone walkabout. After that, I'm not sure. As the curator said, who knows what turns up in people's attics? Maybe our man just got lucky?'

Somehow I didn't think so.

'No. Nothing he does is by chance. Especially not something as important as the blade. I bet it'll turn out to be an original.'

'If it's an original that's been catalogued somewhere, then we'll have a lead. Let's see what turns up.'

Chapter Thirty-Three

30 August – Briefing Room, Fordley Police Station

Frustratingly, but predictably, nothing did turn up. Back in Fordley, I sat in the incident room for a team briefing.

'The Laundy blades are all accounted for,' Callum was saying. 'So no joy there.' He paced the front of the room and looked across the sea of faces. 'Ian?'

DS Drummond stretched forward from his perch on the edge of a desk, squinting at the notes in his hand. 'Lister checks out, boss. So nothing there. We checked hospital phone records, though. When Martha was in the day room, she took a phone call. It came in through the main switchboard and they put him through. He said he was her boyfriend and the call lasted less than two minutes. Telephony say it came from a burner phone.' The telephony team had been tasked with investigating all of Jack's phone activity.

'So we can assume that's when he arranged with Martha to get her out,' Callum said. 'Anything on the actual pickup, Tony?'

'Been checking CCTV, boss. We've got a partial from a bad camera angle near the front of the hospital, less than a minute from the time Martha did her Houdini.'

A grainy image flickered to life and he paused the frame. Everyone shuffled around to get a better look.

'Don't blink or you'll miss it. Overgrown trees block most of the frame, but in the right-hand edge you can just make out a bike going down the drive.'

'You won't get a BAFTA for that one!' some wit joked from the back row.

'Hold on, fat lad,' Tony countered. 'We enlarged the image and captured this bit.'

Everyone strained to see the grainy grey image and tried to make sense of it.

'What the hell is it then, Spielberg?' Ian joked.

Tony took his pen and traced the outline of a shape. 'It's a close-up of the back end of the bike. They think it's a Yamaha YZF-R1, from the partial bit of clip we got. Beth tried for a match on CCTV around the area at the time.'

Beth snorted indignantly. 'I stayed up for two bloody nights looking at CCTV and ANPR from all over Fordley!'

'And?' Callum asked.

'Can't get a number plate, but we're running it through DVLA for owners of the make and model.'

'Right, the boyfriend picked Martha up from Westwood Park on the night she died, and he was the last person to see her alive. So he's our number one priority.' Callum scanned a file on the desk. 'Techies are working on the digitised voice. Nothing so far. But if the caller and the boyfriend *are* one and the same, it begs the question, why bother to digitise his voice?'

'Maybe he knows we'll be bugging the phones by now and his voice is known to us?' Shah offered.

'Or maybe,' Callum said, 'he has an accomplice, so he digitises one voice to hide that fact?' He turned to look at me.

I had considered it, but it did pose problems.

'What you're describing is a folie à deux, or a shared psychotic disorder. Two people share the same delusional system and support each other. In this case, to commit murder.'

'It's happened,' Beth said. 'Look at Hindley and Brady, or Fred and Rose West.'

'But it's rare and it's risky. It's a bond forged in depravity and the levels of trust have to be enormous. The pair have an unusually close relationship, so it's often seen in siblings, or as in the cases you've mentioned, sexual partners. Husband and wife.'

'What are the criteria?' Callum asked.

'There's usually a dominant partner and a more passive secondary. In most cases, females have been the passive subject of an older, more dominant male partner, though it's not unknown for males to act in concert. The dominating player has the original psychosis and they groom their partner. Also, their levels of intelligence are higher than the secondary, so they find it easy to manipulate them. The bond can be familial, sexual or financial.'

'You said it was risky?' Ian said.

'A bond is only as strong as its weakest link. So the secondary might not be able to handle the stress. Especially if they are separated, which is when their confidence drops and their insecurities surface. It's then that they break under questioning or give themselves away during police enquiries. It's hard work for the primary to keep them sustained all the time. They need a lot of supervision, hand-holding. Their psychosis needs constant feeding, whereas the primary subject is naturally compelled to commit the crimes.'

'Do you think we could be dealing with a pair?' Callum asked.

'Maybe,' I hedged. 'But if he's got an accomplice, it's just for support. I stand by my original premise that he lives alone. I don't think he'll have a wife or long-term sexual partner. I think he's digitising his voice to hide the fact that Jack and John are the same person. He wants to create a phantom-like image – the ghost of Jack the Ripper, inhabiting Martha's body and set free during my session. If it's just her boyfriend, then he loses that. When it comes to the actual killing, I'm convinced it's a single hand. Our man and no one else is present at the kill site.'

'That's consistent with forensics,' Callum said, 'which gives us one pair of boot prints, one set of fibres, one sample of DNA. But we'll stay open to it and look for possible connections.' He turned back to the team. 'Anything on Jo's past yearbooks?'

Heslopp shook his bald head. 'Everyone accounted for. Either banged up or dead.'

'None released?'

Heslopp's smile was humourless.

'Most of her customers never get out, boss. Either still serving, topped themselves or died inside. Most are on whole-life tariffs.'

Callum cast me a quick glance.

'Nice company you keep, Jo, but at least that keeps things simple.' He ran his hand over his eyes. 'You don't need a reminder that tomorrow's the thirty-first. That's when Jack potentially will kill again.'

He glanced at the board with its gallery of Martha's torn body. He looked at me.

'Tell us about the next possible, Jo?'

I pulled forward a flip chart with the table of facts I'd written up.

'If our boy's true to form, he'll mimic these details as accurately as possible,' I said, quietly, trying not to slip from academic theory into the horror of what that meant.

'"Polly" Nichols was found in the early hours of the thirty-first of August 1888. So her killer actually began stalking her on the thirtieth.' I shot a glance to my audience. 'Which is tonight.'

'Thank God for that,' muttered Heslopp. 'I thought for a minute there we were on a tight deadline.'

'Her body was discovered at 3.40 a.m.,' I continued, 'in Buck's Row. You've all got a copy of the post-mortem report from the time.' There was a shuffling of papers. 'It's with this murder that Jack developed his MO. This is the first one where he opened up the abdomen. Many experts think Martha was a practice run. The wounds to her were all on the upper part of the body but with Polly, he shifted his attention to her abdomen. This was what gave him his name – the start of the "Ripper phenomenon" – and with each subsequent murder, his ripping and slashing became more violent.'

Callum turned back to the team.

'If our man is true to form, he'll try to match the victimology and location. What've we got?'

'Vice don't know of any girls who go by the name Polly or Nichols. Word has gone out to all the girls to be on their guard or not to go out at all and we've looked at the geography and there's nowhere in Fordley that matches Buck's Row,' Tony said.

'So he could strike anywhere and his victim could be anyone,' Callum said.

'What about the media?' I asked, almost as an afterthought. It had occurred to me that they wouldn't stay quiet much longer. In fact, I thought the police had done well to keep it quiet this long.

Callum turned to me and for the first time I could see the strain showing on his face.

'They'll keep a lid on things for now, but if we get another one . . .'

His voice trailed off and he turned to look out of the window.

If we got another one, there would be no stopping the media feeding frenzy and all hell would be let loose.

Chapter Thirty-Four

31 August

A pulsating haze of blue light from the assembled police vehicles jostled with the purple sunrise to illuminate the lay-by along a quiet country lane on the outskirts of Fordley.

Callum stood with me, watching the CSI team flitting in and out of the small white tent like worker bees around a hive. Beside the tent, a mobile catering van stood with its front hatch open, ready to serve any passing motorist on their way out of town.

I stared at the wooden sign in the shape of a huge teapot above the serving hatch: Polly's Transport Café.

'Polly put the kettle on . . .' I said, almost under my breath. 'The bastard *told* me!' I turned to look at Callum. 'He *sang* it to us, for Christ's sake!'

'I know.'

He raked his fingers through his hair in a gesture of frustration. We walked together to stand beside the open serving hatch. It was just after 5 a.m.

A man sat on a plastic garden chair, a mug of tea untouched on the table at his elbow. His eyes were glazed as he stared straight ahead, his face hollowed out by shock. We walked over to him as Ian stood up to introduce us.

'This is Jim Carter. He found the body when he drove in first thing this morning.'

I nodded a greeting, but the poor man ignored me, still staring at a vacant spot, probably replaying the horror I knew he'd see for the rest of his life.

Callum steered me past him, towards an articulated lorry parked at the edge of the lay-by.

'Carter drives for a firm on the industrial estate,' Callum said. 'Passes here every day around 3.30 a.m. on his way into the depot. He loads the truck, then heads back down here and stops for a brew and a bacon butty. Gets here about 4.15. He's her first customer every morning, so he was the one to find her, poor bastard.'

I glanced at the white tent. 'Who is she?'

'Patsy Channing.' He leaned against the side of the lorry and looked up into the lightening sky. His breath plumed in the early morning chill.

'She owns the van.' He nodded towards the teapot sign. 'But because of the name, the regulars just know her as Polly. She's been running it for a couple of years, apparently. Opens early to catch the truckers coming into the industrial estate. Closes up about two in the afternoon.'

I glanced back at the driver. 'Did he see anything?'

'Said he saw her opening up as usual and gave her a wave. Everything seemed normal. Then at 4.15 he came back. She's normally behind the counter and they chat while she makes his butty. This morning, the brew's there but no sign of her. So he walked round the side of the van and found her.'

'Injuries?'

Callum's eyes met mine in silent confirmation. I knew they'd be the same as Polly Nichols'.

'Bastard slashed her open and almost decapitated her.' His face was drawn, his expression weary. 'We'll learn more after the post-mortem, but we both know what it'll be.'

I nodded. We did know, and the knowledge was terrifying.

1 September

The initial post-mortem findings showed injuries consistent with Polly Nichols' murder in 1888, right down to almost decapitating Patsy. The pathologist also found bruising on her jaw and neck, and his initial assessment was that she'd been strangled before being mutilated. Time of death somewhere between 3.30 and 4.15 a.m. The murder weapon was almost certainly the same as the one used to kill Martha.

I dropped the notes onto Callum's desk. He was watching me silently when I looked up, his expression unreadable. He stood up to pour coffee.

'According to Jack's chronology, the next one's in seven days.'

I took the offered cup, sipping slowly, watching him over the rim.

'I want you at the team briefing.' He ran his hand through his hair. 'They're all familiar with Annie Chapman's murder in 1888, but it'd be useful if you could give us a profile of our copycat?'

'The term "copycat killer" was coined in Victorian London after people mimicked Jack's murders,' I recollected.

Callum paused with the cup halfway to his lips.

'Every day's a school day.' He took a sip. 'Think our man knows that?'

I shrugged. 'Wouldn't be surprised if the irony's not lost on him. Any developments on victims or location?'

'We've got a match on location. There's a Hanbury Street in Fordley, right in the middle of the red-light district.'

'That's too good for him to ignore. He's got to go for that.' I felt certain. 'Annie Chapman was a prostitute who worked the red-light district around Whitechapel. Her body was found in the yard of number twenty-nine Hanbury Street.'

'Well, number twenty-nine isn't a house, it's an Indian takeaway in a row of shops. We've set up surveillance in a flat above the shop opposite, so it's covered like the rest of the area.'

'But?' I sensed his reticence.

'If we put all our resources there and he strikes somewhere else, we'll be caught with our pants down.'

'But what else have you got?' I asked, trying not to push in any particular direction. Not with accusations of flawed profiles still swirling around. 'He's replicating 1888 as closely as he can and you've got a Hanbury Street in the red-light district!'

He rubbed the heels of his palms against his eyes, then focused on a spot over my shoulder, almost talking to himself.

'I know. That's why we've got the community teams and vice warning all the working girls to stay off the streets on the eighth. All the agencies in that area are giving out the same warnings.'

I knew he was referring to the sexual healthcare nurses, needle exchanges and charities that worked to keep the girls safe.

'But that puts the news out there.'

He nodded. 'The media have already got wind of it. They've been contacting the press office but they haven't made the connection to Martha or linked her with Patsy yet.'

But they will, I thought. Soon. And we both knew it.

'Surveillance are already in the area, setting up observation points. High windows. Buildings overlooking the streets where the girls work. In case he comes in on foot.' He sipped his coffee. 'And we've set up mobile CCTV with live feed to ANPR, so we can track any vehicle coming in or out of the area in real time if he drives in. We'll have spotters in the area on the night to pick up and follow any suspects we identify as suspicious.' He ran a hand wearily through his hair. 'Best coverage possible.'

'Isn't Hanbury Street near the university?'

He nodded. 'A rabbit warren. That's why the girls like it. Plenty of dark alleys and side streets to take clients, and plenty of passing trade.'

It was also the centre of student nightlife with curry houses and pubs that stayed open till the small hours. It rarely slept, even on week nights.

'Not easy, but I think we've got it pretty much covered.' He stood up and shrugged on his jacket. 'Let's just hope he doesn't pick somewhere else for his next outing.'

I picked up my notes and followed him to the team briefing.

'So, let's look at *our* Jack.' I wished I had more to give them. 'He falls into the category of a highly organised killer as demonstrated by his knowledge of the original 1888 murders. Also, organised killers don't choose their victims randomly or impulsively, and they bring the murder weapon, and anything else they need to commit the crime, with them. Victorian Jack chose prostitutes because they were readily available and vulnerable. He didn't have to initiate contact with them as they probably approached him. For our Jack, it's different. With Martha, we know he had a relationship with her. He "groomed" her into the correct victimology, persuading her to adopt a false name, etcetera.'

I walked over to the photographs on the whiteboard.

'With Patsy, he would have had to check out the location and become familiar with her routine, probably visited the café prior to the murder and possibly interacted with her without arousing any suspicion. All of that indicates excellent interpersonal and social skills. We know he's male, research would suggest he's white, and the degree of sophistication required to plan these killings places him as older than twenty, probably somewhere between twenty-eight and thirty-eight. Most likely he's a loner, not married or in a long-term relationship. I think you're looking for someone who's regarded by others as studious, even withdrawn at times. Maybe a bit of a bookworm who prefers his own company. He's neat and orderly, may even have a compulsion with tidiness and routine. He's very self-aware and not easily rattled. He's not going to panic and any tactic designed to throw him off balance would have to be carefully planned. He's highly intelligent and obviously tech savvy, as evidenced by his use of technology and the ability to digitise his voice when he calls. I don't think he'll work a nine-to-five job. Martha said he often worked from home, so maybe a freelancer or self-employed. Whatever he does, it gives him a lot of flexibility and autonomy.'

'Motive?' Shah asked.

'Because he's a copycat, we can't assume he's driven by the same compulsions as the original Jack. I also don't think our killer's motive is linked to his choice of victim or location, as those are chosen to match the Victorian murders.'

'So what's that leave us with?' Heslopp asked.

I'd wrestled with this one from the beginning and I was going to have to be honest about it.

'Most theories around copycat killings are that either the killer wants the same notoriety as his chosen role model and the media attention is likely to mean he'll have a film or book written about him. Or that, by taking on the persona of a previous killer, it depersonalises it. Disassociates him from the act, which reduces his inhibitions.'

'So, which is it for our killer?' Callum asked, watching me intently.

'I don't believe it's to lower his inhibitions. I don't think our man has any. I *do* think that the publicity surrounding it is important to him, though.'

'So will the lack of publicity be pissing him off then?' Shah asked.

'Probably. In fact, we could use that to our advantage. His profile suggests he has grandiose ideas about himself. At some level, the publicity feeds his motivations. If we can get the press to cooperate with us, we could develop a strategy that might make him careless. Give us a clue to his motives.'

'But so far you've no idea what they might be?' Heslopp didn't even try to disguise his exasperation.

I chose my words carefully.

'There would be little point in choosing to copy such a high-profile killer if no one made the connection. He needs the publicity, otherwise he's just playing to the police gallery and I think he wants a much bigger stage than that. He relates to Victorian Jack, to his crimes – but that doesn't mean he shares his psychopathy. Something fascinates him. Perhaps the fact that Victorian Jack was the most infamous serial killer of all time? So most certainly the one to emulate. He's somehow managed to practise the mutilations too, so concentrate on access to bodies – human or animal. He knows how to inflict the same wounds in a short amount of time and with great accuracy. He won't get that from a book. He'll have had hands-on experience somehow.'

'What about deviations from the original killings?' Beth asked. 'Does *that* tell us anything more about him?'

'His deviations are in part down to the different era, but yes, they give us some clues. For a start, he's not sticking to prostitutes, which means his motivation doesn't revolve around his victim's character or lifestyle. He uses technology and the fact that he can hide his online footprints so that even your techies are struggling to trace him, means you're looking for someone with advanced technical ability. Maybe he works in that field?'

I paused as I came to the part I personally was most uncomfortable with.

'Also, the fact that he's deviated in one very major way from his role model gives us an important element.'

'What?' Callum asked.

'Yorkshire and not London. That's critical. For him to *not* act these killings out in the one place made notorious by the original, means Yorkshire holds *real* significance for him. Either he's from here, or it's vital to him that it happens here. Maybe because of the connection with the Yorkshire Ripper.'

'Or because *you're* here?' Callum's voice was so quiet it was almost inaudible. 'And he's chosen to put *you* in the middle of this with him.'

Chapter Thirty-Five

6 September – Fordley Police Station

With only forty-eight hours to the next event, police surveillance teams had been in place around Hanbury Street for several days. Manpower and technical resources had been allocated and the team were still frantically trying to get any lead they could to our Jack, which was now 'John's' unofficial name.

I watched as Callum scanned the CSI report from Patsy Channing's murder.

'Tyre tracks found around the site are a match for a Yamaha bike. Can't know for sure that it's Jack's, but it's too much of a coincidence to ignore. I've got the team tracing and eliminating owners of bikes of the same make and model through DVLA.' He chewed his pen as he scanned down. 'Got a boot print that CSI believe to be his. Size eleven. They also got some DNA from Patsy's body, but it doesn't match anything in the database. Not much use unless we get a suspect.' His eyes showed his frustration. 'Not giving us much, is he?'

There was nothing I could say. He was right. Jack was forensically aware and either too careful to leave anything incriminating, or knew his DNA wasn't on the database, so didn't care.

'I've been thinking about the geography.'

I walked over to the large wall map of Fordley, with pins marking the last two murder scenes.

'Geographic or spatial profiling isn't my speciality, so you might want to consult on it, but it may apply in this case.'

Callum came to stand next to me, so close I could feel the heat from his body.

'How?'

'Spatial research says that offenders prefer to operate in a "safe zone", an area that's comfortable for them. The killer usually lives centrally to the radius of his crimes. Victorian Jack killed all his victims within a one-mile radius –'

'His "murder mile"?'

'Yes. All his sites were within walking distance to each other. Our man has already deviated from that, because he's looking for sites that match the original in some way – not because he can freely choose. But the theory might still apply, in reverse.'

I could feel him looking at me. 'You've lost me.'

'Well, usually the killer lives in a fixed place and radiates out from there. But our man planned the locations of his killings in advance. So what if he then *chose* where he lived, so he was central to those murder sites? Then the geographic profiling theory could still work.' I traced a circle around the pins with my finger. 'I think it's unlikely he'll go outside Fordley.'

'But how do we know where the centre of the circle is?'

'Geo profilers look at the distance between the two murders that took place furthest away from one another. Then draw a circle between those two points. They have computer programmes that calculate all the variables and it's been proven to be 89 per cent accurate. It's more problematic when killers dump their victims elsewhere. But our man, like Victorian Jack, leaves them at the murder scene.'

Callum tapped Patsy's location.

'It's only just on the border of Fordley. If you're right and he goes for Hanbury Street in the city centre, then Patsy will be the furthest away to date.' He looked down at me. 'Think it's worth speaking to a specialist?'

I nodded. It couldn't hurt. Fordley was the largest city in the biggest county in England. West Yorkshire had a population of 2.2 million so we needed to narrow down the search area – and the clock was ticking.

Chapter Thirty-Six

7 September – Kingsberry Farm

There was nothing more I could do. Callum and the team were all with the surveillance operation in Fordley and Hoyle had set up camp in the incident room. Annoyingly, Taylor-Caine was with him – no doubt to justify her existence on the payroll. I decided to stay well out of their way and spent the afternoon back at the farm walking Harvey across the fields.

Black fingers of trees at the edge of the woods were silhouetted against the dark blue of the late afternoon sky. Harvey bounded ahead of me, glad to be able to run further afield. I always seemed pressed for time lately and had confined Harvey to a half-hour circuit of our meadows.

Today, though, I needed to decompress, to walk aimlessly, without any particular purpose. My mind felt overcrowded. The usual logical processes were cluttered and overloaded.

My boots scuffed the rough, tufted grass as I walked, taking in the warm scent of late summer flowers. In the distance, the moors rolled away as far as the eye could see, bold in their purple-green majesty, an ever-present backdrop to my walks. High on the fells – so far away that they looked like small white specks – were grazing sheep. I stopped for a moment to admire the distant patchwork quilt of farmers' fields, dissected by the grey lines of drystone walls, then picked up the pace to follow Harvey on his random sniffing expedition. As we went, I pondered the fact that we had far too many unanswered questions.

John Smith, AKA Jack. His choice of victims and locations. Which were *his* signatures and which were elements of his copycatting?

One question haunted me: how did Martha's fractured alter ego present himself to me when she was under hypnosis, and then become a flesh-and-blood killer out here in the real world? There had been just the two of us and now she was dead. How could it happen like that?

Absently, I threw Harvey a stick and listened to him crashing through the undergrowth. A flash of iridescent copper rising into the air startled me as a hiding pheasant took off, the drumming of its wings and indignant crowing shattering the sudden stillness.

Something Martha said to me that day had jarred and now I couldn't recall what it was. At the edges of my mind, I knew it was important and I decided I'd listen to the recording again when I got back. It would give me something else to focus on rather than the endless wait for Callum to ring.

I'd reminded him that the next body had been found at 6 a.m. on the eighth of September. If 'Jack' was true to form, he would stick to that time. Which meant he *could* kill anytime tonight – if he wasn't caught first.

My thoughts were interrupted by Harvey's sudden low growling. He was transfixed by a figure on the other side of the trees. It was too far away for me to make out clearly, but then I saw a hand raised in a familiar greeting.

'It's only George,' I said, more to myself than to Harvey.

I ruffled Harvey's ears playfully. He lowered his guard at my touch, leaning against my leg as we watched the familiar figure climb into his old Land Rover Defender and bounce it out of the gate and down the track towards his farmhouse.

We followed the same direction the Land Rover had taken and five minutes down the disused track it brought us to my empty cottage.

Obviously George had been working there. He'd hung an old door on it just as he'd promised. The paint was peeling and it had seen better days, but it would keep the foxes and the rats out. A wrought-iron horseshoe, cradling the number thirteen, was crudely nailed on and hung at a drunken angle.

The door creaked in protest as I lifted the latch and nudged it open. The single room was tiny. When it was inhabited, there had probably been just enough room for a table and chairs by the open stone hearth opposite the door. It felt crowded with just me and Harvey in it.

He pushed past my legs and barrelled his way round, his nose to the stone flags. He sniffed loudly as he followed the trail of wildlife now long gone. The floor had been swept and the fireplace cleared of the leaves and debris that had been there when I'd last seen it. I was impressed. George had been busy. I made a mental note to take him for a pint down the village pub when I had a free evening.

Harvey's hackles suddenly lifted and he growled softly at nothing in particular, adopting his protective stance beside me. I ruffled his ears.

'Nothing here but ghosts,' I said.

But he wasn't convinced and his hackles stayed up until we were almost back home.

The night dragged. I spent most of it in my office, going over the notes I'd made on Martha's sessions and listening again to the recording when 'Jack' made his first appearance.

But whatever it was she had said that hadn't felt right at the time, it wasn't on the recording. I stared out at the night sky as Harvey snored contentedly at my feet. Perhaps Martha had said it earlier, before I'd started the digital recorder?

I finally switched off the desk lamp. *Enough*. I'd had enough and my brain just wasn't playing. A long soak and an early night were in order. Not that I expected to sleep much tonight, waiting for Callum to ring.

Chapter Thirty-Seven

8 September

Predictably, sleep eluded me. My mind chattered incessantly until I fell into a fitful doze in the early hours. I woke at 5, feeling exhausted, my eyes heavy and gritty. Pulling on my robe I went into the welcoming warmth of the kitchen and let Harvey out while I brewed tea and then carried it down into my office.

I watched Harvey bounding around on the lawn outside my window as I waited for my emails. The 'ping' of incoming mail turned me around to stare at the screen.

My fingers were shaking almost uncontrollably as I called Callum, surprised when he answered on the second ring.

'Sorry, Jo, we're still in the middle of it, but quiet so far. We've had no activity down here yet.'

'Yes you have,' I said, not daring to look away from the horror unfolding on my screen.

'No, Jo, there hasn't been another one.'

'Yes there has . . . I'm looking at her body right now.'

I sat in the incident room, nursing a disgusting cup of vending machine tea, trying to get my thoughts into some kind of order. It felt like I'd stared at my laptop for an eternity before the police arrived to ferry me to the station.

Now I concentrated on a spot on the carpet as I reran the image. A woman lying on her back, her legs drawn towards her.

Her feet resting on the ground with her knees splayed outwards, as if she was preparing for an internal examination. My mind recoiled from the medical analogy. That image had been more like the scene from a slaughterhouse.

Her stomach had been ripped open and eviscerated, her intestines lifted out and placed above her right shoulder. Other parts of her stomach had been put above her left shoulder and her throat had been cut, almost severing her head. But through all the horror, it was her face that haunted me.

Unlike Victorian Annie Chapman, this woman had been pretty. 'Had been', because her face was bloated in death and her swollen tongue protruded between even, white teeth. It was her eyes. Bright blue eyes, that had probably been sparkling and vivid in life, staring blankly towards the camera. Pleading with me . . . just like Martha.

'Jo?' Callum's voice finally penetrated.

'What?' I said. 'Sorry – miles away.'

His eyes were concerned as he took the cup out of my hand and held my elbow.

'Let's go into my office.'

I felt like a spectator in a dream. He sat me in the chair opposite, watching me for a moment.

'If it's any consolation, we all feel the same.' He ran his hand through his hair, his breath escaping him in exasperation. 'We don't know how the hell he got past us. He really is like a bloody phantom.'

'Sorry.' I felt impotent. Useless. 'I don't know what to say. Who was she?'

He tipped back in his chair, staring at a spot on the ceiling.

'Anne Stenson. A prostitute. She's lived in a flat just off Hanbury Street for the last five years. Ironically, she took the warnings from vice and stayed off the streets. Another girl came forward this morning and identified her at the scene, said they'd been working out of Anne's flat lately as they thought it was safer.'

He righted his chair and got up to pour coffee, shaking his head. 'Bloody typical! *They* were the ones being careful. There were plenty of girls out last night and yet *she* copped it.'

'Probably because she fitted the victimology better,' I said. 'Or it was opportune and she was in the wrong place at the right time.' But even as I said it, I was convinced that nothing our killer did was opportune.

'She was found in the backyard behind the newsagent's when the shop owner put the bins out.'

'What number is the shop?'

He turned to hand me a coffee. 'Thirty-one. But it shares the backyard with the curry house, which is number twenty-nine.'

I took the cup and looked into his eyes, which were weary with exhaustion.

'Then it wasn't opportunistic,' I said. 'It was planned. Like everything else he does. Twenty-nine Hanbury Street, exactly the same as Victorian Jack. But how did he avoid the surveillance?'

'The curry house shut at 2 a.m. There's a passage between it and the newsagent next door and we had spotters covering that all night – nothing but a kid taking a pee and some students taking a short cut to the university. A spotter walked down that ginnel at 4.45 and it was empty. At 5 Anne went to the newsagent, as she did every morning, according to the owner.

Apparently, she was always his first customer of the day. She always called in on her way back home for milk and fags as he was opening up. Today was no different, except she'd been in her flat all night. She left her mate there and went to the shop as usual. At 5.45 the owner goes to put the bins out in the yard and finds her body.'

'Habit,' I said, almost to myself.

'What?'

'Routine and habit. I was wondering how "Jack" managed to get her to the right spot at the right time.' I took a sip of coffee, not enjoying it. 'It was her routine. Obviously he's watched her. She matched the victimology – a prostitute called Anne – Annie. She lived near Hanbury Street, but somehow he had to make sure he could get her to the yard at number twenty-nine on the right day at the right time. He probably watched the area for a long time, staking it out to map everyone's routine, and she fell right into it by her routine of calling at the newsagent right next to where he wanted her.'

Callum was watching me as he sipped his coffee.

'Human beings are habitual,' I said, 'some more than others, but for a serial killer, it's a trait they use to their advantage. If their prey is predictable, then it makes the hunt even easier, like a predator staking out a watering hole.'

I ran a hand across my tired eyes, feeling suddenly unaccountably depressed by the premeditated cruelty.

'He probably watched several women over a period of time, to see whether any matched his victimology or lived, worked or frequented the shops near number twenty-nine. Anne just made it easy by having a routine that took her to his killing ground every day.' I looked up into those blue eyes, studying me in silence. 'How did he get her into the backyard?'

He shrugged, slowly shaking his head. 'The team are checking the CCTV. In addition to the mobile units, there are cameras in the street and around some of the shops. So we'll go through all of those to see how the hell he got down there without being seen.'

He started to shrug on his jacket.

'I've got to get back down there. I'll arrange a car to get you back home and I'll let you know what we come up with. What are your plans?'

'Jen's coming up to the farm later. I've got a presentation to give up in Newcastle tomorrow so I'll be doing final prep for that.'

He walked me out into the corridor.

'Well, keep out of trouble. Let me know if anything occurs to you that might help.' He turned, to add, 'Oh, and you might as well know, the media are all over it now. Hoyle's appointed a dedicated press officer to handle all the incoming information requests, so you might get calls.'

I groaned inwardly. *Great, that's all I needed.*

Chapter Thirty-Eight

9 September – Kingsberry Farm

I'd switched off my phones. After what Callum said, I wasn't taking any chances on press intrusion today.

On her way up to the farm, Jen had called to say that reporters were staking out the Fordley practice. She'd been on her way there to pick up my presentation for the conference, but carried on driving when she'd seen the press pack camped outside.

'By the way,' she said, shuffling paperwork, 'the bill's come in from Fosters in Manchester, for James' time at Fordley Police Station.'

'Dare I ask what the damage is?'

'Don't worry – you've got enough in the business to pay for it. Besides,' she said, as she looked at me over the top of her glasses, 'it was money well spent if you ask me. That man is worth his weight in gold. I'm so glad he was on call that day and we got him instead of some junior fee earner. Sent a well-deserved warning shot over Taylor-Caine's scrawny bows.'

I couldn't argue with that one.

She dropped my notes onto the kitchen table.

'Everything you need is there, but I couldn't chance calling at the office, so hope you've got copies of your presentation?'

I sipped my tea, watching her over the rim of my mug as she organised my notes.

'When you called, I accessed the server in Fordley and pulled down a copy. I'd only made a couple of changes, so it'll be more or less right.'

She eyed me impatiently as she clipped my papers together. 'You *should* back up everything you do here with the office server. That way everything's current.'

I rolled my eyes. 'Give me a break, Jen. A few years ago, until Marissa's techie gave me a crash course, I didn't even known what remote access was.'

I took a hurried gulp of tea, realising the time as I stuffed the notes into my briefcase with my laptop presentation.

'Hmm, if your publisher had been local, we'd never have dragged you into the twenty-first century! Should thank her techie someday.'

She was right, I had to admit it. Marissa had been the one to make me embrace remote technology, albeit reluctantly.

'Which reminds me,' she continued, handing me my jacket as I headed for the door, 'Marissa needs confirmation of the date for the new book signing. Can you call her today?'

'Yep.' I leaned in to give her a peck on the cheek. 'Sure you'll be OK here with Harvey till I get back?'

She pushed Harvey behind her with her foot as she ushered me out the door. 'We'll be fine. Babysitting Harvey is a breeze after my grandchildren. He's better house-trained for a start!'

She waved me off in the rear-view mirror as I crunched down the gravel driveway, already dialling Marissa before I lost the signal across the moors.

'So you're OK for the date in December, then?' she was saying, as I navigated my way around a flock of sheep.

'No problem. Oh, by the way: Jen said to thank your techie guy for dragging me into the technological age.'

Marissa laughed. 'Don't have Paul any more. He's left me to set up on his own.'

'Shame.' I meant it – Paul had the patience of a saint.

'Anyway, good luck in Newcastle. Not that you'll need it. I've given access to the *Newcastle Herald*, by the way. They're sending a reporter to cover the event.'

I groaned. 'The press have hardly been friendly lately.'

'I know, I know, but this one's tame, I promise. The journalist's a friend of mine and they've promised not to mention the towpath fiasco. This'll kick over the traces. Give us a springboard into good publicity for the book launch. Trust me!'

Why did my heart sink every time anyone said, 'Trust me'?

The speaking engagement at St James' Park stadium in Newcastle had been booked for over a year and it was an annual event I looked forward to. The audience comprised mainly criminology graduates and students, with a smattering of interested parties from police forces around the country.

I'd been booked to lecture on victim selection – the nonverbal signals people inadvertently sent to a predator that marked them out as vulnerable. I enjoyed mixing with likeminded people, so it was shaping up to be a good day – not least because it took me temporarily away from Fordley and the suffocating immersion in Jack's monstrous mind. I just hoped Marissa had done enough to ensure the press didn't use it as an arena to bait me in.

'Jo, good to see you again!'

Darrell, the event's organiser, shook my hand enthusiastically. His slender fingers flashed purple nail polish and his genuine grin was, as always, as wide as a mile. I grinned back. His energy was always infectious and reminded me why this job was one of the highlights of my calendar.

'Everything you need is in the room back here.' He ushered me down the corridor, linking his arm with mine, like a couple of girly friends reunited after too long. 'Refreshments served in the corporate box just on the right when you're ready.'

His tone was almost sing-song. He took my briefcase and set it on the table in the private room he'd set aside for me. 'You're on from ten till twelve, sweetie. Then thirty minutes' Q & A before we break for lunch.' That beaming smile again. 'Marissa's had your books delivered, so I'll get those set up in the main reception and you're down to do book signings this afternoon. Is that all OK, my darling?' His gestures were big and dramatic – a legacy of the drag act he'd made legendary in the LGBTQ nightclubs when he wasn't working the day job.

'That's great, thanks.' I hesitated before asking, 'What about the press?'

His smile melted away. 'Oh yes, sweet pea, they've really been a bunch of bastards to you lately, haven't they? Don't you worry, they won't maul you here, not on my watch. Besides, the guy from the *Herald* is OK. He's done stuff for me before.' He guided me into the corridor and along to the corporate boxes that overlooked the pitch. 'I've arranged for him to meet with you for a quick interview, just before the book signing and I've reserved seats on the front row for his photographer. He'll get some pictures of your presentation to use on the website. Now then, lovely, let's get your mandatory cup of tea. You must be parched.'

I glanced down at the illuminated clock face nestled between the footlights. It read 12 precisely. Perfect timing. I ended my talk and clicked onto the Q & A slide.

'Any questions?'

The pause that followed gave me just enough time to take a sip of water and cast an eye over the audience.

Just before the lights went down, I'd watched the hall fill steadily until only the seat reserved for the photographer remained empty, but halfway through, the door at the back opened and a figure had crept through the darkness and taken up the space, so I knew I had a full house.

A hand was raised towards the back. 'Is there a cure for psychopathy?'

'Psychopathic personality may be hardwired from birth or influenced by the environment,' I said. 'Each individual is different and it depends on how much of the psychopathic personality is nature and how much is nurture. But once an individual reaches adulthood with these traits, I don't personally believe there is a cure.'

I took another sip of water. 'But you are all aware that not all psychopaths satisfy their need for narcissistic control by committing murder? Thankfully, that's just a small percentage. I've encountered far more psychopaths in business than in prison – they've obviously worked out the financial package is far better there.'

A ripple of laughter went round the room before I took the next question from a young female student.

'What's the best piece of advice you could give to someone who finds themselves confronted by a violent offender?'

'You mean apart from "run like hell"?' I said, half-jokingly. More laughter in the room. 'Well, if you're like me and not built for running, I would say never let yourself be moved from crime scene A to crime scene B. Crime scene A is usually opportune; it's where the offender has to intercept his victim and it's usually not the perfect location. They have to run that risk. But crime scene B will have been prepared. It will most likely be secluded and away from any source of help for the victim. Definitely not a good place to find yourself.'

'But offenders often threaten their victim,' another girl in the audience said. 'So if they jump into your car and threaten to stab you if you don't drive to another location, what you would do then?'

'If it was me, I'd tell them to get on with it.'

'Seriously?'

I nodded.

'Absolutely! Because whatever they threaten you with at crime scene A, will be one hundred times worse when they get you to crime scene B. So you might as well get it over with. Chances are they won't take the risk in an imperfect location like the abduction site – there are too many variables they're not in control of. Remember, like any predator, the two things they fear most are getting caught or getting hurt. In this initial contact, the risks of both are highest. So in many cases where the victim has challenged the offender, they've fled. It's a tactic worth trying because compliance at this stage is only going to put you in a worse position.'

'And if they call your bluff?' the girl persisted.

'Then you're no worse off than you would have been if you'd allowed them to control you and move you. Probably the best of a bad situation.'

The clock read 12.10.

I noticed the dark silhouette of the photographer get up from his seat and go out of the door at the back just as the lights were slowly being brought up.

Darrell moved forward to thank me and the audience broke into enthusiastic applause.

'Jo, this is David from the *Herald*.' Darrell made the introductions as I waited for the book signing. I shook the journalist's hand.

He took a seat. 'I'll start with a few interview questions, if you don't mind?'

Darrell was hovering just over his shoulder, looking agitated.

He glanced at me, then back to David. 'Where's your photographer?'

David frowned up at him. 'Photographer? I don't have a photographer.'

Darrell looked at me bemused, then a wave of nausea swept through me as realisation dawned.

Chapter Thirty-Nine

9 September – A1 southbound

'It's not a crime to blag a seat at an event by posing as a photographer,' Callum said, down the phone. 'But I take your point.'

My point had been that someone had gone to the trouble of ringing Darrell, posing as a photographer, someone who knew the journalist would be there, unaccompanied. He'd arrived after the lights had gone down and left before they came back up again, making sure no one got a look at him. Why would anyone do that?

'Did Darrell ever meet with him?' Callum asked, as I negotiated traffic along the A1 South.

'No, they only spoke over the phone. I talked to the receptionist but she was on her break once the session started, so there was no one in the foyer when he came in.'

'I'll get Northumbria police to check the CCTV and see if we can get a look at him.' I could feel his hesitation as the pause lengthened. 'It's really shaken you, hasn't it?'

My turn to hesitate as I checked in with myself. Had it shaken me?

'Unnerved me, maybe.'

'Why?' His tone was curious. 'It could be someone just wanting a free seat in a seminar.'

'You're right,' I sighed, wearily, even though I knew I didn't believe that. 'But I can't shake the feeling it was him.'

There. I'd said it out loud. Somehow hearing it made me feel worse, not better.

'So let's say you're right,' he said. 'Why would he risk it? He didn't confront you, there were no threats –'

'I know,' I interrupted, feeling foolish but unconvinced. 'It's just a feeling. But if I'm right, there's a chance he's been caught on camera.'

'OK. I'll look into it.'

He paused and I could feel a shift away from the subject of my shadowy audience member.

'Just to let you know,' Callum said. 'Hoyle's briefing the assistant chief constable every day and the team's working round the clock.'

'Any developments?'

'I took your advice about him staking out Hanbury Street on the run-up to the murder. He'd have to watch the comings and goings to select his next victim. So I've had a team checking CCTV to see if we can spot him in the area. Nothing. But we got a break with CCTV from one of the rented houses overlooking the back of the shop on the night. When we piece it together, our man appears to come from the direction of the university. It shows Anne going down the passageway after leaving the shop, and he pulls her backwards into the yard from the alley.'

'So you've got him on camera?' I could hear the hope in my voice.

'Of sorts,' he said. 'It's not the best quality. Plus he's wearing a hoodie and his face is covered, so not great. The techies are trying to enhance it.'

'Well, if he's on camera at the stadium today,' I said, 'that plus your footage might be enough.'

'If it *was* him today.'

'If it was,' I conceded, certain now that it had been.

The A1 was quiet and my mind was drifting as I did eighty on the empty dual carriageway. To my left, the lights from Catterick Garrison lit up a pale crimson sky in an otherwise dark landscape. I'd be back home in the small hours.

Suddenly a call coming through on my mobile cut off the radio and made me jump.

'McCready,' I answered, automatically.

'Doctor.'

The familiar robotic voice made my stomach lurch and sent prickles across my scalp.

'Jack.' The pseudonym was out before I could check myself. 'Or is it John?' I added, quickly.

The robotic chuckle was eerie in the dark, isolated interior of my car.

'Telling you that would take the fun out of the game now, wouldn't it?'

I had to keep him talking. I was still doing eighty along a mercifully empty road. I slowed down, scanning the roadside for a pull-in point as I tried to think.

'Are you enjoying my work?'

'"Enjoy" wouldn't be the word I'd use.'

I finally pulled into a dark lay-by.

'But you're an interesting study,' I said, deciding to use the strategy I'd planned if he called again.

'You'll have a lot more material to study as we play our game. I'm so glad I have you to share it with this time,' he whispered, intimately.

'It was you at the stadium today, wasn't it?' I chanced. 'You should have introduced yourself instead of skulking about in the shadows.'

'I hope you liked the picture of Annie?' He pointedly ignored my question.

'About that,' I decided to go along, 'why did you choose her?'

He laughed. A metallic, harsh sound that grated.

'She chose me.' He sounded triumphant. 'Like they all do . . . they're born to be prey. Cattle for slaughter.'

'Is that how you see them, John?' I chose the name deliberately.

'*Jack!*' He spat the word, raising his voice. Irritated as I'd hoped he would be.

'I'm sorry,' I said, insincerely, 'I'm forgetting. There are two of you, aren't there?'

There was a long pause and I let it ride to see what happened. He didn't speak so I pressed the advantage I felt I had. 'That's why you have to disguise your voice, isn't it? You're not Martha's fractured alter ego, are you, John?'

His laugh was unamused. There was an unmistakeable undercurrent of anger – as I'd intended.

'John is weak!' he spat. 'I'm *Jack*. We're not one and the same. Not at all. Two very different animals, doctor, and believing otherwise is a dangerous assumption.'

I decided to change tack, keep him off balance if I could.

'Why do you identify with Jack?' I needled. 'What is it about him you admire so much that you have to copy him? Aren't you creative enough to be an original?'

He laughed, his tone soft, almost gentle. 'Don't demean your-self, or me, with such obvious tactics. I'm not emulating him . . . I *am* him. Have always been him.'

I closed my eyes, forcing myself to concentrate on his vocal patterns. The digitised voice robbed me of the fine nuances of tone that often gave clues to a person's true feelings. But I still had tempo, pitch and some inflection in there if I listened hard enough.

'When we last spoke, you said it *had* to be me, John.' I deliberately didn't call him Jack. 'Why me?'

'It has to be you who unlocks my story.' The words were spoken almost lovingly.

'Tell me your story, then. I'm listening.'

'That would be too easy, wouldn't it? I want you to work for it this time.'

'This time? Have you spoken to me before?' A brief hesitation said I was right.

'You have to share it with me this time.' He made it sound almost sexual.

'You have no one, do you, John?'

I softened my tone to match his, speaking quietly, gently.

'No one else to share things with. No woman in your life.' I could hear his breathing. He stayed silent, so I pressed further. 'You've always been lonely, haven't you? Feeling out of step with everyone else? Even as a child, John, you never fitted in, did you?'

I concentrated harder and could sense his breathing quicken a little.

'But I have you now,' he said, quietly, confirming I was right.

I took the advantage before he regained his footing.

'Is that why you kill women, John, because they treated you so badly? Do you hate them all, or just your mother?'

Did I hear his sharp intake of breath, or imagine it? I wasn't sure, but I gave him silence to see what reaction I'd get. He paused for only a heartbeat.

'I'm not in therapy, doctor.'

His voice wasn't as strong. I'd punctured his defences, if only slightly. But it was a start. The metallic voice grated down the phone as he recovered himself.

'I admire your tactics, but don't waste our time like –'

'OK, then,' I interrupted. 'Instead, tell me why you're being so inconsistent?'

'Inconsistent?' He sounded irritated.

'You didn't send me a picture from Polly's café. That's very sloppy, John. For someone trying to be so meticulous.'

I chose the word 'trying' deliberately, to goad a response.

'I had no time.' He was aggravated. 'The trucker arrived earlier than usual. I had to leave. I'll make it up to you next time, I promise. I hope you're looking forward to it? Perhaps I'll give you a present as a symbol of our bond? A special gift. From me to you.'

I decided to change my questioning to try to get some answers.

'The Laundy blades are a nice touch, John. Where did you find those?'

'They're mine. I've had them for over a hundred years. They worked so well on the Victorian whores, I brought them out again.'

'These women aren't all whores,' I said, prodding him. 'That's another inconsistency.'

He laughed. 'All women are whores. At least prostitutes are more honest about it.'

I changed tack again, wanting to keep him off balance with different questions, not allow him to control the conversation. He liked being in control. I wanted to take that from him.

'It must be frustrating, John, wanting to tell your story, but getting no attention from the media . . . All your hard work and not a mention in the news. Victorian Jack had much more coverage, even a hundred years ago.' I paused. 'John . . .?'

But he'd hung up.

I sat in the darkness, suddenly feeling vulnerable even inside my locked car. As I pulled out onto the empty road, my heart was hammering and my insides felt as though they were trembling.

In an automatic reflex, I switched on the radio. I needed to feel less alone in the dark, with the remnants of 'Jack's' toxic voice filling my safe space.

The *Shipping Forecast* was on.

I listened to the velvet tones of the male voice, reciting in rhythmic poetry the familiar roll call: '*Cromarty, Forth, Tyne and Humber.*'

Reassuringly solid, banishing mythical monsters and grounding me back into the real world.

Memories from childhood of Mamma kneading pasta dough in the warmth of the kitchen on a Sunday evening, Dad sitting in the armchair by the fire, polishing his shoes over newspaper on the floor, ready for work on Monday morning.

'*Viking, Forties, Fisher and Bailey.*'

It soothed my nerves. No room here for monsters and murderers. Cosy. Comforting. Protecting me from the tormented seas inside Jack's psyche and bringing me back to safe harbour.

Chapter Forty

26 September – Briefing Room, Fordley Police Station

It had been almost three weeks since the Newcastle seminar and the team had been chasing every lead. The cell-site data showed that Jack's last call to me on my drive down the A1 had pinged from a mast close to the football ground in Newcastle. Confirming – in my mind at least – that it had been Jack at the stadium that night.

I'd listened as the telephony team briefed everyone on their findings so far. As usual, it appeared Jack had used a burner phone to make that call, probably disposing of it straight afterwards, but at least it gave the team a lead.

'Northumbria Police sent us the CCTV footage from the stadium,' Tony was saying, from his seat on the front row. 'It shows a figure walking through the stadium at various points. He seemed to know where the cameras were, though, and made sure he obscured his face with a baseball cap pulled down low.' He flicked through his notes.

'We've compared those images with the ones taken around Hanbury Street on the night of Anne's murder. Both figures are the same height and build, and gait analysis suggests they both move with the same bearing and posture. So there's a high probability it's the same individual.'

'Nice one, Tony,' Callum said.

Callum had already told me that all the data coming in had been collated and put into the Home Office Large Major Enquiry System. Poignantly, the HOLMES computer had been developed after the Yorkshire Ripper enquiry – the irony of which wasn't lost on anyone.

During that enquiry, back in the eighties, handling the overwhelming mass of information had presented the police with some serious challenges. All the information had been kept on index cards and the weight of evidence had literally weakened the floor of Millgarth Police Station.

Since then, Sherlock's computerised namesake now processed all the information, to make sure vital links and clues weren't overlooked. The actions generated were passed to the growing number of officers in the major incident rooms, which now occupied two floors of Fordley nick. The police knew just about everything there was to know about Jack, except his real name, address and postcode.

I sat and made notes as Callum went through everything to date.

On the whiteboard, photos of Anne had joined the others. The belongings she'd carried that morning had been laid out at her feet, just as Victorian Jack had done with Annie Chapman. But instead of two combs and a piece of muslin, our victim had some loose change, a carton of milk and a packet of cigarettes.

'The pathologist's report confirms it's the same weapon used in the other murders,' Callum was saying. 'We've also got more trace fibres that they believe come from the killer's clothing, and hair strands with follicles. Which means we've now got his blood group and DNA. He isn't in the system, but we can use it for a match, going forward, if we get a suspect. Anne had also been wearing two rings like these when she left the flat.' Callum pointed to a picture of two thin gold bands. 'But they were missing when the body was found, just like Annie Chapman, whose rings were kept by her killer.'

He pointed to the gory post-mortem photographs on the board.

'Along with all the other injuries listed in the post-mortem report, the pathologist also confirmed Anne's uterus was missing.' He turned back to the team. 'Just like Jack the Ripper's MO in 1888.'

'If he cut her up *and* carried away her uterus, he must've been covered in blood,' said Beth. 'How could he exit the ginnel and walk through the street into town without attracting attention?'

'The same question they asked in 1888,' I said.

'Could've changed clothing?' Shah said. 'He's carrying a backpack on the CCTV footage.'

'Possibly,' Callum said. 'We now know he's got the uterus in there, along with different clothing perhaps. We need to trace his potential route to see where he might have gone to change – if that's what he did.'

Beth shuffled the paperwork on her knee.

'No sign of him after the ginnel,' she said. 'Checking CCTV to see if we can pick him up in different clothes.'

'Update on the DNA testing,' Heslopp said. 'Officers going door to door to take mouth swabs. Jo estimates he's aged between twenty-eight and thirty-eight, so we've broadened it to take samples from males aged between twenty-five and forty to give us a margin. Just over five thousand tests in so far, cards being left if people aren't at home, inviting them to attend clinics. Obviously it's voluntary, but anyone refusing will be implicated and we'll take another look.'

'OK,' Callum said, nodding in my direction. 'Jo?'

'"Jack's" call gave me a few interesting bits of info. He says he wants his story told and he seems to think I should be the one to tell it, so that's why he's involving me. He also implied he's tried to speak to me before, but I'm pretty sure I've not seen him as a patient, at least not in a criminal context.'

'So what then?' Ian asked.

'Maybe a witness I've interviewed or a patient who at the time had nothing to do with a criminal case at all,' I said, 'in a ward or clinical setting. I'll keep working through it – see if I can come up with a name.'

'He also told Jo that he owned the Laundy blades,' Callum added. 'So although we didn't find any leads with those first time round, we need to go back to the drawing board. Antique shops, auction sites, collectors, anywhere someone might pick them up. Also look back at robberies where anything like that might be listed as unrecovered.' He raked his hand through his hair again. 'The next event is set for the thirtieth. Four days from now.' He turned to me. 'What can you tell us about the next one, Jo?'

'Thirtieth September 1888. Prostitutes Elizabeth Stride and Catherine Eddowes are murdered forty-five minutes apart in what's become known as the "double event". Stride's body was found at 1 a.m. in Dutfield's Yard along Berner Street behind the International Working Men's Club, which was frequented by Polish and Russian immigrants. Her throat was cut but no other injuries sustained, and the theory is the Ripper was disturbed and couldn't carry out the usual mutilations.'

I walked over to the flip chart where I'd written up the main facts.

'During the chaos surrounding *that* discovery, the murderer slipped away unnoticed and went to Mitre Square – about twelve minutes' walk away. Here he murdered Catherine Eddowes, whose body was discovered at 1.45 a.m. It's believed she was killed at about 1.30. Her body was extensively mutilated.'

I held up the printed sheets that had been handed out. 'You've all got copies of the post-mortem reports from the time and photographs of the bodies. But to summarise: Catherine Eddowes was eviscerated. Like the others, she was rendered unconscious by strangulation prior to being mutilated, preventing her from screaming. Death was caused by haemorrhage from severing the carotid artery. She was opened from breastbone to groin and her intestines were lifted out and placed over her right shoulder.'

I paused to take a sip of water, trying to keep this a professional litany. '"Jack" also mutilated the face, this time. Cutting off her nose and slitting her eyelids and cheeks. There are lots of theories as to why he did that. Knowing what we do now about serial killers, it shows an increased confidence and escalation in brutality. The theory suggests he was attempting to remove her face. But I suppose we'll never know for sure now.'

When I finished, Callum broke the silence in the room by walking over to the area map.

'So far, there are no matches to any of the historical place names, but we know how creative "Jack" can be. HOLMES hasn't made any connections yet either. So unlike the last one, we don't have an area to stake out. We've been allocated extra manpower and we've got vice issuing the usual warnings to all the working girls but, as we know, he's not restricting himself to prostitutes.'

'So he could literally strike anywhere?' Beth said, echoing the frustration of everyone on the team.

Callum raked his fingers through his hair. 'Potentially, yes. But although we don't have any location names that match, we'll have plain-clothed officers on the streets around the red-light district. Also, we'll have surveillance set-up along the main routes in and out of town. We're also getting observation posts put on working men's clubs.'

A knock on the door paused proceedings and Callum ushered in a man I hadn't seen before.

'Right on cue,' Callum said. 'This is Professor Astley from Liverpool University. As we were just saying, "Jack's" killing ground could be just about anywhere this time, and he might not stick to the city centre. With Polly, he went to the edge of Fordley, so there's that possibility again and we haven't got the resources to cover all county borders but Professor Astley might be able to help us out. He specialises in geographic profiling, which is why we've asked for his input on this.'

While Callum introduced the team, Tony set up the professor's laptop and pulled down the projector screen. Callum had said that after our conversation he'd contacted a spatial profiler, but I didn't know they'd engaged one or what the man might have found. I supposed I was going to hear it now along with everyone else.

'If psychological profiling is the "who",' Astley began, flicking up the first slide in what was obviously a well-rehearsed presentation, 'then geographic profiling is the "where".' He acknowledged my presence with a slight nod. 'So Dr McCready's field and my own complement each other.'

Subtext: *Relax, I'm not here to tread on your toes.*

'Geographic profiling is an investigative tool that focuses on the geography of the crime and was developed in response to solving serial offences. The journeys offenders take determine the spatial range of criminal activity,' he continued. 'These areas are the predator's comfort zone and, by mapping the murder sites, we can assess – with a fair degree of accuracy – the area in which an offender lives. However, there is also a buffer zone an offender will avoid too close to home, to avoid identification.'

'So they don't shit on their own doorstep?' Tony quipped, causing a ripple of laughter around the room.

Astley never looked away from his slides. 'Hmm, indeed,' he said, without humour.

'Our offender is copying the crimes of a historic series,' Heslopp said, diplomatically avoiding any mention of Jack the Ripper. It was something we wanted to keep out of the press for as long as possible. 'He's not choosing these sites at random, so will this still apply?'

Astley adjusted his glasses as he considered the question. 'It will have a bearing on the analysis, but we've input that into the computer algorithm to account for the variables.'

Heslopp looked as if he wished he hadn't asked.

'In cases where the site of the offence is dictated by considerations other than free choice, the offender will often locate himself close to his base of operation,' Astley said. 'For example, terrorists targeting a strategic objective will recce the area and might rent rooms nearby, embedding themselves into the local area and thereby creating a comfort zone.'

He paused, and as there were no questions, continued, 'The criminal geographic targeting software, or CGT, analyses the geographic coordinates and produces a 3-D probability surface or colour map that shows the most likely area of the offender's home or search base.'

Astley turned to his laptop and began to call up the image he'd programmed. Every eye in the room was glued to the screen in anticipation, just as the door opened and Hoyle and Taylor-Caine walked in.

Astley's hand hovered over the 'enter' key.

Chief Superintendent Hoyle glanced at me with an expression of undisguised distaste, then walked into the centre of the room. Taylor-Caine stood beside Callum, but her eyes stayed on me.

'I need to have word with the team,' Hoyle said, to no one in particular.

'Yes, sir,' Callum said, stepping back slightly to give Hoyle centre stage.

'But not in the presence of unauthorised personnel.' Hoyle looked directly at me and paused for dramatic effect.

For a moment I considered being a hard-ass and staying put, playing dumb and making him spell it out. But the desire to not put Callum's head even further in the noose won out and I slipped from the edge of the desk and grabbed my briefcase as I headed for the door. There was nothing I could say that wouldn't have sounded petty in that moment.

Taylor-Caine, on the other hand, had no such qualms.

'Best leave it to the professionals.' She didn't even try to hide the smirk that pulled at the corner of her mouth.

The team shuffled in collective discomfort and the room felt suddenly very still. Beth jumped up to get the door for me and shot me a sympathetic look and a regretful half-smile.

I walked down the corridor, feeling my face burn with embarrassment, resisting the urge to barge back into the room and wipe that smug expression off Taylor-Caine's face with the back of my hand. My stomach was in knots and I felt sick on a cocktail of humiliation and resentment.

I called Jen from the car, like a hurt child wanting to vent about the bullies at school and offloaded to her as I drove, without really thinking, towards Fordley.

'What a bitch!' she said with uncharacteristic venom, but it felt good. Coming from someone whose opinion was usually so balanced, it validated my feelings somehow. 'They deserve each other,' she carried on, 'her and Hoyle. A dysfunctional, self-aggrandising double act!'

That made me smile despite myself.

'You should be a behavioural analyst with insight like that.'

'Only if "arseholes" is a clinical term I can use,' she said, still spitting.

'It's a collective noun.' I laughed as I navigated the afternoon traffic. It was only as I turned the corner that I realised where I was. 'Oh, shit!'

'What? What's the matter?' Jen stopped mid-rant, suddenly concerned.

'Just realised I've driven to the practice without thinking.'

The sight of dozens of reporters and an outside-broadcast van blocking the route made me stop in the middle of traffic. I indicated back out into the flow and drove on before they spotted me.

'Where are you now?' I asked.

'At home. I *did* warn you about the office.'

'I know. I wasn't thinking. Meet me up at the farm tonight. I think we need to set up a temporary office for the duration. This is getting ridiculous!'

Chapter Forty-One

26 September, late afternoon

Instead of going back to the farm, I drove down to Hanbury Street and parked a few minutes' walk from the row of shops where Anne Stenson's body had been found.

It had been almost three weeks since the murder and, to the uninitiated, there were barely any tell-tale signs of those events now.

I stood in the street opposite the curry house, with my back to the flat where the surveillance team had been. The curry house was closed, but the newsagent next door was a hive of activity.

I stood for a while, observing the people coming and going. Students walked down the street, some took the shortcut through the ginnel between the newsagent's and the adjacent houses; shoppers and school kids made their way home; people got off the bus at the stop down the street and went on their way.

I'd learned long ago, from walking crime scenes, that if I watched an area long enough, I could see patterns emerging – routes people took, shortcuts they made, the areas most frequented and those that people seemed to avoid, the ebb and flow of the population as they interacted with their geography.

After a few minutes I crossed the street and entered the ginnel that ran down the side of the newsagent, trying to picture it as the killer had seen it that early morning, three weeks before.

The dark stone walls towered three floors above my head, the roofs of the buildings on either side almost meeting in the middle, creating a long, dark and damp corridor that opened out about sixty yards ahead of me into the bright sunlight of an autumn day.

To my right was a ten-foot-high wooden fence surrounding the yard behind the shops. I stopped and considered it for a moment, turning to look back the way I'd just come. I was alone in the ginnel, the high, thick stone walls muffling the sounds coming from the busy street I'd just left, and the light from above barely penetrated down here.

As I pushed the creaky wooden gate open, I noticed the remnants of the blue-and-white police tape still attached to the posts, and the dark, silver-grey smudges from the aluminium fingerprint powder that had been dusted everywhere. The yard was a bit brighter, but not much, still towered over as it was by the high buildings around it.

I began to put myself in the killer's mind. *He'd arrived ahead of time and hidden in here waiting for his prey.* I turned and pushed the gate to, but not on the latch. The wooden slats were old and had spaces in between, enough to see through. I put my eye to the gap and imagined him watching, waiting for Anne to come past this spot as she did every morning.

I could hear my own breathing, feel my heartbeat. The muted soundtrack of the city beyond was just a background hum. It would have been easy enough to hold the gate ajar with his foot, just enough to spring out and grab Anne as the CCTV from the house opposite had shown.

I could just see the partially obscured camera at the corner of the house above. But as Callum had said, it didn't cover the yard completely, so it was left to the imagination to paint the horror that had happened once he'd dragged her in here.

Crime scene B – always worse.

I looked back at the spot where her body had been found. Faint bloodstains were splashed along the fence, still visible on the stone flags. I breathed in the stale, damp stench of the place. He'd breathed this air, looked at the same spot, stood where I was standing now.

And then what? After the horror. After the mutilation. His heart would have been pounding, his breathing quickening as the adrenalin coursed through him, heightening every animal sense in his body.

I cautiously opened the gate slightly and waited, listening intently, as he would have done, for any sign that he'd been overheard – nothing. I pushed the gate open just enough to go through and turned to my right as the CCTV showed he'd done, and walked quickly towards the street beyond.

He'd been carrying a backpack containing Anne's womb. I could imagine him feeling elated. Exhilarated. Excited by the thrill of the kill. Not wracked by guilt or fear or horror at what he'd just done, but revelling in the fulfilment of another fantasy. Another victory over the inferior police officers trying to catch him.

'Cattle to the slaughter.'

The end of the ginnel opened out into a surprisingly wide area. Shops along the high street backed onto the space to my left. If he'd walked straight ahead, he would have come out in the city centre, with its imposing town hall and wide-paved pedestrian square with ornamental fountains and colourful flower beds. Even at that early hour there would have been people about. He would have risked being seen and, depending on the amount of blood on his clothing, would have perhaps attracted attention.

I stood and considered his options. To my right was a wide grass verge and a footpath that led to the back of more commercial buildings – not as public or open, and not covered by any CCTV cameras that I could spot.

I turned right and walked slowly along the path, noticing how few people there were. I stopped and looked up, turning through 360 degrees, seeing the skyline, the rooftops, the buildings. Ahead, towering above the other structures, the large glass edifice of Fordley University looked back at me.

I checked the time and then picked up the pace, following the path quickly now. He wouldn't have wanted to attract attention to himself by running. He would have looked like someone hurrying to work, maybe? Head down, striding with purpose.

In exactly seven minutes, the path brought me to the back of the university complex. A high, green chain-link fence marked the boundary. There was a warren of delivery bays and loading areas at the back of the building. A barrier protected the entrance to an underground staff car park, with signs that declared it to be for 'Permit holders only'.

I followed the footpath, noting the swipe-card protected locks that guarded access from this side of the building. Seemingly deserted. Not a route many pedestrians would take ... It took another five minutes to walk around the edge of the university and come out at the front main entrance.

I took the time to stand and look around. To my right, Manchester Road snaked its way up the hill out of town and I could see the towering blocks of flats along its route. George House, where Martha's body had been found, was clearly visible. Just a few minutes' walk away. Less than a mile – a murder mile.

Chapter Forty-Two

26 September – Kingsberry Farm

Jen arrived at the farm in a car loaded down with equipment and files. We set up another desk in my office and arranged things the best we could. Jen got things sorted while I called Callum.

'Jo, I'm sorry about earlier at the briefing,' he said, as soon as he picked up. 'Hoyle's a complete –'

'Never mind that,' I cut across him. 'I walked the scene today at Hanbury Street.'

This statement was met with silence, so I ploughed on.

'I think the university might be your link.' I said it hurriedly before he could cut me off. 'It fits the geography of the murder and the killer's profile.'

'Go on.'

'The university is almost on a direct route from the ginnel in Hanbury Street. In seven minutes he could have been at the back of the university. It's a rabbit warren of delivery bays and staff entrances, offices and security blocks.' I was saving the best till last. 'And it's just ten minutes' walk from George House'.

'OK. That's the location link – what about "Jack"? Is it feasible he's connected to the university? I mean, does that fit with your profile of him?'

'Your techies said that his IP address was being routed through proxy servers in universities or companies around the world. So that would fit. Yes, I think our man could be an employee there; that would give him access to the university buildings.'

'Not a student?'

'No. His age range doesn't fit.'

'Mature student?'

'I don't think so. He's too polished. His intellect and disposition have a maturity that makes me think he's more likely to be a lecturer or on staff somehow. My profile of him has always been that he is intelligent, educated. He's calm and unruffled. He's a linear thinker, a strategist who plans every minute detail. He's not reactive and has highly developed impulse control. He's also used to being in charge so I think he has a position of authority – is used to people following his instructions. That fits with a lecturer or senior member of staff rather than a student, even a mature one. Plus, if he's on staff, he would have more freedom to come and go at odd times of the day and not attract attention. It would account for how he could disappear into the ginnel and not reappear in town. It would give him a place to change clothes or dump his bag – whatever.'

'OK,' Callum said, and I got the sense he was making notes.

'And *don't* pass this on to Taylor-Caine.' I knew it sounded petulant, but I couldn't have cared less.

'You don't have to worry.' He sounded distracted. 'She took a call just after you left the briefing. Seemed in a rush to leave after that and booked off for the day. Rumour has it she's been seeing someone, which pissed Hoyle off even more.'

'Shame,' I said, without sincerity. 'So, back to the job at hand. Given the technical wizardry, maybe look at the computer sciences department?'

'I'll get onto it – we've only got a few days to the next one.'

'Sooner rather than later then,' came my rather unhelpful parting shot.

I was more determined than ever to see this through, despite Hoyle's resistance. I owed it to Martha. More than that, I owed it to the other girls who had died, and to the ones I knew would go on to die if we didn't catch him.

'Jack' had all but told me that somehow I knew him, or knew of him. Somewhere, our paths had crossed and whatever his motivations now, he was driven to make sure I was involved. I couldn't step away from this, even if I wanted to. If the police didn't want my help, fine. But it didn't stop me working on this on my own. Callum could help me or not, that was up to him. But I had a feeling he wouldn't stop feeding me information and if we had to use back channels to communicate rather than the front door, then that's what we'd do.

Jen sat down in the armchair across from my desk, looking at me as she took a sip of coffee. We'd finally managed to create some order out of the chaos of boxes and it was getting late.

'I think I should move in,' she announced, simply.

'What?' My surprise showed.

'If we're going to base the office here until all this is over, it's easier than commuting from mine every day.'

A million reasons why this wouldn't work went through my mind. The silence lengthened as I tried to diplomatically pick the one I thought would dissuade her most effectively and hurt her feelings the least.

She pounced on my hesitation. 'We can't use the practice in town because of the press, and if I travel in from home there's every chance some journalist will follow me up here. So far, they don't know where you live.'

That was true. The nature of my work meant I'd been careful to keep my home address and my private life just that: private. The phone numbers here weren't listed and I'd chosen the farm partly because of its seclusion. Only close family and the local police knew how to find me here.

'What about Henry?' Her husband was legendary for his annoyance with her late night, early morning work ethic, and protective of their family time.

'He'll cope,' she snorted. 'He might realise just how much I *do* if I'm not there. He'll suddenly realise the fridge isn't self-filling or the dishwasher self-emptying. And as for changing the loo roll . . .'

'Bit harsh, Jen.'

I was struggling to come up with a reason that wouldn't offend her. After all these years of living alone, I didn't know if I could share my space with anyone else.

Those sharp blue eyes seemed to see right inside my head.

'Remember, I've known you forever,' she said. 'I know all your moods. That you're as grumpy as hell if you don't get enough sleep, or enough tea. And you snap like a Rottweiler when you're distracted from your work. Not to mention the fact that you don't eat when you're stressed out. If you're left up here to work this on your own, all of the above will apply, and I'm not allowing that to happen.'

She stood up abruptly and put her cup down on my desk like a full stop. 'I've already told Henry, so don't worry about him.'

Her expression softened and she placed her hand on mine. 'This case is as big as it gets, Jo, and I'm not leaving you on your own. We're a winning team, remember?'

I was shocked to feel my eyes welling up. I slipped my hand from beneath hers and patted her wrist as a diversion.

'Sounds like you've got it all planned,' I said, trying not to let my emotions get the better of me. I never could cope when people were unexpectedly nice to me.

'I have. My case is in the car and I'll sort out the spare room. I'm cooking tonight, so you can work till it's ready, OK?'

I nodded, surprised and relieved to have an ally in what was starting to feel like a very lonely battle.

Chapter Forty-Three

28 September, morning – Kingsberry Farm

The house phone was ringing. I could hear it from my office.

'Jen!' I yelled. 'Jen! Can you get that?'

It kept ringing.

Irritated, I dragged my attention from the computer and walked the corridor to the kitchen. As I got nearer, I noticed that the porch door was open and there was no sign of Jen or Harvey. She'd probably taken him out for a walk.

'Hello?'

'Jo?' James' familiar voice crackled. It sounded like he was calling from the car.

'Hi. Where are you?'

'I *was* driving to your office. I called to make sure you'd be there but it went to voicemail. Tried your mobile too. This was my last resort. I guessed you might be at home.'

'Sorry,' I said, holding the phone under my chin as I filled the kettle. 'We're not at the office because of the press. Jen's diverted office calls to her mobile, but it looks like she's out with Harvey and there's no signal across the fields.'

'Is it OK for me to come up there then?' His tone was tight. Businesslike.

'Of course. What's wrong?' I could hear the infectious tension leaking into my own voice now.

'I'll tell you when I get there.'

James sat across from me at my desk. His usual relaxed demeanour was missing and he seemed tense as he talked me through recent events.

'I should have gone back to London yesterday,' he said, 'but it's taken me a few days longer than I thought to tie things up in Manchester. However, the staff are up and running now, so I'm not needed here any longer. Then this morning, as I was getting ready to drive south, I received some information that I thought you should be made aware of.'

My stomach plummeted. How did I know I wasn't going to like what came next?

'What?'

'After you left the last briefing at Fordley nick, Astley showed the team his results from the spatial analysis. Hoyle and Taylor-Caine didn't want you to see the results with the rest of the team because, apparently, they'd been given an advanced preview at Hoyle's insistence.'

'And?'

'The map showed the killer's location as here,' he said, simply.

His eyes were studying mine for some kind of reaction, but what he said didn't register with me at first.

'Here?' I mimicked stupidly. 'You mean in Fordley?'

He reached for the inside pocket of his immaculate suit jacket, shaking his head as he pulled out a neatly folded sheet of paper.

'No, Jo. *Here.*'

He spread the paper out on my desk and rotated the image so I could see it.

It showed a colour contour map of Kingsberry with all the familiar landmarks. At the centre was the unmistakeable image of my farm, as if taken from the air. I could see the lane and my farm, and George's property and outlying buildings further down the track. A portion of land at the edge of our adjoining fields was coloured in red and raised out of the image in 3-D.

I frowned. 'But this doesn't make sense,' I said. 'Are you telling me that –'

'Yes,' he interrupted. 'Exactly. It shows the killer's most likely residence is *here.*'

I stared again at the map, as if looking at it harder would somehow change it. When I looked back, he was watching me from across the desk. His eyes unreadable.

'Is there anything you want to tell me?' he asked, quietly.

'Are you *mad?*' I said. 'Are you *seriously* implying that you think for one minute . . .?'

He shook his head.

'No. Not at all.' He sat back in his chair, studying me intently. 'I *know* you're not implicated, Jo. I got you off that hook already, remember? Plus, you have a solid alibi for Martha, as we both know. But maybe there's something else? Something you haven't thought of?'

'Like *what*, for Christ's sake?'

He shrugged, his eyes never leaving mine. His stare was making me feel uncomfortable and I was beginning to sense what his opposition must experience in court.

'There's a theory that perhaps "Jack" has an accomplice?'

He saw me bristle and held his hand up as I opened my mouth.

'Maybe someone who's *unaware* they're helping him,' he said, quickly. 'Before you rip into me, just try to be rational for a minute and see how this might look to the police.'

'I don't give a *shit* how it looks!' I knew I was raising my voice, but I didn't care. 'I was the one who suggested using spatial analysis in the *first* place. Why would I do that if I knew it would implicate me? And who would entertain a half-arsed theory that puts me in the frame anyway?'

Even as the words left my mouth, I knew the answer. I nearly knocked my chair over as I stood up and went to stare unseeingly at the view across the fields. 'Oh, spare me! That bloody woman! And let me guess, she came up with that theory *after* Astley showed them his findings?'

'Is there someone, Jo, *anyone* who's been staying here with you? Your son maybe –'

I rounded on him before he could even finish the sentence.

'*Alex?* Thank God he's still in India, or that stupid cow would no doubt frame *him* for it.'

Anger was coiling round my innards with a reptilian fury that I couldn't even begin to verbalise. For once in my life, I was speechless with rage.

'This is . . . it's . . . argh!'

The papers flew off the desk with a sweep of my arm.

'Calm down!' he shouted, startling me.

He was suddenly standing, facing me, his body language taut with anger. Unexpectedly, I saw fury flash through his blue eyes. But as fast as I saw it, it was gone as he regained his professional composure.

'Maybe someone you haven't thought of?' he continued, as if my outburst had never happened.

His tone was calm again, changing so quickly it caught me off guard. I was so busy marvelling at the volte-face, I had to force myself to concentrate on his question.

'Travellers staying on the land somewhere? Holiday lets? Anything?'

I shook my head, sitting back at my desk. 'No. Just me and George, and he lives alone.'

'George?'

'George Theakston. He's my neighbour, a mile down the track.' Then another thought occurred to me. 'How do you know all this, anyway?' I indicated the map now on the floor with the rest of my papers. 'And how did you get hold of that?'

I watched his back as he bent down and picked the papers off the floor. He began to stack them into neat piles on my desk.

'I have sources.'

'Someone on the enquiry team?' I asked, as my mind ran through the possibilities. None fitted.

'No.' He finally looked at me. 'Someone I've known for years in the West Yorkshire force.'

There was that disarming smile again. It was as if my outburst and his angry response had never happened.

'Fosters have contacts in all the major forces, Jo. That's how it works. Why do you think we're as successful as we are?' He shrugged as he took his seat again and crossed his legs, flicking an imaginary speck of lint from his knee. 'It's a reciprocal arrangement. They help us from time to time and we return the favour every now and again – sharing information, or giving them a heads-up when we get a sniff of something they might find useful.'

'As long as it doesn't give them an edge over you in court?' I suggested, with more than a hint of sarcasm. I couldn't quite relax back into our conversation somehow. Was it his inference about Alex that had raised my hackles, or something else?

'Something like that.' He smiled again and regarded me with more patience this time. 'I'm sorry, Jo,' he said, quietly, as if reading my thoughts. 'I didn't mean to offend you when I asked about Alex.' His eyes glittered with unexpected amusement as he smiled. 'You really must learn to control your emotions, you know? That temper of yours will get you into serious trouble one day.'

'Believe me, it has,' I reflected without amusement. 'Saved my skin on more than one occasion too, so I'll leave it as it is. If it's all the same to you?'

He shrugged. 'That's the Irish gene, I suppose.' He smiled. 'Goes with the package. Listen, Jo, I was only fishing when I asked about Alex. I suppose what I meant was: is there anyone not local to the area who comes to mind?'

'Jen moved in with me a couple of days ago, but suspecting her is even more ridiculous.' I shook my head. 'I can't imagine how the computer could throw this location up. Can you?'

He pursed his lips thoughtfully. 'No. But then I'm not a spatial analyst. I'm a lawyer and right now my only concern is protecting you from whatever fallout this causes.'

Something in his tone alerted me that there was more. 'Such as?'

He shifted in his seat. 'My source tells me that you should expect a visit.' He nodded towards the map. 'As a result of that – and Taylor-Caine's assessment.'

I resisted the temptation to actually grind my teeth.

'So she postulates that I might be implicated when she sees Astley's analysis, and the enquiry team just *accept* it?' I was incredulous. Especially as I knew Callum well enough to know that he would discount it.

'Didn't they speculate in 1888 that Victorian Jack might have been more than one offender?'

'Yes. But he certainly isn't now,' I said with conviction. 'Our man kills alone. If he's the kind of character I think he is, then he won't trust anyone enough to involve them that closely. Like you said, they may even be unaware they're assisting him. If he has help, it's purely peripheral and probably unwitting on the part of the person he enlists.'

'But you *can* see how they might think you're implicated somehow?' The simplicity with which he said this incensed me.

'What would be my motive?' I raised my voice again, despite his warning look to keep a hold on my 'Irish' temper.

He shrugged. 'For what it's worth, I don't think Callum and the team believe it either.' He flicked the map with his finger. 'But they can't ignore this, Jo. Now it's come up, they have to action it.'

We both looked up as the office door was nudged open and Jen appeared.

'Tea?'

'Your timing is flawless,' I said, showing her the map and bringing her up to speed.

'Well, that accounts for your visitor then.' I raised an enquiring eyebrow.

'Callum's car is pulling down the lane,' she said, going down to the kitchen as we all heard the doorbell.

Chapter Forty-Four

28 September – Kingsberry Farm

'So that's the long and short of it, Jo. I'm sorry.'

Callum looked tired and I could tell this was difficult for him.

'Well, appreciate you coming. You could have just called.'

He ran a hand across the stubble on his chin. 'I could have, but I knew how you'd feel about a search.'

He took a gulp of tea, which emptied the fine china teacup in one go. Jen had found it in the cupboard and regarded it as more 'proper' than my half-pint mugs. He placed it back on the delicate saucer with a 'clack'.

'When should I expect them?' I asked.

James turned from the window he'd been staring out of ever since Callum had arrived. Apart from exchanging nods, neither had spoken. It was evident that Callum had drawn his own conclusions as to why James was here first thing in the morning. He was obviously wrong about any relationship between us, but I didn't have the energy to put him straight. It wasn't lost on James either, but he was enjoying Callum's discomfort far too much to disabuse him.

'They're here now,' James said, pointedly. 'Your guardian angel couldn't give too much advanced notice, Jo, in case you disposed of the evidence.' When he smiled at Callum, it didn't reach his eyes. 'Isn't that right, chief inspector?'

Callum stood up. 'I'd like to think you practise being such a complete bastard, Turner,' he said, as he went to the door, 'but you really are a natural.'

James was unfazed. 'Coming from you, Ferguson,' he smiled, 'I'll take that as a compliment.'

James persuaded me to walk with him across the fields while the police searched the farm. I reluctantly left them to it, knowing Jen would keep an eye on things.

Harvey tagged along, much to James' discomfort.

'I've never been OK with dogs, and they seem to sense it,' he said. 'But then we never owned one when I was growing up. Maybe that's why I'm no good around them.'

I made sure I walked between him and Harvey, who kept up a low, grumbling growl.

'I think all kids should grow up around dogs. Teaches them a lot about responsibility, compassion, love.'

'Love?' He sounded bewildered. Or was his tone just curious? I couldn't decide.

'Only a dog gives you unconditional love and devotion,' I said, absently rubbing Harvey's silky ears as he walked beside me.

'Keeping a dog wouldn't have been practical for us.' He held a farm gate open for me. 'My brother and I were sent to boarding school and my parents were abroad a lot.'

I watched him close the gate, stepping carefully round a cowpat in his immaculately shiny shoes.

'You're not really dressed for this, are you?' I laughed. 'You're messing up your suit.'

'You're worth the cleaning bill,' he said and grinned.

He could charm anyone he wanted, I reflected. No doubt a vital ingredient for success in his chosen profession – equal measures of charm and intellectual aggression, served up with precise logic and razor-sharp wit.

'So you have a brother? I can't imagine another one like you.'

'Oh, believe me,' he said, seriously, 'my brother is *nothing* like me.'

'Is he a lawyer?'

He shook his head. 'Thoracic surgeon. Works in London.'

'Done well for himself, then.'

'Well, he's fifteen years older than me, so he had a bit of a head start,' he said and laughed.

'What about your parents?'

He frowned. 'Feel like I'm on the therapy couch, telling you all about my childhood. Isn't that what you shrinks believe is the root of all screw-ups?'

I laughed. 'It usually is.'

I threw a stick for Harvey to distract him from James.

'My mother died when I was young. Originally she studied Russian literature at Cambridge and then made a career out of being married to my father who was a QC at a chambers in London at the time.'

'Russian literature? Exotic choice.'

'Not really,' he laughed, 'considering her family were Russian. She lived in Saint Petersburg until she was twelve years old. Then the family came to England. She spoke fluent Russian, so Russian literature wasn't too much of a stretch. My grandmother was a big influence in her childhood. She kept the Russian traditions and language alive – believed it was important for my mother to know where she came from, what her history was. I suppose that's where the interest started.'

'So, a choice between medicine and law then?'

'Something like that,' he said. 'I considered medicine for a while and my brother arranged for me to spend one summer at the hospital, getting some work experience.' We stopped and leaned against a drystone wall, watching Harvey run around the meadow. 'It could have gone either way, but after my mother died, it was just me and my father, so I suppose his influence won out.'

'And the rest, as they say, is history?' I leaned back on the wall to look at him.

He shrugged. 'I've done OK, I suppose. Made partner at Fosters by thirty-five. Youngest they'd ever had. Made my father proud at least.'

That last sentence chimed in my head, like the toll of a distant bell. A muffled sound echoing all the way back to his childhood.

I watched his profile. He'd gone suddenly still, as if he sensed the laser focus of my damage-detectors homing in on him.

He was staring straight ahead. Waiting to see whether I would pursue the thing he'd inadvertently revealed. The pain from his childhood that the therapist in me had zeroed in on, like spotting a half-hidden child in the thick undergrowth of adult camouflage.

Usually I couldn't resist picking up pain that people dropped at my feet, almost daring me to open that Pandora's box of childhood hurt and suffering.

I debated for a second whether to go for it. Then I let the laser dot of my aim slide past him, letting him know that today wasn't the day I'd take that shot.

He relaxed beside me as I pretended instead to concentrate on Harvey. I wasn't looking at James but I felt the tension leave his body – and we both knew he would never allow his vulnerability to become a visible target again.

I picked up instead on the humble tone he'd used when speaking about his achievement at making partner at Fosters. It lacked sincerity, and he knew it.

'Oh, admit it.' My tone was deliberately teasing. 'You love the reputation you've got. Hard-assed defence lawyer? First port of call for the rich, famous and corrupt.'

'Er, not to mention celebrity forensic psychologists in the middle of the biggest serial murder case since Jack the Ripper.'

He tugged my arm playfully, pulling me a little closer so that I could smell his cologne. His smile was teasing, but his eyes were looking deep into mine with a sudden intensity that seemed to still the air around us. His fingers felt warm on my wrist, pressing just enough to hold me close and I felt his breath warm against my face as his head dipped towards mine. Intuitively, I turned my face at the last moment and his lips brushed my cheek.

He looked bemused.

'What's wrong?'

I hesitated, watching his eyes, genuinely not knowing how to vocalise an ephemeral reaction to him that had taken me as much by surprise as it obviously had him.

'I don't know,' I said, smiling slightly to take the sting out of the rejection. 'Bad timing, maybe.'

I went to pull my hand away, but he held on to my wrist. I could feel my pulse fluttering beneath his thumb. He was looking into my eyes with an intensity that was almost mesmerising.

I smiled again, gently pulling away from his touch. 'A complication I don't need right now. Nothing personal.'

He let my hand go and we both looked up as the clatter of the police helicopter shattered the rural peace.

'No expense spared,' James muttered.

'Standard procedure, I suppose.'

'Don't keep holding on to him, Jo,' he said, quietly, still watching the helicopter. 'He doesn't value you.'

'Who?' We both knew, but I asked anyway.

'Callum.'

'And how would you know that?' I asked, studying his profile, looking for tell-tale signs of jealousy. Manipulation? He wasn't giving anything away. The muscles bunched in his jaw, as if trying to hold on to something he didn't want to tell me.

'Like I said.' He turned to me with a half-smile. 'I have sources.'

I felt a coldness spreading through my stomach.

'And what do your sources tell you?' I asked, quietly, almost holding my breath.

He shrugged again as he regarded me for a moment, as if debating whether to tell me more. His smile was almost regretful.

'He uses you, Jo. And when it's expedient, he'll throw you to the wolves just like he did after the Woodhouse business.' He put his hands on my shoulders, turning me to face him, looking down at me like a parent breaking bad news to a child. 'You know I'm right. You've felt it, but you don't want to admit it to yourself.'

I thought he was going to say more, but then he seemed to catch himself and stopped, looking beyond me to a point in the distance. His hands dropped and he turned to lean back on the wall.

'Anyway, you're a big girl and I'm sure you know what you're doing.' He turned his head to look down at me. 'I'm driving back to London tonight to prep for a major case, so I'll have to leave you with it, I'm afraid.'

'Will you be coming back?'

I was puzzled at the unaccountable sense of relief I felt. Was it because it removed a potential complication, or because I was struggling to read James – a feeling I wasn't used to?

He shrugged. 'Being up here was only ever supposed to be temporary while I supervised setting up the new office.' He smiled. 'But then I picked up Jen's call and got, er . . . distracted. Maybe, if I thought I had a reason to come back . . .'

That was my prompt, but I couldn't think of anything to say that wouldn't launch me right back into the complication I'd just avoided. And I wasn't about to be drawn into reciprocating just to spare his feelings.

I suddenly saw how good he was at using that mechanism in people, that need to 'dance' in our social interactions with others, to respond automatically and by rote in a way that finds us painting ourselves into corners, then wondering why we agreed to something we didn't really want to do.

Even though I knew how it worked, and used it myself to gain a foothold with a patient or get an edge in an interview, it was difficult not to respond to his cues. He was skilled, all right. I supposed it was something he used in his job. I looked down at my feet to break the moment.

'You can reach me on my mobile any time,' he said. His warm hand cupped my chin and he turned my face towards his. I had to resist the urge to pull away. I couldn't meet his eyes for some reason, so I closed mine.

'Any time, Jo.' I heard him say. 'I mean it.' He hesitated for a heartbeat before adding, 'Not just for work, either. I mean, if Callum –'

'I know,' I interrupted him, not really wanting to hear any more, despite the clawing curiosity about what else his 'sources' might have said. I couldn't face having my illusions shattered right now. It felt as though everything I'd held on to lately, everything I'd believed was solid and real in my life was on shifting sand, and at this moment I needed to focus.

We started back to the farm and I let him carry the conversation. My mind was too busy processing the things he'd said, sifting through the unfinished sentences and halting delivery that gave me the sense he knew more than he was sharing. Or had he designed it that way? To keep me off balance and whet my appetite? To draw me in? If so, it was a divisive technique designed to distance me from Callum, to make me question the relationship I thought we had and destroy my trust in him. Or maybe I was overthinking it? The curse of the analyst was to overanalyse everything and create shadows and hidden motives that often weren't there.

The paranoia of the professional inquisitor. Maybe everything he was warning me about was true and he genuinely cared?

'So I've given notice on the flat in Salford Quays,' he was saying. 'Can't see I'll be coming back in the foreseeable future. There's too much work back in London at the moment.' He laughed. 'Unless they've found a body in your basement while we've been away? That would keep me busy for a while.'

Chapter Forty-Five

28 September – Kingsberry Farm

Thankfully there were no corpses in my basement or anywhere else for that matter, and the team were leaving by the time we got back. Callum waited by his open car door when he saw me.

'I hope you didn't upset George?' I heard the serrated tone in my voice but couldn't stop it.

It wasn't lost on Callum either and he shot a look across my shoulder to James, who had hung back. I wasn't sure what was irritating me the most. The fact that he automatically attributed my mood to the time I'd spent with James, or the fact that he might be right?

'He wasn't home,' Callum said. 'His door was unlocked and there'd been a fire in the grate. The Land Rover was on the yard with the keys in, but no sign of him. Looked like he'd just gone out on the farm somewhere.'

That was typical of George. 'He never locks his doors.'

Callum looked down at me as I stood by the car. 'If you give me his mobile number, I can call him.'

'He doesn't own one. I'm amazed he even has a landline. I hope he's not going to come back to a mess?' I sounded irritable. I couldn't help it.

His expression was a mixture of exasperation and hurt. He kept glancing behind me to James, who I knew, without looking, was watching us from the doorway.

'No mess. We left a copy of the warrant on his kitchen table so he knows we've been and I left a card with the direct number for the enquiry team, so he can call us if he needs to.'

'No Laundy blades or spare wombs lying around then?' I really couldn't help myself.

Callum sighed and got in his car.

'If you need anything, Jo, you know where I am.' He sounded resigned and tired, but I was being too bloody-minded to back off. Fuming as much at myself as him, I turned and walked back to the house.

28 September, evening – Kingsberry Farm

The press were in a feeding frenzy. Apparently, in the early hours of the previous day, Sky News had received a call, purporting to be from 'Jack' himself. He'd claimed responsibility for all three murders and gave information only the killer would know, such as taking Anne's womb – a fact the police had held back.

All the news channels were carrying the story now and the ticker-tape banner at the bottom of the screen updated hourly.

Hoyle's face stared back at me from every TV channel, alongside the assistant chief constable. The press briefings assured the public that every resource was being given to the enquiry and that the major investigation team were working round the clock.

The murders had inevitably drawn comparisons with the Yorkshire Ripper – in this county, the press couldn't resist citing that history, but it was an uncomfortable association the police didn't want to encourage.

The newspapers too were full of the murders in every gory detail, with journalists hungry to track down anyone who knew the victims – no matter how tenuous the connection.

The dedicated press officer walked a very fine line between feeding a hungry press pack enough information to keep the public informed and encourage witnesses to come forward, and holding back vital facts that might compromise the investigation.

I was happy to lie low and stay away from locations where the press were gathered, which now included all three murder sites, as well as the Fordley practice and the police station. I was thankful I'd walked the Hanbury Street scene before it had become a place of such morbid fascination.

It wasn't lost on me that it was on exactly the same date that Victorian Jack had sent his 'Dear boss' letter to the Central News Agency in London in 1888. That letter had been signed 'Jack the Ripper', giving him his legendary name.

Our 'Jack' was obviously a man of his time, using the power of the twenty-four-hour news cycle to capture for himself the global infamy spawned by his predecessor.

So far he was sticking to the timetable in every detail and I had no reason to suppose that would change for the anniversary of the 'double event' in just two days' time.

Chapter Forty-Six

29 September – Kingsberry Farm

I sipped my tea and looked out of the office window as Harvey bounded around outside. It was cooler, with glowering grey skies that weren't helping my mood.

I'd heard nothing from Callum and while the logical part of my mind reasoned that was down to the pace of the investigation and the hundreds of actions being generated by HOLMES, I couldn't get James' remarks out of my mind.

I instinctively felt a coldness settling over our relationship. Callum was distancing himself and I reasoned it was because he didn't trust me any more.

I looked at my desk and the endless printouts of possible suspects from my clinical files. None of the profiles fitted 'Jack'.

As I turned back to the view, my thoughts returned to Martha. There was something in our conversation that didn't fit, an inconsistency that was nagging at me. Somehow I knew there was a clue in something she'd said, but I just couldn't get hold of it.

I decided to do what I always did at times like this: walk. Walk aimlessly and endlessly to clear my mind of clutter and talk myself along a logical, rational timeline; go back over my conversations with Martha, line by line, moment by moment, hope that something would click into place.

Harvey ran ahead, stopping every few hundred yards to look back and make sure I was there, but my mind was elsewhere.

I was recalling my interview with Martha, replaying it in as much detail as I could; the light, the sound, the smell of the hospital room, the grey stains of tears splashing onto her hospital gown.

She had talked about how much John had protected her, how he had helped her get off drugs. And then she'd shown me his method of 'stroking' her to relax her during the rattles of her withdrawal.

I focused on a point in the distance as I replayed what she'd said. It felt as if I was reaching in the air for the string of a balloon floating just out of reach above my head. It was there, I could feel it. That missing piece. What was it?

I closed my eyes and listened to her small voice. The halting delivery as she relayed what John had done to help her kick the habit . . .

'Yes, John did it . . . He said he could and he did. I don't take nothin' no more . . .'

My fingers stretched higher. I was almost touching it.

'Yes, John did it . . . it worked . . .'

Mentally, I strained to reach it. My fingertips brushed the string, focusing hard to recall every detail, every nuance, every word.

And then I understood.

'He had to repress me 'n everything, he said he could and he did . . . it worked.'

That was it!

I opened my eyes as Harvey pushed his cold nose into my hand, nudging me in frustration at my lack of attention.

'Repress.' She said he repressed her.

That had been the piece that jarred. At the time it meant nothing and now it explained everything.

Martha's IQ was that of a ten-year-old and her vocabulary reflected it. Repression wasn't a word she would use or even understand. And if that *had* been the nature of her relationship with John, she wouldn't have had the ability to vocalise it that way.

She had misused a word she'd heard but not understood, mixing up the context. She hadn't meant that he'd *repressed* her. But if she'd meant something else entirely, then it unlocked it all.

It gave me the answer to the questions that had haunted me. How could the killer know what had been said in that room between Martha and me? How could 'Jack', the alter ego locked in Martha's mind, come out to become a flesh-and-blood killer and commit the murders only Martha and I knew we had discussed? How could 'Jack', the phantom, be made real?

I raced back to the farm with Harvey at my heels, barely aware of him, of anything except the urgency to test my theory that unlocked the mystery of what we were dealing with. And maybe even the vital clue to 'Jack's' true identity.

29 September, evening

I scanned my notes on repressed memory retrieval, the basis of my first book.

Lister had said what a good hypnotic subject Martha was. When John used to 'stroke' her to help her through her withdrawal, he was obviously inducing a hypnotic state.

Was it possible that while under hypnosis – in the fragile and vulnerable mental state that Martha's drug withdrawal had created – John had gone even further?

I barely noticed the clattering of dishes coming from the kitchen as Jen cleared up after supper. Closing my eyes instead, I mentally replayed my conversation with Lister.

'*She was tormented by memories of a period when she believed she'd committed serious crimes. She was having nightmares and believed they were flashbacks to real events . . . She thought she had committed murder . . . more than once. She thought she had stabbed other prostitutes.*'

'Making progress?' I was so deep in thought, Jen made me jump.

I indicated the chair opposite my desk and Jen sat down. I paused for a moment, trying to get my thoughts into logical order before pitching my theory.

'Remember the Gail Dobson case?'

'How could I forget? The woman was a bunny boiler.' She frowned as she remembered the events a few years before that had landed us in the middle of a legal mess. 'It was a complete shitstorm.'

'That about sums it up,' I agreed.

Gail Dobson had been a psychotherapist treating a business-man for anxiety and depression and during their sessions she supposedly uncovered repressed memories of sexual abuse he'd committed against his daughter when she'd been just a child. The daughter was in her twenties by this time and the revelations had come as a complete shock to her as well as to the rest of his family.

'That was actually the first time we used Fosters,' Jen recalled. 'Marissa put us on to them when Dobson tried to sue *us*.'

'It wasn't James Turner, though. It was before his time at the firm. Can't remember the guy we used. Think he's retired now, anyway.'

I'd initially been called in by the man's wife and daughter, who were adamant that the abuse had never happened. But the businessman was so wracked with guilt once the memories had been 'unlocked' that he'd made a full confession to the police. Gail Dobson had given police statements that supported his claim.

We'd become engaged in a battle between the poor man's own confession and the 'victims' – who were fighting to prove his innocence.

I assessed him privately and the report I produced meant the CPS dropped the case before it went to court. The family took out a private prosecution against Dobson, but she didn't go down without a fight and actually tried to discredit me during the case. She lost and was eventually struck off.

For months afterwards, we got anonymous hate mail and a sustained vitriolic campaign on social media but with the help of Marissa's technical wizard, we eventually traced the hate campaign back to Dobson and handed the case over to the police.

'I remember the case well, but what's this got to do with anything?' Jen frowned.

'I think the boyfriend installed false memories into Martha, to make her believe she'd committed those murders in Manchester,' I said, as if that explained everything.

'Why?' Jen asked, going straight to the heart of it. 'To what end?'

I might be the clinician, but Jen had spent her entire career working with some of the best forensic psychologists in the field. She may not have had the qualification, but she knew more about the subject than some 'specialists' I'd met in my time.

I valued her input and her opinion, which was why I bounced my theories off her. If she thought I was wide of the mark, she'd tell me and, just as she had now, she would pin me down until my logic passed her scrutiny. It was a great method for testing our argument before presenting evidence at trial. We'd perfected it over the years and I knew if my theory stood up to Jen's devil's advocacy, then I could confidently face any QC in court.

'For some reason "Jack" wants me as a central player in all this, which is why he's staged his crimes here and not in London. I think Martha was the bait to draw me in.'

'So he'd planned all along to leave her at Westwood Park? And called us to make sure you knew she was there?'

I nodded, watching her expression as she thought it all through, testing it from all the angles.

'Lister said they'd tried to regress her back to the time in Manchester,' I carried on, 'but every time they got near, it triggered her severe abreaction.'

'So?' Jen probed.

'So, when he installed the false memory, he put a tripwire in there so that as soon as a clinician tried to probe into those events using the usual techniques, she'd freak out and they'd not get past it. By calling me and getting me to see her, he was banking on the fact that I *would* be able to bypass the abreaction and uncover the "repressed memory" of her "crimes".'

'Rewind,' Jen said. 'So far so good. He's baited the hook with an intriguing case that gets you to see her at Westwood. Let's say you're right and he's installed a tripwire to trigger an abreaction that probably only you can bypass. But you said Martha was like a child. I mean, would she have had the mental capacity to pull it off?'

'That's just the point, Jen. Martha wasn't complicit in the deceit, any more than our businessman was. She wasn't trying to pull anything off – she *truly* believed she'd committed the murders, just like the businessman was convinced he'd abused his daughter. You remember how he was after that whole thing? Even after I'd proved to him that it had never happened, he clung on to it. He needed months of reconstructive therapy to rationalise that what he'd experienced was false memory installation by Dobson.'

'Hmm – like brainwashing.'

'In the Dobson case, the father was a highly suggestible subject,' I said, looking at my notes on the laptop. 'As a teenager, he'd fantasised about having sex with young girls. He wasn't a paedophile – it was adolescent fantasy. He never acted on it and he outgrew it. But when the therapist "uncovered" the event, he was convinced he might have given in to those early sexual drives.'

'Felt he could have been capable of it?'

'Exactly. There are three factors needed to successfully install false memory,' I said, as much to run through it for my benefit as hers. 'The subject has to perceive the event as plausible, just like our businessman did because of his fantasies. Then the installer has to make them believe it's *likely* to have happened. And thirdly, they have to interpret the events as actual memories, which can be done by an authoritative figure claiming to *know* it actually happened. In his case, that was Dobson.'

'Were those ingredients present in Martha's case?'

'Yes. The boyfriend picked Susie Scott to groom her for the role as "Jack's" first victim. He changed her name, exploited her vulnerability while she was in withdrawal from heroin, and her memory lapses fell right into his hands. He installed false memories of murders she'd committed. Lister said the boyfriend was an authority figure to her, that she looked up to him. If *he'd* said he *knew* she'd done it, then she would believe him. She *knew* it was plausible or even likely she'd stabbed someone to death because she'd been arrested for stabbing her pimp, so it would have been easy to manipulate her. He created himself as her rescuer, who would get her off drugs, get her away from Manchester and cover up her crimes, give her a new life here in Fordley.'

We looked at each other in silence for a moment, letting the thought percolate.

Jen scratched her head with the end of her pencil. 'How do you explain "Jack", the alter ego you "met" when you went into her head?'

'We know the unconscious mind runs strategies for everything, from routine tasks to elaborate behaviours.' Jen nodded but gave me the silence to continue. 'An external trigger happens and fires the strategy, the behaviour or the verbal script that we just run automatically.'

I'd explained it often enough to patients who said they habitually fell into a behaviour and 'couldn't help themselves', even though they wanted to stop. Like launching into a tirade of verbal abuse if someone cut them up in traffic. It happens so automatically they can't help it, and then are ashamed of themselves afterwards.

'It's only an extension of the techniques we use to "uninstall" those unhelpful behaviours,' I said. 'We identify the external trigger that "fires" the automatic response, then neutralise it. Done in reverse, you could *create* a response and install a script that runs once it's triggered by an external stimulus.'

'So "Jack" is "installed" into Martha's mind along with a script that she would just repeat as soon as the "play button" was pressed?' Jen said.

'Exactly. The "play button" for the appearance of "Jack" would be a key word that I would use during my hypnotic induction. I've listened to the recording of that session, Jen. It's not a conversation, it's a script delivered by rote. The vocabulary wasn't Martha's – it was too advanced for her. It was *installed*, Jen, so I'd feel as if I'd encountered an alter ego – Jack the Ripper. It felt like I was in a dialogue – but you could take me out of the conversation and it would run the same and still make sense.'

I leaned forward, tapping my notes. 'If I was the clinician that bypassed the abreaction, then it was going to be *me* that encountered "Jack" – nobody else. If no one could get far enough with Martha to access the false memory of the fictional murders in Manchester, then nobody was going to hit the button that played "Jack's" script. No one would ever hear that but me and that's just the way he designed it to happen. After that, the rest was easy. He kills Martha and replicates Jack's murders. He knows the script – knows what I've heard and can "share" that conversation when he – the phantom that's been released from the locked room of Martha's mind – contacts me.'

'He created the lock and you presented the key,' Jen said, sitting back in her chair. She looked at me for a long moment. 'Would a layman be able to install something so elaborate?'

'No. Either he's got the ability to do it . . .' My eyes met Jen's. 'Or he's working with someone who does.'

Chapter Forty-Seven

29 September, late evening

I dialled Callum's number and was surprised when a woman answered.

'Callum's phone.'

'This is Dr McCready.'

'Hi, Jo, it's Beth.' There was an uncomfortable pause. Just a heartbeat, but enough of a 'tell' for me to know that Callum was there. He just didn't want to speak to me. 'The boss is tied up at the moment. It's mad here tonight – can I help?'

I ran through my theory, while she made notes.

'So do you think "Jack" and Gail Dobson might be acting together in this?'

'I'm not saying that exactly, Beth. I mean, I don't even know where Dobson is now. Last we knew, she was in London.'

'Her practice was in London when the original case happened?'

'Yes, but she was struck off after the tribunal by the governing body, so she won't have a practice now. At least, she shouldn't have.'

'OK . . .' Beth was speaking slowly, thinking out loud. 'We've always suspected it was someone from your past, Jo, but we've concentrated on offenders, not clinicians. Sounds like she harboured a serious grudge. Good work coming up with her as a person of interest – it's definitely a line of enquiry. Would it fit the profile if "Jack" was her boyfriend or husband?'

'Possibly.' But even as I said it, I wasn't sure. 'It would fit with folie à deux and the accomplice theory. Martha said that the boyfriend had taken her to London to see a therapist for treatment but she couldn't remember the therapist's name. Said it was a woman though, so that fits. But if it *is* Dobson, she's probably not involved in the actual murders – I mean present at the scene. Her character doesn't fit that kind of psychopathy.'

I ended by adding, 'I still think the university is at the heart of it somehow too.'

'That's great, Jo, thanks for this. We'll follow it up.'

I glanced at the clock. It was almost 8 p.m.

'Time's tight – he'll be on the hunt already. First victim of the double event is dead by 1 a.m. –'

30 September – Kingsberry Farm

Neither Jen nor I had slept. I'd watched 1 a.m. come and go, sitting by my phone with the news channel on all night. I knew if anything happened, the media wouldn't pick it up until morning, but it was the only connection to the unfolding events that I had.

Part of me hoped Callum would call just as he had after all the others, or even during the night – but nothing. There was no doubt that he was cutting me out of the loop. Ever since they'd searched the farm, I'd known I was being kept firmly on the outside of the investigation.

Jen stuck her head round my office door.

'Scrambled eggs on toast for breakfast?'

'You been shopping?'

I was surprised. Our fridge was running seriously low as we'd been on lockdown at the farm for the past couple of days.

'Found this on the porch door handle this morning.' She grinned, holding up a carrier bag. 'A dozen fresh duck eggs and some milk, courtesy of George.'

I smiled. He often left eggs and produce from his veg patch on my doorstep in the early morning. Said he couldn't keep up with his ducks when they were laying well, so shared the extra bounty with me.

I went down to the kitchen and sat at the table as Jen poured tea and buttered the toast. The clock above the Aga said 6 a.m. If the double event had happened, they'd know by now.

'Stop clock-watching,' Jen said.

'Why hasn't he called?' I took a mouthful of eggs that I really couldn't stomach. 'Even if it's to say nothing's happened, I should have heard by now.'

'You don't want to hear this, but you're not naïve, Jo.' She looked at me over the rim of her cup. 'You're out in the cold and Callum's not going to call. None of the team are. It ended with Astley's report. That, coupled with "Jack's" calls, are putting you too close to events. If you're not a suspect, then at best you're a material witness whose involvement is unclear and Hoyle wants you kept as far away from the major incident room as possible.' She took another sip before adding, carefully, 'And for what it's worth, the way Callum feels about James hasn't helped.'

She was right – I didn't want to hear it. But I knew it was true.

'Well,' I said, wearily into my teacup, 'James is back in London, so that's one complication out of the way I suppose.'

We both jumped when my work mobile rang. It had been switched off, but I'd put it back on the night before, to give Callum as many options for reaching me as possible.

'Hello, Dr McCready?' It was a voice I didn't recognise. 'I'm the on-call crime reporter for the *Herald*. I'm calling for your comments on the discovery of Lizzie Taylor-Caine's body this morning?'

The reporter kept talking, but I wasn't processing what he was saying. I put it on loudspeaker so Jen could hear and we stared at each other, dumbfounded.

Lizzie Taylor-Caine.

A million jumbled thoughts raced through my mind, jockeying for position in the likely scenario stakes. Had she been with the surveillance teams last night? Had there been an accident?

'How?' I finally managed, sounding lame even to my own ears. 'When?'

'Her body was discovered by police just after 1 this morning,' he said, matter-of-factly. 'Her throat had been cut. Any comment before the news agencies run it on Breakfast TV?'

Jen took the phone off me and spoke to him, but I was no longer listening.

In 1888, Liz Stride had been discovered at 1 a.m. behind the International Working Men's Club, used by Polish Jews. She'd had her throat cut.

Liz Taylor-Caine . . .? Was it possible?

'Where?' I asked.

Jen paused as we waited for the answer. The reporter's disembodied voice echoed through my kitchen.

'Behind the Polski Klub, Charles Street, in Fordley. Sounds like this is the first you've heard of it?' He sounded surprised. 'Aren't you working with the investigating team?'

'Was there a second body found last night?' I asked, flatly.

'The police aren't releasing any information at this time, doctor. We picked this up from residents posting the activity on social media, and an overheard broadcast over a police radio at the scene. We were hoping you could . . .'

I gestured for Jen to end the call. I'd heard enough.

As soon as she hung up, it began ringing again. I let her field the first few calls – all the same, from journalists and reporters – until eventually she switched the phone off. I stared at my mobile, willing Callum to call, knowing he wouldn't.

We both jumped again when the bell above the Aga shrieked. The press didn't have the number of the phone in my study.

Chapter Forty-Eight

30 September – Kingsberry Farm

'Doctor . . .'

'Jack.' I felt bile churning in my empty stomach. 'I was expecting your call.' I sounded far calmer than I felt.

I cradled the phone under my chin as I booted up my computer. Had he sent me an accompanying photo of his latest victim?

'You've heard?' I could hear the smile in his voice.

'Yes,' I said, watching the screen in sick anticipation. 'Have you sent me a picture?'

'Not this time.' He sounded disappointed. 'No time. It was a very busy night.' He laughed. 'Do you like the irony?'

'Of what?'

I wanted him to say it. If the police were still bugging my phone, I needed him to say it.

That metallic laugh again, making my skin crawl. 'Lizzie. Not Stride this time . . . Taylor-Caine.' He couldn't keep the triumph out of his voice. 'I said I would give you a token . . . a gift, from me to you.'

'What do you want? *Thanks?*' I was gritting my teeth. '*Why?* Why her?' The volume of my voice was rising, but I couldn't keep my composure. The enormity of it was beyond shocking.

He laughed, enjoying the reaction he provoked. 'Admit it, you're pleased she's dead, that thorn in your side. If you could have done it yourself, you would ha—'

'No!'

Jen was beside me, making gestures for me to stay calm, but I'd gone beyond that. The pressure in my forehead was building, as if it might explode any minute.

'Don't lay this one at my feet,' I said, through clenched teeth. 'You sick bastard!'

'Doctor, doctor, where's your composure?' He was laughing at me – enjoying the fact that he'd got under my skin. 'It's a fine line you walk on the other side of that abyss, isn't it?' His tone was intimate. 'It would be so easy for you to cross over, wouldn't it? You look into the minds of monsters and understand them because your own is wired the same way. It wouldn't take that much, would it? For you to act out those drives you understand so well? That you can see in yourself as well as in people like me?'

I held my breath and squeezed my eyes shut, not trusting myself to speak. He took hold of my silence.

'Appreciate the gift,' he whispered, 'the most precious gift one can give another – a life. I shared the most intimate moment of all with her. More erotic than sex. More intimate than making love. I felt her last breath against my lips . . . felt the last beat of her heart under my hand. Saw that light leave her eyes . . . for you.'

I sat on the corner of my desk, my free hand gripping the edge, willing my voice to become calm again.

'What about the second victim?'

I chanced it. Would he realise I knew nothing about last night's events? Whether there had even *been* a second?

'A whore,' he said, dismissively, as if he was bored by the second event. 'Not as special to us as Lizzie. I hope you enjoy your jewellery,' he said, enigmatically, before the line went dead.

Chapter Forty-Nine

1 October – Kingsberry Farm

'I wasted my chance when he called.'

Beth and Ian were at my kitchen table, sitting down to the tea and biscuits Jen had laid out. They'd arrived that morning to bring me up to speed and to interview me. They were doing it subtly, but it was an interview, nonetheless. It was painfully obvious that a sea change had taken place in the way I was being viewed by the senior investigating team and I had to work hard not to show that it mattered.

'In what way?' Beth asked.

'I'd pre-planned my strategy if he called,' I said, trying not to sound as if I was defending myself. 'I wanted to throw him by telling him I'd worked out how he'd implanted the false memory with Martha, see if I could get him to give me something more – maybe implicate whoever had helped him.' I shrugged. 'But I suppose he threw *me* with his choice of victim. So my strategy went to ratshit.'

'Understandable.' Ian was sympathetic. 'Totally unexpected. The last time any of us saw Lizzie was at Astley's briefing. She booked off after that and just dropped off the grid.' He sipped his tea. 'You say you didn't see or hear from her after that either?'

I shook my head. 'We were hardly friends. No reason she *would* contact me.'

'And you've been here at the farm for the last few days? Just you and Jen?'

I nodded. 'But I'm sure you've checked the cell-site data for my phone too,' I couldn't keep some acid out of my tone, 'so you already know that.'

He didn't miss a beat.

'That proves your *phone* was here – not that you were with it.'

Even though he smiled slightly as he said it, I could feel the iron beneath the velvet.

I did my best not to bite. 'Indeed.'

He carried on. 'We found Lizzie's mobile at her flat. Looks like she simply walked out without it. So there's no cell-site data to plot her whereabouts before her body was found last night. The call she took at the briefing is listed on her phone as an unknown number and the Telephony team think it was from a burner phone.'

'Jack' had completed the 'double event' true to schedule, and simply melted away.

Unlike the last time, the police hadn't had a specific area to cover. He could have struck anywhere in one of the biggest cities in the largest county in England. As it happened, despite the increased police presence in the area – on foot and in patrol cars – he'd struck at the edge of the red-light district. And no one had seen or heard a thing.

A Polish couple leaving a lock-in at the Polski Klub had found Lizzie's body dumped alongside the railings and raised the alarm at just after 1 a.m.

Fifty minutes later, while police were dealing with that discovery, a 999 call had come in from a group of students who'd stumbled across the second victim when they'd taken a shortcut through the churchyard of the Polish Catholic church. It was just fifteen minutes' walk away from the first murder scene.

'How did she come into contact with "Jack"?' I said. 'Obviously, from what he said to me, he planned for her to be the fourth victim all along. But *how* did he get to her? Surely that's not an area she would have gone to normally?'

Beth glanced down at her notebook. 'We're checking to see who she called and where she went, but like Ian says, she just disappeared. Her car was left at her flat, so we can't track that on CCTV, and neighbours say the last time they saw her was on the day of the briefing.'

'Any lead on Gail Dobson?' I asked.

'We ran her through PNC after speaking with you,' Beth said, looking briefly to Ian, who nodded imperceptibly. 'She committed suicide last year at her flat in London. Overdosed on prescription pills and vodka.'

I looked down into my cup. Strangely, I didn't feel anything. The woman had caused Jen and I all sorts of pain a few years before, but I wouldn't have wished her dead.

'She didn't strike me as the kind to take her own life,' I said, slowly sipping my tea. 'Totally narcissistic, deflected responsibility onto everyone else for the situations she found herself in. I can't imagine her feeling deeply enough about anything or anyone to push her to suicide.'

Ian helped himself to another biscuit. 'Well, it wasn't totally cut and dried,' he said, dunking the biscuit. 'The coroner recorded an open verdict.'

That piqued my interest. 'Why?'

He shrugged. 'There was some doubt thrown on her suicide at the time. Friends and relatives said she'd been planning a holiday, was generally happy, got her life back on track –'

'Plus,' Beth put in, 'officers investigating weren't totally happy about the circumstances around it either, but there was nothing conclusive at the post-mortem. The pathologist couldn't find evidence to say it was anything other than suicide, but because of the officer's concerns, returned an open verdict.'

I nodded, thinking beyond Dobson to 'Jack's' earlier call.

'"Jack" said something to me about jewellery?'

'I was coming to that.' Ian slipped a photograph out of his jacket pocket and pushed it across the table.

It was a picture of something inside a clear plastic evidence bag. It took a moment for me to work out what I was looking at. Two thin gold rings, joined together with bloodstained twine. I looked at Ian, my expression obviously begging a million questions.

'The two gold rings that Anne Stenson was wearing when she was murdered,' he said.

'They were missing when her body was found, weren't they?' I looked at them both. 'We assumed the killer took them as trophies – just as Victorian Jack did with Annie Chapman's rings.'

'He did,' Beth said. 'They were found in the wound to Lizzie's throat.'

'Jesus . . .' I managed.

Ian cleared his throat. 'I know. The other end of the string was attached to this . . .'

He pushed across another photo. It showed a heavily bloodstained floral gift tag with the words: "Jo, from me to you – Jack. Xx."

I could feel a pulse behind my eyes. 'So after cutting her throat, he . . .'

Beth nodded. 'Pushed those into the wound and left the tag hanging out so we'd find them.'

I couldn't speak. I just stared at the pictures and shook my head. Jen discreetly poured everyone more tea.

'We're waiting for the full post-mortem report,' Ian was saying. 'But at first glance, it doesn't look like Lizzie was killed at the scene.'

I gave him the silence to continue.

He was flipping through his notebook.

'The pathologist thinks she was killed elsewhere. He thinks she'd been dead as long as two days, before being dumped behind the Polski Klub. She also doesn't appear to have been killed like the others. No bruising to the jaw, or signs of strangulation. She had ligature marks on her wrists. She was bound prior to death, unlike any of the others.' He paused for a moment before adding. 'She had marks on her body that would suggest she'd been tortured.'

'Tortured?' I was surprised. 'He's deviating from the script. Liz Stride had no marks on her – apart from having her throat cut.'

I sipped my tea to buy some thinking time.

'Victorian Jack committed the two murders forty-five minutes apart,' I said. 'Theory has it that the reason Liz Stride only had her throat cut was because he was disturbed and fled the scene, but was in such a heightened state he wanted to finish what he'd started and almost stumbled across Catherine Eddowes twelve minutes later. Her attack was more frenzied, with the removal of part of her womb and her left kidney. Difficult to replicate

307

that scenario, though, especially if you're picking victims randomly. Not plausible that he'd get Taylor-Caine to the site at just the right time. More likely he killed her first, somewhere else, then dumped her body that night before killing his second victim.' I looked at them both. 'What do you know about the second one?'

'Kate Lawson,' Beth said, flipping through her notebook. 'Thirty-five, a prostitute working the area. Apparently she took punters into the churchyard, which is where she was found. The wounds inflicted on her are identical to those of Catherine Eddowes, including removal of a portion of her womb and her left kidney – neither of which were found at the scene, so he must have taken them with him. Other girls who usually worked with her had taken recent warnings seriously and most of them were off the streets, so Kate was on her own. So far no one's come forward to say they saw or heard anything and there's no CCTV around the churchyard. We've got a team looking at footage from the area to see if we can piece her movements together.'

'Mitre Square was the Victorian murder scene,' I said, thoughtfully. 'Suppose a Catholic church is a close enough reference.' I looked across at Ian. 'That isn't far from town?'

He shook his head. 'Few minutes' walk.' He paused before adding, 'Not far from the university either. Less than a mile.'

'The university is at the heart of this, I'm sure of it. If I'm right, "Jack's" profile fits with a lecturer or someone who works there in a professional capacity. It's central to most of the murder sites and it would give him a bolthole after the murders – to change clothes or dump his trophies, so he's not spotted walking the streets covered in blood. Your techies say he's using proxy servers in universities around the globe to kick over his electronic footprints – it fits.'

'We're on it,' Beth said. 'There are so many lines of enquiry now. HOLMES is generating hundreds of actions, but we're getting through them. Eventually we *will* get a breakthrough.'

Chapter Fifty

8 October – Kingsberry Farm

A breakthrough couldn't come soon enough.

The media were in meltdown. The murders had sparked the biggest manhunt in UK criminal history and coverage was extensive The twenty-four-hour news was constantly on in the office, with the sound muted, but I kept an eye on the ticker-tape updates scrolling along the bottom of the screen.

There were so many lines of enquiry that extra manpower from other forces had been drafted in and the chief constable's face was all over the media as he appealed for calm, reassuring the public that everything possible was being done.

The fact that one of the last victims had been 'one of their own', fed into the horror of the narrative.

'Jack' had killed West Yorkshire Police's own criminal profiler, giving a defiant two fingers to the police and assuring his infamy as one of the most audacious serial killers in British history.

This Ripper wasn't confining his victims to prostitutes. He was a threat to *everybody*. With Fordley swamped with a new intake of students for Fresher's week, protest marches of worried students and parents swept through the city, calling for a curfew for men in the city, and demanding more police presence on the streets. For those who had lived through the nightmare years of the Yorkshire Ripper, it was all too familiar.

I still hadn't heard anything from Callum and, as I pulled on my boots in the porch, I told myself to accept that it marked the end of whatever we'd had going.

The thought left me feeling empty and hollow – and desperately lonely. I'd lost my friend and my confidant, that missing piece I'd finally come to need.

Harvey stood expectantly by the door, eager to get out, both of us needing to walk off the tension. The air was turning autumnal, with a fresh bite to the breeze and a threat of rain in the darkening sky.

I waved as George's Land Rover swept past my gate on the way down to his farmhouse, and he raised a hand through his open window. Harvey chased after him until the bend in the road, then came panting back to me.

I was using our walks to get some clarity, to try and untangle all the threads running through the enquiry.

I'd not matched any of my patients to 'Jack's' profile. The only person who came to mind with a motive had been Gail Dobson, and her death eliminated her immediate involvement. But I was certain she had been the therapist Martha's boyfriend had used in London. She'd been a tenuous link at first, but once I became convinced that my encounter with 'Jack' was the result of false memory installation, Dobson was the only one who fitted.

So where did it leave me now?

I *still* believed the university was at the heart of it, maybe someone in the computer science or psychology department.

Beth told me that they could find no connection between Taylor-Caine and Gail Dobson. Or to anyone at Fordley University, for that matter. So how did 'Jack' get to her?

I suspected that he'd abducted and murdered her not long after Astley's briefing, then planted her body on the night of the double event. That would fit with her being kept bound somewhere before being killed. But it was circumstantial and I had no proof beyond my own glimpses into his monstrous mind.

Torturing her was a deviation that continued to bother me too. 'Jack' was undoubtedly a psychopath who would enjoy inflicting pain and terror onto a helpless victim, but he was also coldly precise and methodical in his devoted following of Jack the Ripper's original killings. He must have had a serious reason to deviate from that MO with Lizzie Taylor-Caine.

As we neared the farm, Jen came to the door, frantically waving the office phone.

'It's Beth!' she said, breathlessly, as I took the phone off her.

'Hi,' I said. 'Any news?'

'Just wanted to let you know, we've had a break.'

'Go on . . .'

'An anonymous call from a student, saying that someone asked him to take the DNA test for him –'

'Who?'

'The IT consultant from Fordley University. The team are going to pick him up now.'

Chapter Fifty-One

9 October – Fordley Police Station

'Paul Harrison,' Callum said. 'We've got him, Jo. It's over.'

I was numb with shock. Harrison was the techie Marissa had used in London, the one who'd installed all the software on my computer at the farm and taught me how to access the servers remotely and dial into my messages and email. Part of me simply couldn't believe that the quiet, patient young man who'd treated me with such politeness, and our modern day Jack the Ripper, could be one and the same.

I stared at Callum across his desk. He'd sent for me as soon as they'd had confirmation.

Teams of police had raided Harrison's office at the university and his address in Fordley simultaneously the previous day. His office had been empty, but what they found at his apartment left little doubt they had their man.

Callum pushed CSI photographs across the desk.

'The flat looked innocent enough, until they got to the spare bedroom. He used it as an office and apart from the two large split-screen monitors and laptops on the desk, they found a drawer containing several new pay-as-you-go mobile phones and sim cards. Techies are still going through it all,' Callum said. 'But that lot includes a voice digitiser, and this . . .' he pushed another photograph across '. . . was the back wall of his office.'

I was looking at dozens of photographs of myself.

A whole gallery taken from news articles, magazines and, more eerily, surveillance photos obviously snapped covertly.

There was one of me parking my car at the Fordley practice. Another, entering and leaving the police station. Even one showing me walking into St James' Park in Newcastle on the day of the speaking engagement.

I couldn't think of anything to say.

'His bedroom's a treasure trove,' Callum was saying. 'Forensics are still working the scene, but already there's evidence that Susie Scott – Martha – was there.'

I looked again at the photo gallery on his wall as Martha's voice echoed to me.

'*Don't I know you? I've seen you before . . . pictures of you.*'

'This was in the fridge.'

He pushed photos across the desk. They showed Tupperware boxes with their lids opened, revealing their grizzly contents.

'A complete womb in one and a partial in another.'

'What about the kidney taken from Kate Lawson?' I asked.

'No sign of it yet.'

'What has Harrison said?'

'Not a lot,' Callum said. 'He's dead.'

'*What?*'

'Harrison was a freelancer, employed to look after the university computer system. He repaired the IT infrastructure and rarely spent time in his office, but was mostly in the server rooms in the basement. When the team at the university searched the place, that's where they found him. He'd hanged himself.'

Callum spoke with his back to me as he poured yet another coffee from the eternal pot in his office.

'Hanged?' I repeated lamely, as much to make it sink in, as to confirm it to myself, as if saying it out loud would make me believe it.

'He wanted to make sure.' He ran a hand over his eyes before taking a deep mouthful of strong black coffee. 'So he slit his wrists as well.'

He looked more exhausted than I'd ever seen him and I found myself wondering how much sleep he'd had in the past months.

'Why?' I said. 'Why would he top himself now?'

Callum shrugged. 'Maybe he knew we'd been tipped off about the DNA swab? Maybe he could feel we were getting closer? He wouldn't be the first serial killer to take that option rather than face justice. Raoul Moat, Fred West . . .' He drained his coffee. 'The ultimate two fingers to the law – the last way to take back control and let their secrets die with them, to deny us the answers and them the humiliation of a public trial.'

The 'Jack' I'd encountered seemed unlikely to kill himself if the police were closing in. But he was right about the precedent for it. I couldn't argue that others had done it before.

'The "Jack" I profiled wouldn't commit suicide, Cal. It doesn't feel right.'

'We found the Yamaha bike in a staff bay in the underground car park at the university. He'd hidden it under a dust cover, so even though we were circulating its description, a concealed bike in a car park where the general public never went, didn't attract any attention. Out of sight out of mind. Forensics are crawling all over it, but we're pretty certain it matches the tyre prints at Polly's café. And now we know what we're looking for, I'm sure we'll link him to it through DVLA records.'

He rubbed his eyes and stretched out the knots in his shoulders. He'd probably been living on a diet of junk food and caffeine for weeks.

I stated the obvious. 'You need to get some sleep.'

'Fat chance. Finding him has generated almost more actions than hunting for him did.' He grimaced as he attempted to uncrick his neck. 'Techies have seized his computers, but they already know he installed remote links to your office computer at the Fordley practice *and* the farm. Along with all your unlisted phone numbers.' He looked at me, his dark eyes unfathomable. 'It's him, Jo, no doubt about it.'

I nodded slowly, taking in all the photographs spilled across his desk. The evidence was overwhelming, that was certain, but the Harrison I'd met and the killer I'd interacted with were such poles apart. I simply couldn't make the connection in my mind.

'No doubting the evidence,' I said.

'But?' He was watching me carefully in that way he so often did, as though he was looking directly into my thoughts.

'Maybe there's *too much* evidence? Like you say, it's overwhelming.'

'You sound like that's a bad thing. What exactly *are* you saying, Jo?'

I opened my mouth, but I couldn't verbalise it. I couldn't give logic and rationale to something that was, at this point, just gut feeling. Finally I shook my head.

'Oh, I don't know. Just . . . I'm not arrogant enough to say that my profile's infallible, Cal . . .' I looked up and let our eyes meet for just a moment – enough to add weight to what I was saying. 'But Paul Harrison is *so* far away from "Jack" in every conceivable way.'

I shook my head slowly. 'Despite all the evidence you've found, I can't make him fit what we've been dealing with – he just *doesn't.*'

It was his turn to shrug. 'I'm just a copper, Jo. I follow the evidence. Forensics will fill in the gaps and we'll go from there. But given this lot . . .' He nodded towards the photos.

'I know,' I conceded. But it still jarred.

Chapter Fifty-Two

23 October – Kingsberry Farm

It had been two weeks since Paul Harrison had been found hanged at Fordley University, but the story was still dominating the news, with journalists tracking down anyone who had even the slightest association with him. His family had been so hounded by the media, they'd gone into hiding. Journalists were trying to track me down too, so Jen and I had been laying low at the farm.

The previous week we'd watched the TV coverage of Lizzie Taylor-Caine's funeral. The people of Fordley turned out in their hundreds to pay their respects, as uniformed officers from West Yorkshire police lined the route of the funeral cortege, on its way to Fordley cathedral. The Chief Constable gave the reading at the service, which was attended by Callum and the rest of the team.

My publisher, Marissa, had been as shocked as we were when she'd heard about Paul Harrison. We'd spoken on the phone almost daily since the news broke, as each new piece of evidence that nailed the case to him was released and picked up by a voracious media.

'It's been a nightmare down here,' she said. 'I've had to abandon the office. I'm camped out at my cousin's holiday cottage to avoid the bloody press.'

'Know what you mean,' I sympathised.

'I still can't believe it.' I could hear the hurt in her voice. She'd liked him. We both had. 'The police have been grilling me for days about what I knew of his movements after he left me, but I can't tell them anything. It was three years ago for God's sake!'

'And you had no idea what he was going to do work-wise?' I asked. 'I mean, what about references?'

'There was no need for references.' Her voice echoed over the loudspeaker as Jen and I listened in my office. 'He was going freelance.'

'And you never heard from him after that?'

'He said he'd been headhunted by a big firm in the city, on a consultancy basis. I always knew he was too good to stay with me for long, and I was pleased for him. Think they offered him the big bucks, so it funded his start-up. I know he'd been offered a contract to look after the computer networks of several universities, but didn't know where.'

I stared out of the office window, deep in thought. 'Did you *ever* have an inkling about him? About anything that might give us a motive?'

I could almost hear her shrug. 'You're the shrink, Jo, not me. But no, he never struck me as being odd, unhinged – whatever you'd call it. But then not all psychos foam at the mouth, do they? I mean, look at Ted Bundy, or Harold Shipman. They were educated, professional. Held down good jobs – who knew?'

Who knew? Indeed.

'Paul knew about Gail Dobson,' Jen said, across the loud-speaker. 'That connects him to her too.'

'The police asked the same thing,' she said, thoughtfully. 'I told them he was here when you had all that trouble with her. He tracked all those emails she'd sent and gave the police what he'd found at the time. He helped build the case against her, for God's sake. I can't imagine she was a big fan of his, can you? They already knew as much anyway – it was all a matter of record. But they were interested to know whether he'd ever met her. I said he hadn't. Not while he was working for me – to my knowledge at least.'

But he had known about her, I thought, as I listened to Jen and Marissa pick over the bones of it. *He'd known what she'd done. Which he could have used to his advantage later on if he'd needed someone who knew how to manipulate Martha. It was a connection that tied him even tighter to the murders.*

But, for me, he *still* didn't fit the 'Jack' that I'd been dealing with.

Chapter Fifty-Three

1 November – Fordley Police Station

In the three weeks since Harrison's name had been released, things had moved quickly. Forensic evidence was still coming in, but what the team had so far was damning and conclusive, and more than enough to convince everyone they had their man.

As the enquiry began to wind down, Callum seemed less stressed. But whenever I saw him, I felt a distance between us that I couldn't span. He was civil and formal, which in some ways made it feel even worse. Perhaps too much had happened for it to ever be the same?

He watched me as I scanned the paperwork he'd pushed across his desk.

'Forensics confirmed there was soil on the bike that matched that found at Polly's café,' he said. 'The blond hairs found on the victims are Harrison's and they found his DNA matched the blood spot on Anne Stenson.'

He tapped the pictures of the contents of his fridge. 'The womb came from Anne Stenson, and the partial womb belonged to Kate Lawson. Still no sign of her kidney, though.'

'On 16 October 1888, Victorian Jack sent Catherine Eddowes's kidney to George Lusk, who was running a vigilante group in London at the time. That's probably what he was keeping it for – to post it to someone – but was dead before he could send it on the right date.'

'I bet he would have sent that to you, if he'd had the chance,' he said, watching me across the desk.

I looked up from reading the post-mortem report on Lizzie Taylor-Caine.

'I can't imagine what I would have felt, getting that through the post. *This* was brutal enough,' I said, quietly, pointing to the image of the gold rings, with their grizzly message, pushed into the throat wound that had almost decapitated her.

He nodded. 'There were traces of her all over his flat in Fordley. Not to mention we found her handbag and the keys to her apartment there. CCTV shows her leaving her place on the day of the briefing. Then, the next morning, it picks up her car going back to the underground car park at her apartment block. There's no coverage inside the garage. But we're assuming it was Harrison who took her car back there. He probably let himself into the flat with her keys, then left them – and her mobile – on the table, dropped the latch and let himself out. That accounts for all her belongings being at home when we got there. Made it look like she'd just walked out and disappeared into thin air.'

'Any CCTV of him leaving her flat?'

He shook his head. 'No, but the cameras at the front had been vandalised. Could be a coincidence, or maybe he'd taken care of them earlier, knowing he was planning to go there. Maintenance say they'd been broken the week before, but it would take them weeks to get round to fixing them.'

He offered me a coffee. I shook my head and watched him pour another for himself.

'In the bin in his kitchen they recovered tape with her hair and skin cells stuck to it,' he said. 'Looks like he kept her there before killing and dumping her at the back of the Polski Klub in the early morning of the thirtieth.'

'How did he move her?' I asked. 'He could hardly have taken her body on the bike. He'd need a car or a van, surely?'

'We're working on that. He must have had access to some kind of vehicle – probably stolen. There's nothing registered to him, but we'll find it.' He arched his back and stretched. 'The techies found access to your computer at the farm from the computer at the university. The pictures of Susie – or Martha as you knew her – and Anne are on there. The dates on which they were sent to you match up. There's also lots of activity on all his computers, accessing your remote server and your messaging service.'

I nodded, unable to find holes in any of the evidence. When I looked up, he was watching me.

'But?' he asked, quietly.

I shrugged. 'All the physical evidence fits,' I said. 'But that's not the evidence *I* need.'

'Which is what?'

'The evidence in his mind. I don't see "Jack" in Harrison,' I said, simply.

'You met him over three years ago, Jo, and only for a few days spread over a period of weeks.'

I shrugged. 'It can be enough.'

'But not always,' he reasoned. 'They don't all present that obviously. You've said yourself, there are more psychopaths in business than in prison, holding down professional jobs, with partners, families. We've all come across them.'

'True,' I conceded.

Maybe it was professional pride – not wanting to admit that I hadn't picked up on anything when I'd been with him. One thing was bothering me, though. 'The Laundy blades – any sign of them?'

'Not yet. Have to say, that *is* a loose end that concerns me.'

It concerned me too. 'He attached great value to those,' I said. 'He wouldn't discard them. Why would he use the kitchen knife you found with his body and not a Laundy blade when they're such a big part of his killing ritual?'

He shook his head. 'Maybe that's the point? They *were* so valuable to him, he wouldn't want them falling into our hands – would rather dispose of them?'

'No. I don't think so,' I said with conviction. 'My profile might not have been right about everything, but I'm sure on this one. Those blades are a vital part of his signature. He wouldn't dispose of them and he *would* have used them in his own suicide. If that's what he did.'

I still couldn't convince myself that 'Jack' had killed himself. It was a massive piece that didn't fit.

'We'll keep looking,' he said. 'I've got less of a team now, though, and the chief constable is pulling back the resources.'

I'd seen evidence of that when I'd walked through the incident room that day. Previously, as the body count had risen, so had the number of officers involved. There wasn't a square inch of space at Fordley nick that didn't have a desk and a computer squeezed into it. Over three floors of the station had been taken up by the major incident team, with officers drafted in from other forces. But in the last few weeks the team had been stripped back to almost its original size.

The press were still hungry for anything connected to the victims or to anyone who knew Harrison, and the coverage was relentless. As if reading my mind, Callum tossed over the latest edition of the *Fordley Express*.

'At least we don't have to brace ourselves for that one,' he said, indicating the banner headline.

WHAT THE RIPPER HAD PLANNED FOR HIS FINAL VICTIM

It had a sickening image of the remains of Mary Kelly, discovered on the morning of 9 November 1888 in her own house at thirteen Miller's Court, Whitechapel.

I looked at the black-and-white image, taken in the early days of crime scene photography. It was one of the most horrific and gruesome murders in the annals of serial killings.

The remains barely looked human, such was the ferocity with which Jack the Ripper had brutalised the young Irish girl's body. Both breasts had been cut off and placed beneath her body and she had been totally eviscerated and her organs placed around the room. Her heart was missing, but there had been a fire set in the grate of the small cramped room during the night, and there was evidence that the Ripper had destroyed her heart in the flames. All the features of her face had been cut off; the rest had been hacked to pieces and was unrecognisable. He had also stripped the flesh from her thighs.

'Cause of death was the severing of her carotid artery,' I said. 'Hopefully, for her sake, before he carried out the rest of the mutilations.'

'Why do you think she was treated so much worse than the others?'

'Lots of theories. Some say he knew her – had some sort of personal grudge with her. Others think that it was simply because he had all night with her in the privacy of her own home so he could indulge in all of his fantasies with her body without fear of interruption. She was the only one of his victims not killed in the street.'

'What's *your* theory?'

I looked again at the barely recognisable remains of what had, by all accounts at the time, been a pretty girl.

'I think she knew him. She obviously felt comfortable enough to take him back to her home. Neighbours said they saw her going into the house with a man voluntarily and they heard her singing during the evening while she was with him. They ate together; the remains of her last meal were still in her stomach at the post-mortem. A familiar punter, maybe? I think she'd entertained him before and was comfortable with him.'

'And yet, he could do *that* to her – to someone he knew?'

'A natural escalation of his deviance. Classic, really. They get better as they practise their craft.'

'Well, thank God we stopped Harrison perfecting *his* craft before he got to that victim.'

Chapter Fifty-Four

8 November – Kingsberry Farm

'You're *selling*?' Jen seemed shocked by the idea.

'It's not realistic to use the Fordley practice any more, is it?'
I reasoned. 'Even when the dust settles, I don't really want to
go back there. Too many people know it's our place now. It
wouldn't afford us the privacy we need.'

'I suppose clients might be reluctant to go there now it's
been splashed all over the news.' She cleared the supper dishes
from the kitchen table. 'We could still work up here though,
couldn't we?'

We'd agreed it was time for her to move back home and her
bags were in the porch, waiting to load into her car. I'd become
used to having her around, despite my initial misgivings. It had
been nice to have the company and the extra help around the
place, but I couldn't keep her from Henry any longer.

'Certainly more convenient than the commute into town,'
I said. 'For me, that is. You'd still have to travel on the days you
were here, though.'

She shrugged, opening the porch door with her foot to let
Harvey out.

'Same travel time as going into Fordley for me, but less
traffic and Henry is happier that I'd be working from home
a few days a week. Still, feels like the end of an era selling the
practice.'

I knew what she meant. But I felt it was time for changes all round. The publicity surrounding 'Jack's' murder spree had been double-edged. On the one hand we were inundated with requests for TV appearances and interviews as the press picked over the facts of what had happened and why – hungry for more insight into the mind of a serial killer and fascinated by my connection to the case. That had also fuelled interest in the launch of my next book, due out at Christmas, so we were frantic with engagements with Marissa too.

On the other hand, calls for my expertise on the criminal justice side of things had stopped coming. The circus surrounding my connection with 'Jack' made me persona non grata on the court circuit for now so my work as an expert witness used by police forces and the crown prosecution service had dried up.

Jen gave me a peck on the cheek as I hauled her case into the car.

'Give me a call tomorrow and we'll sort out the diary.'

'Will do.'

I caught Harvey's collar and watched as she reversed out. She paused to let George's ancient Land Rover go past the gate as he went on his habitual trip for a pint at the local, and then followed him down the darkening lane on her way into Fordley.

'Just you and me now, boy,' I said, as he whimpered at her retreating tail lights.

Chapter Fifty-Five

8 November, 11 p.m. – Kingsberry Farm

Back in my study, I sat and looked at the reams of notes I'd made on 'Jack', alongside my assessment of Paul Harrison. It was two different jigsaw puzzles that just didn't fit together.

A soft silence settled through the house, broken only by the sound of Harvey's snoring and the gentle ticking of the clock. I tapped a pencil against my teeth as I went through my notes again.

Motive? As far as I could see, Paul Harrison didn't have one.

Because of the picture gallery at his flat, the police theorised that Harrison had become obsessed with me, then enacted 'Jack's' crimes in some sort of twisted role play of *UK's most infamous serial killer versus famous criminal profiler*.

But obsessive behaviour doesn't spring from a void. There has to be a catalyst for it. As I replayed all the interactions we'd had while he was with me at the farm, I couldn't find one.

I jumped when the shrill of my mobile shattered the silence.

'Hello?'

'Jo ...?' I could barely hear the hoarse whisper down the phone, despite the silence in the room.

'Hello?'

'Help me! Jo ...' The voice was barely audible. I glanced at the caller ID – George's farm.

'George?' I could hear the alarm in my own voice as a cold panic began to grip my stomach. 'George, are you OK? What's wrong?'

'Think . . . oh God, Jo . . . think I'm having . . .'

I barely heard the soft groan and then a faint 'thud' that could only be a body hitting the floor. 'George? George!'

I was already reaching for my car keys as I headed for the door. Harvey was on my heels as I pulled open the door of the Audi that had no room for him.

'Sorry, boy.'

The gravel sprayed behind the rear tyres as I accelerated out of the drive and bounced out of the gate and onto the lane. As I jounced over the potholes, I could see Harvey in the rear-view mirror racing along behind me, barking over the roar of the engine.

It was only a mile of rough track, but never had it felt so long. I had the headlights on full beam as I recklessly negotiated the narrow lane. Turning the last bend, I lost sight of Harvey but I knew he'd still be galloping down the track behind me.

I swung the car through the gate of George's farm, barely stopping before I flung open the door and ran towards the house. I pushed open the unlocked front door and ran in.

The small parlour was bathed in the honeyed glow of a fire-side lamp. The only sound above my laboured breathing was the mellow ticking of the old grandfather clock in the corner.

The handset of his ancient telephone was swinging from its wire, dangling over the edge of the Welsh dresser. I stopped and stared at the empty spot in front of the dresser where I'd expected George to be.

I walked over and slowly returned the handset to its cradle, scanning the room for any clue as to what might have happened to him. There was an open box beside the phone, its contents of gift tags spilling out as if they'd been tipped out in a hurry. I recognised the pattern – they were the same tags found in Liz Taylor-Caine's severed throat.

'George?' I yelled, already moving to the back of the house.

I stood in the middle of the kitchen, willing my heart rate to slow down so I could listen for sounds above the thundering of the blood in my ears.

His coat hung on its peg by the door, his muddy boots were on the mat.

Everything seemed in its place apart from a sliver of light spilling out onto the stone flags from the partially open fridge. As I went to close it, I noticed a red stain along the bottom of the door. My eyes followed the sticky red trail to a Tupperware box on one of the glass shelves. My fingers shook as I unclipped the lid.

'Shit!'

As I dropped the box, the bloodied human kidney hit the floor, splashing my shoes in sticky gore. I stared at it in shock, frozen to the spot.

Kate Lawson's kidney? The one 'Jack' hadn't had time to post?

I heard Harvey barking in the yard, then a high-pitched squeal as the unmistakeable crack of a gunshot reverberated around the house.

When I ran onto the yard, Harvey was lying in the circle of light cast by my car headlights, his side bloody and matted. He raised his head slightly and whined when he saw me, then fell back with a low whimper.

'Harvey!' I rushed towards him.

It was then I saw, out of the corner of my eye, the barrel of George's shotgun to my left. In pure reflex I caught hold of it as the figure holding the gun stepped out of the shadows and stood in front of me.

My brain froze, momentarily unable to process what I was seeing.

'You!'

The cold metal of the barrel was ripped from my grasp as a strong arm brought the hard wooden stock round to hit me across the face and, with a sickening 'crack', the ground came up to meet me.

Chapter Fifty-Six

8 November, 12 a.m.

I swam towards consciousness, as if following air bubbles to the surface of a dark sea.

'Welcome to crime scene B.'

The words triggered an alarm inside my head, flooding my body with adrenalin, the surge of cortisol sending shots of electricity through my skin and tripping my heart to hammer against my ribcage like a terrified bird fluttering against the bars of a cage.

This couldn't be real. I was waking from a nightmare.

I tried to sit up but pain seared through my neck and shoulders. Something was holding me down and it was stiflingly hot, hard to breathe. The metallic taste of blood was in my mouth.

I willed my eyes to open, focusing on the face inches from mine.

'No!' My voice was hoarse.

James looked down at me.

I was lying on a mattress, my arms outstretched, wrists tied to the brass bedhead of a narrow single bed. I twisted to one side, trying to raise my knees, then looked down to my naked ankles tied to the ornate metal foot of the bed.

His fingers traced the line of my jaw where he'd hit me with the butt of the shotgun.

'Sorry about that, but I heard your seminar in Newcastle, so I knew you'd never allow yourself to be moved from crime scene A without a little encouragement.'

I tried to order my thoughts, which were racing in panicked chaos. I squeezed my eyelids shut, then opened them again as if that might erase this nightmare and replace it with something that actually made sense. It didn't.

'The ninth of November,' he said, softly, running his hand across my naked body. 'Mary Kelly. Little Irish girl. My final and most beautiful piece of work.'

The horrific image of the mutilated remains of Mary Kelly flashed through my mind. I twisted uselessly against the tight cords that were biting into my wrists and ankles.

I finally oriented myself – we were in my cottage in the woods, the cottage with the old door George had hung a few months before, the number thirteen cradled in its rusty horseshoe . . .

Number thirteen Miller's Court, the scene of Jack the Ripper's final killing.

'Where's George?' I dreaded the answer.

'Dead,' he said, simply. 'I dropped his body in the septic tank. No disturbed earth for the searchers to see, no grave to find. I've been living at his farm since September – the day you nearly caught me cleaning this place. I added the number thirteen to the door George had put in – nice touch, don't you think? I've been wearing his clothes, driving his Land Rover. Hiding in plain sight. People see what they expect to see . . . I've waved to you and Jen a dozen times across the fields these past few weeks.'

Shivers prickled across my skin. Of course, Harvey had always known what James was. That's why he'd behaved as he did at the cottage that day. He'd known James had been in there.

He dipped his head, trailing his lips across my neck, down my shoulders.

'Did you know your boyfriend had a CROP set up at your place the day they searched the farm, as well as putting a lump on your car?'

A covert rural observation post – surveillance officers literally hiding in my bushes. A 'lump' – a tracking device. Could Callum have suspected my involvement seriously enough to have gone that far?

'The morning of the double event, I came to deliver the eggs on my way back to George's. I wanted to keep up his usual routines, to keep him alive in your mind. Coming to your door in the early morning, seeing you and Jen around the place – knowing you never suspected a thing as you waved to me in the distance. I almost stumbled across the surveillance officer. Then I watched while the CROP was ordered to stand down. He removed the tracker on your car before he left.' His lips trailed across my collarbone as he spoke. 'If he'd stayed another ten minutes, he would have seen me come to your door – how lucky was I?'

A million thoughts fragmenting into hot metal shards seared through my mind. My words were my tools, my only weapons.

'*Why*?' was the best I could manage. 'What motive . . .?'

He smiled, like an indulgent parent with a stupid child.

'My grandmother was Jane Lubnowski.' He watched. Waiting for me to catch up.

My brain crawled sluggishly through the database of Ripper facts.

'Aaron Kosminski,' I said, slowly, 'the prime suspect for Jack the Ripper in 1888. He had a sister, Matilda, who married Morris Lubnowski.'

'My grandmother was Kosminski's niece.' He lowered his head and brushed his lips across my neck, whispering against my skin. 'I *am* Jack the Ripper. I always felt his presence inside me. When my grandmother told me about my heritage, it explained everything. All the feelings.'

His hand followed the trail of his lips, skimming my collarbone, finally resting across my throat. 'All those thoughts, all the things I'd dreamed of doing.' His grip tightened slightly.

'You're insane.' I arched my neck to slacken his grip.

He closed his fingers more tightly.

'Perhaps. Or maybe I'm fulfilling my genetic destiny?' His face was filled with a cruelty I *had* seen before, that I'd caught a glimpse of that day in my office when he'd momentarily lost his temper. 'But you didn't want to help me when I asked the first time. So here we are.'

'You *asked?*'

He nodded, but his eyes were on my stomach. His hand followed his gaze as he spoke.

'I was twenty-two. At university. I watched your documentary about serial killers. The UK's leading expert, they said. You talked about Jack in the film. I knew then that you were the one. I wrote to you, but you never replied.' His hand lingered, gently stroking. 'I wrote that I was a descendant of Jack, that I felt *his* hungers ... *his* drives ... *his* needs. I wanted you to help me.'

His hand slid again around my throat and his grip cut off my breath. 'But you didn't even bother to reply.'

'I never re . . . ceived . . .' I gasped, twisting my head frantically, trying to draw more air into my lungs.

Suddenly he let go. I drew in a ragged breath, straining to claw in as much air as I could, before he could grip my throat again. Instead, he got up and turned his back to me as he busied himself at the small bedside table.

The light in the room was coming from a coal fire in the grate, causing James' shadow to flicker in grotesquely gigantic proportions across the whitewashed walls. The heat in the small space was suffocating.

Unwanted details from the Victorian police report into Mary Kelly's death ran like a reel of film in my head. I squeezed my eyes shut to try to stop them.

'*Inspector Abberline explored the ashes in the grate of Mary's room. The fire had been so fierce, it melted the spout off the kettle . . .*'

I could feel the heat from the grate. All-consuming . . .

'*Both breasts were removed by circular incisions. The pericardium was open below and the heart absent . . . Mary's heart had been cut out and burned in the fire . . .*'

I felt the bed dip as James sat back on the edge.

'Open your eyes.' He grabbed a handful of my hair, jerking my head around so that I had to look at him. In his other hand, he was holding the knife. 'You've been looking for this.'

'*Don't.*' I hated the pleading tone I couldn't keep out of my voice.

He wasn't listening. His eyes travelled to my breasts, lingering for a moment before he lowered the knife. I felt the cold tip of the blade as he held it against my ribs.

'No!' I felt the searing cold pain as he lightly drew the surgically thin edge across my skin, just deep enough to draw a delicate line of blood.

'Razor sharp,' he whispered, 'only the slightest pressure needed.'

'W-wait . . .' My breath was coming in short, shallow gasps.

I had to make him stop. Make him listen. Try something – anything.

'You said you wanted to stop, when you were twenty-two?' I was speaking too fast. I took a breath, trying to slow my words. 'When was the first time you killed?'

He stared at me. 'Why?'

'I need to know.'

I felt the knife lift as he released the pressure. Then he lowered his hand. Resting the bloodied blade against his thigh.

'My mother,' he said, quietly. 'I was fourteen.'

'Why?'

'I hated her,' he said, simply. 'There was a fifteen-year gap between me and the golden boy and I always knew I was her menopause mistake. She blamed me for her being trapped in a loveless marriage with my father. She used to entertain her male "friends" at the house when my father was away in London and I threatened to tell him if she didn't stop. She beat me. She said he'd never believe me and he would hate me for telling lies about her. I was sent to boarding school at five-years-old, was barely tolerated during the holidays, so I stayed with my grandmother whenever I could.'

He turned the blade slowly in his hand. 'My grandmother gave me the knives as part of the family inheritance, told me who they'd belonged to. My mother thought they were obscene. She hated them, was ashamed of their history and made my father keep our ownership of them a secret. He wanted to loan them to a museum – especially given their provenance. As a lawyer, he found their story fascinating. But she was horrified people would find out about her family's connection to Jack, so she wouldn't let him.'

Chapter Fifty-Seven

9 November, 1 a.m.

I followed his gaze to the green leather case, open on the bedside table.

His focus came back to me. 'That night, they'd rowed again. She got drunk after my father left the house and I told her how much I hated the way she treated him – treated *me*. She slipped onto the rug, so drunk she couldn't get up and I strangled her with the fabric belt from her dress.' He took a deep breath and his eyes refocused.

'But you got away with it?'

'She was petite – weighed nothing. It was easy to drag her onto her knees. I tied the belt to the door handle, then stood and watched her for a while. I didn't know enough back then to be certain she was dead. So I slit her wrists, just to be sure. That was the first time I used Jack's blade. Appropriate she should die by it, considering how she felt.' He smiled. The memory of it pleased him. 'It was recorded as a suicide and no one was surprised. She'd threatened to do it often enough when she was drinking.'

'You were a child,' I said, with a calmness I didn't feel. 'Emotional abuse leaves scars deeper than physical.' I shifted, trying to ease the burning tension in my arms and shoulders. 'It's not too late,' I said, quietly. 'I let you down before because I never received your letter – but I can help you now.'

He looked at me quietly for just a second, giving me a glimmer of hope. Then laughed.

'I think you'll find you're the one on *my* couch now, doctor.' He held the side of the blade flat against my cheek, the tip of it touching the corner of my eye. 'The victim no one can save this time.' His fingers dug into my chin, tilting my face towards his. 'Your knight in shining armour thought it was all over so the cavalry have packed up and gone home. Nobody is coming to help you. It's just us for the grand finale.'

His knuckles blanched white as he tightened his grip on the knife, moving it from my face, lowering it to my belly.

'Wait!' My stomach tightened as I felt it touch my abdomen. 'If this is how it's going to end, then at least give me some answers first. Please?'

The muscles bunched in his cheek as he considered for a second. Then he nodded.

I took advantage of his silence. At least talking bought me some time. Maybe I could find a chink in his psyche? Find enough space between his delusions and reality to salvage something – *anything*?

'Martha?'

He smiled. 'Susie. Pretty little thing. Trusting – like a child.'

'She loved you.' I could feel tears pricking my eyes and marvelled at the human ability to feel such compassion even at this moment – facing the monster with no such empathy, who had ended her life.

'Almost a shame,' he said, but I could see no emotion behind his eyes. 'I chose her for her role – right from the start.'

'Where did you keep her? They could never find out where she lived with "John". I take it you *were* John?'

346

He nodded. 'She only ever knew me as "John" – her boy-friend.' He laughed again. The thought of her childlike naïveté amused him. 'I kept her in my apartment at Salford Quays. I told her the police were looking for her – for the murders she'd committed in Manchester.'

'For the period she couldn't remember because of her drug use?'

'Yes. She never questioned what I told her. I was keeping her safe, hiding her secret. But it meant she knew to stay out of sight when I left her alone. Knew to keep the blinds closed – not go out or answer the door. No one ever knew she was there. My flat was full of traces of her, evidence I later planted at Harrison's apartment.'

'Tell me about Paul Harrison?'

He rested the blade on his knee. I had to force myself to concentrate on his face.

'I knew you used Fosters – I'd seen the publicity for the Gail Dobson case at the time of the court case. I applied to the firm when I qualified and used the position to find out everything about you. It was easy enough to meet Harrison. His name came up in Dobson's case files.' His hand absently stroked my stomach as he talked. 'Everyone has a weakness, you know that,' he said, quietly. 'For some it's money or power, for others it's attention, affection – love.'

His eyes met mine and held my gaze. And for a second I glimpsed that mesmeric charisma I'd seen when we'd first met. 'People starved of love recognise each other – don't we, Jo?'

He would have sounded seductive if it hadn't been for the circumstances.

'Harrison wanted independence. His talent was stifled with Marissa, but he didn't have the resources to go it alone.'

'So you helped him?'

He nodded. 'I got close to him. Then I waited. My chance came when I was made partner and Fosters asked me to recruit for the new Manchester office.'

I flinched when his fingers reached up to my face, but he simply brushed a damp tendril of hair from my forehead. His fingers gently traced the curve of my jaw, like a tender lover.

'We needed an IT consultant, so I offered Harrison a contract that would give him enough to finally set up on his own and that put him in my debt. I used my contacts to get him some university contracts – Manchester, Newcastle, Fordley so he moved here. I told him the firm were paying for his flat, but I took care of it. He didn't know that, but it meant there was no record of it.' He smiled as his fingers caressed the rope around my wrists. 'Financial handcuffs, you might say.'

'But the police didn't find a connection between Harrison and Fosters?'

'I never put his invoices through the books. I paid him myself. But he never knew that and Fosters didn't even know he existed. I gave him a dummy contract.'

'You thought of everything.'

I winced as his finger traced the shallow incision he'd made around the curve of my breast.

'I've had a lot of time to plan.' He licked my blood from his finger, his eyes never leaving mine. 'I told him Fosters needed access to your computer and messaging service – that it was company practice. I said the firm routinely monitored email

348

and messages, in case our clients were doing anything that could damage us or come back to bite us in court. He believed he was hiding his electronic footprint to protect the firm. He knew it wasn't strictly legal but he needed the money.'

'What about the burner phones and the voice digitiser? Surely he must have smelled a rat when you needed those?'

'My client base, like yours, are criminals. Easy enough to learn their tradecraft. I sorted those out myself. Harrison never knew about them and he used the computer in the university basement to access your computers. I'd had copies made of his keys and his passes. So when I needed to send you photographs of Martha and Polly, I'd go there at night after he left and send them myself.'

'He never suspected?'

He shook his head slowly. 'I arranged for a lock-up near his flat so he could keep his bike there.'

'And you had keys, so you could take the bike whenever you needed it? You used it to get Martha away from Westwood – and later at Polly's café?'

'Bravo!' He raised his eyebrows, mockingly impressed. 'After Hanbury Street, Harrison had expended his usefulness. By then he'd set up the electronic maze that kept the police from tracing the IP addresses. The only use I had for him then was to harvest his DNA.'

I took a shaky breath, trying to keep my tone even. 'So you took strands of his hair and trace evidence from his flat to plant on the bodies.'

'His toothbrush, hairbrush. Easy, really. Then I arranged to meet him in the computer room at the university.' He spoke

349

matter-of-factly – as if he was talking about a day at the office. 'I strangled him with the noose, then hung him by it.' He laughed. 'He was so passive – hardly put up a fight.'

I remembered Paul. That polite, gentle boy who had shown me such patience, and my throat tightened.

'Then I made the "anonymous" call to the police, saying he'd asked me – his student friend – to take the DNA test for him. So they'd find him there – with all the evidence they needed.'

I could feel a tension travelling through him. His hunger was building, like a starving predator tiring of tormenting its prey.

'How did you install false memories in Martha?' I asked, quickly.

'I used Gail Dobson.'

'She didn't know who you were?'

He shook his head. 'She thought I was a patient of yours when I took Martha to see her. A patient with a grudge. It was easy to convince her to help me set you up, to install "Jack's" script and the false memories. She thought I was going to get you involved in a fake case and then humiliate you in the press.'

'You killed her too?'

'I would have done eventually – to tie up the loose end. But she saved me the trouble. Stupid bitch actually fell in love – thought we were in some grand romance. She threatened to kill herself when I ended it and I turned the knife, metaphorically speaking. I knew which cracks to leverage, to make sure I'd destroyed her enough. Then I left the flat.' He laughed. 'She called me to say she was going to do it if I didn't go back that night and I told her to get on with it.'

I swallowed hard, but I had no saliva. The calculated callousness of it was horrific.

'I waited a few hours then went back. I still had a key.' He caressed my neck as he spoke. 'She'd taken an overdose of sleeping pills and painkillers – all washed down with nearly a whole bottle of vodka. She was conscious enough to know I was there.' He licked his lips. 'So I helped her along – slit her wrists and watched her die. Not *across* the wrist, you understand.' His finger traced a line from my wrist to my elbow. 'But down the arm. That's the mistake people make – going across the wrist rather than up the arm . . . far more effective. I learned that from working with my brother that summer at the hospital.'

'And Taylor-Caine?' I asked, trying to distract him from my wrists as I tested the knots.

He glanced down at the blade in his hand. 'Ah, saving the best for last. She was so easy to play. I called her, posing as a journalist. Said I had information about you that she would find useful. She wanted to destroy you so badly, she didn't even question it. She was almost *too* keen to meet with me.'

'The day of Astley's briefing? It was you she went to meet?'

'In woodland – not far from the farm. Of course she recognised me as soon as she saw me, but it was too late by then.' His face was a mask, devoid of all emotion.

He was reliving the images he'd harvested and stored for his own pleasure, to run again whenever he wanted to remember the sick gratification her pain and terror had given him.

'I moved her to George's place. Crime scene B, nice and secluded. Held her there for a few days. She provided some entertainment, while I found out what she knew.'

'Your "source" in the police?'

He nodded. 'That's how I knew about the farm searches a few days before they actually happened. Would have been awkward if I hadn't got that out of her. I had to get my car out of George's barn and get rid of anything that showed I'd stayed there. I killed her just before I came to your place.'

I thought about how quickly he'd arrived at mine. It made sense – he hadn't had that far to travel.

'When your boyfriend turned up with the search team, I actually had her body in the boot of my car.' He couldn't disguise the triumph in his voice. One up on the police – on Callum in particular.

He caressed my face gently as he spoke. 'My gift of her to you. Did you like that?'

I gave the impression I was struggling with the morality of it.

'I was shocked at first.' I looked into his eyes, trying to forge a common bond that would make him hesitate to kill me. 'But if I'm honest . . .'

'You *wanted* her dead – didn't you?' I felt his hand tremble against my skin.

I nodded slightly. Turning my face away as though ashamed. He took my chin in his fingers, turning my face back to his.

'It's OK to admit it,' he said, softly and I forced myself to endure it when his lips lightly brushed mine.

I chose my words carefully. 'You said once that you knew it would be easy for me to cross that line.' I looked deep into his eyes. 'And you were right . . . but I didn't have your courage.'

I felt him tense and his lips froze over mine. As he looked down at me, his eyes narrowed. 'Of all the things you could admit to, that's the one I really *don't* believe. I *know* you.' His words echoed the sentiment of the robotic, digitised voice I'd first heard on the phone. 'I've studied you for *years*. We both know that's not true.'

I felt my momentary advantage slipping out of reach.

'It *is* true.' I talked fast, my mind racing. I wished my hand was free so I could touch him – create a physical anchor for my words. Anything to buy myself extra time. 'But I didn't have your strength to cross that line. To actually kill –'

'No!' He spat the word in my face. 'You breathe a rarefied air, standing on your moral high ground, you and Ferguson, building careers out of examining specimens like me. Like insects in a test tube. You prod and poke at our psyche and decide whether we're insane or not. Your judgements play God with people's lives.'

His jaw tightened and his breathing became erratic. Beads of sweat stood out on his forehead. 'But you don't have the guts to play God for real – to hold life and death in your hands.'

Firelight glittered across the blade as it flashed past my face. I screamed at the searing pain as he drove it deep into my right shoulder.

I'm going to die . . . Alex! Oh, God. My son is going to have to see my body. See what he's done to me – like Mary Kelly. I'm never going to see Alex again . . .

The images of Mary Kelly's mutilated body exploded in my head. Pain shot through my jaw as his fingers tightened their grip on my chin, forcing me to look at him.

'Severing the carotid artery is how you *should* die,' he said, through clenched teeth. 'How Mary died. But that's over far too quickly.'

The edge of the mattress lifted as he got off the bed. His eyes never left mine as he took off his shirt. His torso was slick with sweat. He threw the shirt into the corner of the room and picked the knife up from the table.

'You don't have to do this . . . My God, please – no!'

'Yes!' he snarled. 'Right here . . . right now . . . I *am* God!'

He sat beside me, grabbing my hair in his fist. My eyes were transfixed onto the blade as he placed it against my groin. He applied the slightest pressure and a droplet of blood appeared on my skin.

'The femoral artery.' He pressed the tip of the blade a little further.

I sucked my breath in through gritted teeth as pain shot through my groin and spasms tightened the muscles in my stomach.

'This takes longer for you to bleed out.' He was a predator scenting the kill.

I tugged at the cords, trying to turn away, but there was nowhere to go. Pain coiled through my shoulder and around the curve of my ribcage. Rivulets of sweat slid down my arms, causing the cords to bite deeper into my wrists.

'Beg me.' He said it so quietly, I hardly heard it. 'Beg me for your life.'

His face glowed in the surreal light cast by the fire and when I looked into his eyes, they were black dots, lacking all that was human.

In that instant I felt a certainty that was deeper than my terror or my pain. A knowledge that whatever I said, whatever I did, I could never reach him now. His fractured psyche was being driven by a hunger that had dragged him into the depths of depravity, from which there was no way back.

Begging for my life would fuel his sadistic need to inflict pain. Seeing fear in my eyes would feed the monster inside him, like the thrashing of a wounded fish excites a feeding frenzy of sharks, pushing them to greater extremes of savagery.

A calmness suddenly descended on me. 'I'd tell you to go to hell,' I said, quietly. 'But you're already there.'

His face contorted. 'Bitch!' He pushed the blade into my thigh.

I screamed as a bolt of unimaginable pain ripped through me, convulsing me against the ties, arching my body like a bow off the mattress. I felt him push me back down onto the bed.

'It'll take a few minutes for you to bleed out, depending on how fast your heart is beating.' His fingers gripped my face, making me look into his eyes. 'I'll feel your last breath on my lips, taste your tears on my tongue – and just before you slip into unconsciousness, I'll cut out your heart!'

'Your father,' I said, between ragged gasps for breath. 'Your brother . . .did they ever know . . .?'

He shook his head, watching the blood slowly staining the mattress in a darkly spreading pool. A droplet of saliva appeared at the corner of his mouth as his breathing became more shallow in his excitement.

Shivers ran through me despite the heat from the fire.

He reached out to gently stroke my cheek. 'Not long now.'

I willed myself to breathe slower, to keep my heart rate down but my body wasn't responding to my mind any more. The pain was receding and my limbs felt leaden – I couldn't move them. Even my head was too heavy for my neck to lift now.

His face was starting to blur.

'Please . . .' I managed, but my words slurred.

'Shhhh.' He lowered his head and I felt his lips brush mine. He put his hand on my chest and I could feel the thud of my heart against his palm.

'That day we walked across the fields, I held your wrist. I felt your heart beat beneath my fingers and I fantasised about this moment. You sensed it.'

His kiss was warm against my ice-cold lips. 'Your heightened response to a predator. I tried to make you think it was sexual attraction, but I knew I couldn't fool your instincts for long. So I said I was leaving.' He stroked my hair. 'I knew I wouldn't have to wait long before we could share tonight.'

Darkness invaded my peripheral vision.

I wasn't cold anymore and it was difficult to keep my eyes open. His voice was echoing from so far away, I could barely hear him.

Finally, he sat back. He raised the knife and held it over my heart. I braced myself for the final, deadly blow – and then everything seemed to happen at once.

The door burst open. James half turned as a figure filled the doorway.

I vaguely heard a shout and James stood up. He looked down at me, his hand raised high. The knife blade glinted in the firelight as he brought it down, just as thunder crashed into the room, deafening me.

James seemed suspended in mid-air for just a second, before spinning around in slow motion, to slam against the wall. I felt his weight across my legs and then Callum's face filled my vision.

He was holding George's shotgun as he looked down at me.

He mouthed my name, but there was no sound. His eyes were filled with a visceral fear I'd never seen before. He reached out to me as the blackness finally closed in.

Chapter Fifty-Eight

14 November – Fordley General Hospital

'Lucky for us, he couldn't resist it.' Callum carefully put the glass of water into my left hand – my upper torso, right arm and shoulder were immobile, wrapped in mummifying bandages. 'One last call to torment us with the fact that "Jack" was still out there, determined to finish what he'd started and tell us we couldn't stop him.'

'So he called you – just like the calls he made to me? With his voice digitised?'

Callum nodded as he sat back on the chair beside my hospital bed.

'But how did you know *where* we'd be?'

'If he hadn't made that call, I wouldn't have.'

I tried to shift to a more comfortable position and winced as the ache in my left thigh reminded me that moving had consequences.

'You're going to have to run through that night again,' I said, running a hand wearily across my eyes.

I was only just beginning to piece it all together and this was the first chance Callum had had to come and see me, to talk to me properly when my brain wasn't flying morphine kites.

'You couldn't have known then that it was James – or that I'd be his next victim.'

'You're right – I didn't know for sure, but I had my suspicions.' He took a sip of vending-machine coffee and grimaced.

I made a clumsy attempt to put my glass on the bedside table and groaned when the stitches snagged.

Callum took the glass from me with a disapproving look. 'Are you *deliberately* trying to undo all my hard work? Take it easy, for God's sake.'

I couldn't help smiling at him – my lips were one of the few things that didn't hurt if I moved them.

'*Your* hard work? *You* didn't put my stitches in!'

'No – I just had to use the belt off my trousers to stop you bleeding to death.' He plumped my pillows before taking his seat again, but I could tell he was trying hard to maintain the stern look.

The Yorkshire Air Ambulance crew had said that his improvised tourniquet had not only prevented me from bleeding out, but had probably saved my leg.

'Remember when we searched the farms? I came to see you before we left and you were all standing in the yard when I made a point of telling you that I'd left a card at George's place, with a direct number to the enquiry team.'

I nodded.

'As far as we were concerned at the time, only four people, apart from my team, knew about that card. You, Jen, Turner and George – we thought then he was still alive, of course. But it wasn't the incident room number. It was one I'd had set up and it diverted directly to my mobile. The only way anyone could have access to that number was if they'd been inside George's farmhouse.'

I looked at him as the implications of what he'd said sank in. He sat in silence while I processed it. When I finally spoke, I chose my words carefully.

'So you were baiting a hook. But we were the only fish in the pond?'

He nodded slowly, his eyes never leaving mine.

'George could have just called it to ask about the search and that wouldn't have added a damn thing to the investigation. But if "Jack" used it to contact us, it would have narrowed things down.'

'You had a CROP set up outside my home and a tracker put on my car,' I said, quietly.

He went very still and looked at me for what seemed an eternity. Then ran his hand through his hair.

'You have to remember, Jo, Astley's geographic profile pointed squarely to that location. I was the SIO. I couldn't simply ignore that.'

He paused, expecting me to say something. When I didn't, his breath escaped in a low sigh. 'I had to be seen to cover all the bases. No, I didn't *really* believe you were involved. But it would either implicate or eliminate you as a suspect. Which it did.' He lifted his eyes to look squarely into mine. 'The night Taylor-Caine was murdered, the CROP gave you a cast-iron alibi.' He was watching me steadily. 'The card left at George's place was never set as bait for you.'

'Jen, then?' I couldn't disguise the sarcasm.

He shrugged again. 'George, possibly, or Turner. Or someone unknown to us who had access to the farmhouse.' He stretched his legs and looked down at his shoes. 'It was a long shot. It could have led me precisely nowhere.' He looked up and his eyes met mine again. 'But it paid off – didn't it?'

'But once Paul Harrison was dead, why would you assume "Jack" would call? Everyone thought it was all over. Why wasn't the number just disconnected?'

'Despite what you thought – what you might *still* think – I trusted you. After Harrison's death, you were adamant he couldn't be "Jack". If you were so sure that his personality was totally incompatible with our killer, then I believed you. But we had to follow the evidence and we didn't have a concrete lead to anyone other than Harrison.'

'But Hoyle was disbanding the major incident team, shutting down all the resources. He thought it was over.'

He nodded slowly and I suddenly realised how exhausted he looked. His eyes had a weariness in them when he looked across at me.

'He was winding things down. The extra officers we'd drafted in were sent back, but I still had my original team. So I kept some lines of enquiry open. We had loose ends to tie up and it was still an active enquiry, despite our prime suspect chilling in the mortuary. How I allocated the remaining resources was up to me, so I kept that phone line open. What Hoyle didn't know wouldn't hurt him.'

'And when "Jack" called that night, the call came in on that number? But surely that only told you he'd somehow got the number from George's? It didn't tell you *where* he was. He could have been calling from anywhere.'

'I had Shah with the telephony team monitoring all the numbers "Jack" had used previously. We assumed he'd been destroying the burner phones, but some were never recovered, so there was a chance he might still be using one of those.'

'And he did?'

Callum nodded. 'And the signal from his phone pinged off the Kingsberry mast, so I knew he was near the farm when he called. I couldn't reach you on any of your numbers. So I drove up to your place and called out the cavalry en route. You weren't there and your car had gone. But you'd left without locking up, so I knew you hadn't gone far. Obviously my next stop was George's.'

We sat in silence for a moment, both thinking about the odds that had been beaten that night. But I still had pieces missing.

'How did you know where he'd taken me?'

'Harvey told me.'

Chapter Fifty-Nine

14 November – Fordley General Hospital

Callum sat forward in the chair. 'When I got to George's, there was just your car there with the driver's door open and your mobile phone on the seat. In the headlights, I could see blood on the yard. I thought it was your blood.' He paused and had to clear his throat before he could carry on. 'The blood trail went away from the house, so I followed it down the track to the cottage.'

'But I assumed James took me to the cottage in George's Land Rover?' I was being slow on the uptake.

'He did, and as I got to the cottage I saw the Land Rover parked outside. It wasn't *your* blood trail I'd followed, Jo. It was Harvey's.'

I felt tears stinging my eyes as I thought of Harvey struggling to follow as I was driven to the cottage – still trying to protect me, despite being wounded.

'Harvey had collapsed beside the Land Rover,' Callum continued. 'He'd obviously not got enough in him to go any further. George's shotgun was in the passenger footwell – I picked it up before I entered the cottage.'

'So when you burst through the door, did you expect to see George?'

Callum's head was down, looking at the floor. I knew his eyes held a pain he didn't want me to see.

'Didn't know what I'd see.' He looked up and his eyes were moist. 'I knew what I dreaded, though. That I'd be too late . . .'

The lump in my throat blocked my words.

He shook his head and took a deep breath.

'Despite all the circumstantial evidence that night, no, I didn't expect it to be George. For one thing, I trusted your profile of "Jack", and George was a million miles away from being like that. But I can say that I wasn't surprised to see Turner.'

I looked at him steadily, debating whether to ask my next question. But I needed to know.

'Did you mean to kill him?'

'I meant to stop him.'

He looked at me in silence, then lowered his head as he spoke, looking down at the floor again.

'I've never killed anyone. Can't say it feels good – even though it *was* the second coming of Jack the Ripper.' He lifted his head and his eyes met mine and held my gaze. 'I didn't have time to think. When I came through the door, I saw him. Saw the knife. I shouted a warning but he ignored it – brought the knife down. He was going to kill you, Jo.'

I couldn't meet his eyes any more. The images from that night were something I didn't want in my head. Callum was the only person alive who could see what I could, could share the connection of what happened. The experience of that night had changed us both forever, in ways we probably couldn't yet imagine – but we both knew it had.

'Are you glad he's dead?'

He looked back down. 'As a copper, I wanted him to face justice for what he'd done, to give the victims' families some answers.' He looked back at me. 'But that night? I was just glad I'd stopped him, and when I saw what he'd done to you, Jo . . .' He slowly shook his head. 'Yes – I was glad, and if the bastard had moved a muscle, I would have enjoyed shooting him again.'

'Thank you,' I said. 'For everything you did that night.'

He nodded and we sat in silence for a while. I could feel the dull ache of fatigue spreading like molten lead through my limbs, but I still had questions to ask.

I shifted, trying to ease the ache in my leg. 'You never liked him. But that's not enough to make the leap that he was "Jack".'

'Not a leap – more a confirmation of suspicions.'

'Well, you were better than me then – he was the *last* person I expected to see that night.'

'Don't be too hard on yourself. My suspicions were based on things the team began to piece together. But only *after* Harrison's death, things you weren't privy to. But you're right – I didn't like him. He made his reputation getting the bad guys off the hook, people we *knew* were bang to rights. "Mister Loophole" would usually find a technicality – or miraculously produce an alibi.'

'Was he bent – as a lawyer, I mean?'

'Not crooked exactly – too clever for that. But I always felt that if he'd swallowed a nail, he'd shit a corkscrew. There had always been something about him that tweaked my copper instincts. I thought he might have been implicated in all this, but I didn't have enough to get authorisation to breach his legal privilege.'

'So what, then?'

He shrugged. 'I did a bit of digging into his background. His brother was head of thoracic surgery at a teaching hospital in

London and he arranged work experience there for Turner one summer –'

'I know, he told me that.'

Callum raised an eyebrow. 'Bet he didn't tell you how it ended though, did he?'

It was my turn to look curious.

Callum drained the last of his coffee and pulled another face at the taste.

'Apparently there was an "incident" in the hospital mortuary. From what I can gather, his brother hushed it up and sent him home. Most of the people involved are either retired or dead now and the brother's saying nothing. There was never an official record of it, so Turner managed to airbrush it from history. But I learned enough to believe that's where he practised inflicting "Jack's" wounds with an amputation knife.'

'I said he would have had some anatomical knowledge. He replicated the wounds from the Victorian victims too precisely. We knew he would have had to practise somehow.'

'Apart from that, his name kept cropping up too often. Coincidences that I didn't like –'

'Such as?'

'He worked for Fosters and they were the same law firm that represented you during the court case with Gail Dobson. Turner didn't work for them then, so there was no connection during that time. But a few years later, while he *was* there, she committed suicide. I got the intel team to dig into that one. The cause of death was recorded as an overdose. Dug a bit more and it turns out she'd slit her wrists – but that didn't cause her death. One of the unusual aspects, though, was the way she'd done it.'

'Up the arm, rather than across?'

He shot me a look. 'That's not a lucky guess, right?'

'Let's just say he shared some confidences that night.'

Callum visibly shuddered. 'Dread to think. But what *really* got my baton twitching was that that was the same method Harrison supposedly used on himself . . .'

I couldn't help laughing – despite the subject matter. 'You don't carry a baton any more!'

'The ghost of it *still* twitches.'

'Wasn't Gail Dobson's death enough to get authorisation to go after James?'

'Circumstantial. Nothing a good lawyer like Turner couldn't wriggle out of. The team were also trying to find his car. That triggered a hit on an ANPR camera near Taylor-Caine's flat the day she left the briefing. Then we lost it and it seemed to have disappeared off the face of the earth. We know now, he had it in George's barn – but we didn't know that then.'

'Like you say – too many coincidences pointing to him.' I put my head back and closed my eyes. Fatigue was beginning to dull my thinking.

He stretched his legs out and eased tension from his shoulders. 'When we searched Harrison's flat and the university, you said we almost had *too* much evidence. You were right. It bothered me that we had photographs, DNA, computer kit – everything we needed to link the murders to Harrison; and yet the one thing we couldn't find was the murder weapon. You'd insisted it was key to the crimes. He'd used it in all the killings, yet he cut his own wrists with a kitchen knife? As you said – that didn't make sense. And what had Harrison done with the murder weapon?'

'It was symbolic for him,' I said, with my eyes still closed, 'mythical in its status. It linked him to his history with Jack. He would never have disposed of it – even to prevent you from finding it. After all, what would it have mattered once he was dead? But then I never believed "Jack" would commit suicide. That's another reason why I didn't believe it was Harrison.'

'It was something your favourite detective, Frank Heslopp, turned up that gave us the break we needed.'

I looked up then and raised an impressed eyebrow. 'Remind me to buy him a pint when I finally get out of here.'

'Finding the Laundy blades was one of the actions I kept open and I tasked that to Frank. All catalogued examples were accounted for, but he was talking to collectors, antique shops, dealers. Not just in Fordley but nationally.'

He pulled a sheet of paper from his inside pocket and scanned down it.

'Frank transferred to us from the Met and he's still got contacts down there. A crime reporter for the BBC in London heard from a Met copper about Frank's enquiries. The reporter's hobby was collecting true crime memorabilia and he told us he'd heard a whisper around ten years ago about a family who owned a complete set of Laundy amputation knives that might have had a connection to Jack the Ripper. He'd tracked the family down to Sussex, but they wouldn't speak to him. So he asked a prominent art dealer in London to approach them on his behalf.'

'Let me guess. They wouldn't entertain the dealer either?'

'Wouldn't even set up a meeting. They said the collection wasn't for sale. But the reporter was more interested in the story. After all, if this family could prove the provenance of the collection, it might reveal the identity of the most legendary serial killer in history.'

'The one who got away . . .'

Was it my imagination, or was discussing 'Jack' making my wounds ache even more? I shifted uncomfortably and winced.

'As we got near the night of the ninth of November, the team worked flat out,' Callum said. 'No one went home. All the lines of enquiry were being followed up to the last minute and I *still* couldn't implicate Turner. He was a person of interest but I didn't have anything I could arrest him for. I had people out looking for him – even if it was just to tail him and keep tabs on him that night. Because, whoever "Jack" was, we knew if he was still out there, we'd hear from him. There was no way he'd miss that date.'

'But you couldn't know where he'd strike or who he'd target.' My voice sounded weary even to me.

'Turner had gone to ground. Fosters said he'd taken annual leave but we couldn't find out where he'd gone. He'd given up his flat in Salford and disappeared. Then fate seemed to favour us and things happened all at the same time. I got a call from Beth. The name of the family in Sussex was Lubnowski –'

'James' maternal grandmother.'

'Can't help showing off, can you?'

My eyes were closed, but I could hear the smile in his voice.

'I might have tried to get a warrant based on that, but I didn't get the chance because the call from Beth was interrupted by "Jack" ringing the bat phone. You know the rest –'

A young PC stationed outside my room to keep the press away knocked and stuck his head round the door. 'Visitor for you.'

I opened my eyes to see him holding Harvey, who was straining at his lead to get to me, despite the bandage wrapped tightly round his shoulders.

'How did you get him in here?' Suddenly the fatigue had gone.

It hurt to laugh, but I couldn't help it at the sight of the ridiculous high-vis dog jacket they'd put on him.

'He's in uniform,' Callum laughed. 'We told them he was a police dog.'

Harvey put his huge paws on the edge of my bed and tried to lick me, despite Callum's best efforts to keep the dog saliva off my pristine bandages. We were all distracted from the chaos by another knock at the door.

'This'll be the nurse coming to throw us all out.' Callum pulled open the door.

Jen stepped in, beaming. 'Look what the cat dragged in!'

'Alex!'

I couldn't stop the tears as my son jostled for position with Harvey on my bed. I buried my face in his neck and breathed in the precious scent of him as he held me.

Acknowledgements

I would like to thank everyone at RCW Literary Agency and in particular my agent Jon Wood. I am extremely grateful for your faith in me and for your endless patience, help and support, in what has been an amazing journey. Thanks must also go to Betsy Reavley and Bloodhound Books, who discovered me and gave me my initial break. Without you, none of this would have happened.

Huge thanks to Zaffre, for seeing the potential of my work as a series and giving Jo McCready a whole new lease of life. In particular, my editor, Ben Willis, deserves a medal for his patience and dedication to making my words infinitely better.

Thanks also to my good friend Maria Sigley, for all her help in reworking the book and keeping me on track with continuity issues. Your hard work and eagle-eyed attention to detail was priceless. To my police advisors, for their input and advice into the procedural elements of the book, many thanks. If there are any errors, they are all mine.

I am eternally grateful also to the family and friends who participated in the brainstorming sessions, encouraging me to keep going and never losing faith in my abilities – you know who you are and I couldn't have done it without you. You never flinched when I explored various methods of body disposal!

Finally, to my partner Ian, who has given me the space to write – both emotionally and literally. You built me an amazing creative space and tolerate the unsociable hours I spend in it. Thank you for your love and encouragement.

If you enjoyed *The Murder Mile*, don't miss the
thrilling next instalment in the series . . .

The Killing Song

Keep reading for an exclusive extract . . .

Chapter One

The horror was nameless, faceless – but I knew I was fighting for my life. I struggled, tried to free myself, but my limbs wouldn't move. I opened my mouth to scream but no sound came. My throat was tight, constricted as I fought to breathe.

Dark, grotesque shadows flickered across the walls, and the heat from a fire I couldn't see suffocated me. My heels pushed hard against the mattress to stop him pulling me back to where I didn't want to go; clawing hands held me down, hurting me. I pedalled my legs harder, desperate to get away, until my back was against a wall. I had nowhere to go – I couldn't escape. I was going to die.

I forced my eyes open as my breath came in sharp gasps, sending spasms of pain across my chest. My arms wrapped tightly around my body, squeezing me awake. I was pressed against the headboard of my bed, my legs drawn up in a tangle of damp sheets. Heart hammering against my ribs like a terrified animal banging against the bars of its cage.

I squeezed my eyes shut, then opened them again as sanity slowly returned, allowing me to make out the dim shape of familiar surroundings. Forcing myself to breathe more slowly, I willed my heart rate to descend from the heights of terror.

My hands were shaking as I untangled the sheets and put my feet on the floor. A sharp jolt of pain shot through my left thigh, and I cursed as my leg threatened to give way underneath me, forcing me to sit back down on the edge of the bed.

I gingerly massaged the ridge of scar tissue that ran from my thigh into my groin, gritting my teeth at the jagged shards of pain that threatened to send my muscles into a protest of cramp. The bedside clock said 4 a.m. Grief and hopelessness rolled all over me and I cried silently in the dark.

* * *

Kingsberry Farm, Fordley – Monday morning

'But it's the sixth time he's called.' Jen, my PA, peered at me over the top of her reading glasses and pursed her lips in that way she had when I was getting on her last remaining nerve.

'Tough!' My patience was already paper thin – a legacy of being woken by my recurring nightmares.

She handed me a mug of tea, reading my mood all too easily. 'Someone woke up grumpy.'

'Broken sleep . . . leg playing up, that's all,' I lied.

Jen sighed. 'There's no shame in admitting the last case got to you, Jo.' She indicated my leg with a nod of her head. 'If not psychologically, then physically. Getting attacked like that is enough to give anyone night terrors.'

I shrugged, trying to make light of it. 'You know me, Jen – hard as nails.'

'Hmm.' She didn't look convinced. 'It's *me* you're talking to, remember?'

I waved the message slip at her, moving the topic on to less uncomfortable ground. 'Anyway. What's the point in having a "gatekeeper", if you don't keep people away from my bloody gate?'

'I will and I do . . . but I really think you should talk to him.'

'Why?' I flipped through the messages while I perched on the corner of her desk. 'I'm not getting involved in police cases anymore.'

'Technically it's not a *live* case—'

'Death usually isn't.'

'Very funny.' She took the cup out of my hand and replaced it with the phone. 'Call him, Jo.' She raised an eyebrow as I looked down at her, trying to think of a plausible reason for not calling Charles Fielding. The father of a dead son, who continued to campaign for the case to be re-examined. The coroner's ruling that death had occurred under suspicious circumstances, meant an 'open verdict' – something the Fielding family had struggled to accept for years now.

'If for no other reason than to stop him mithering you.' Jen persisted. 'I've spoken to him, Jo . . . he's convinced *you* can help.'

'Why me? I'm a forensic psychologist, not a cop. West Yorkshire Police are looking at it, even if it *is* in the cold case files. Let them deal with it.'

She studied me for a moment before adding quietly, 'What if it was Alex?'

'Low blow, Jen.'

'You're a mother . . . you wouldn't give up either.' She raised an expressive eyebrow. 'Unless you speak to him, he's just going to keep on calling.'

'How did he seem? When you spoke to him?'

'Frustrated, Angry. All the things I suppose you'd feel if your son's dead and no one seems to care.'

The last sentiment did it – just as she knew it would. 'OK . . .' I said, resigned. 'I'll call him – but only to get rid of him.'

'Good.' She didn't even try to hide the smug look.

'But mostly to get *you* off my back.'

'Very wise.' She smiled sweetly, handing me the number.

* * *

Fordley – Later that morning

I pressed the button to crack open the window of my car and let in the early May breeze. I'd parked in a part of Fordley known as Little Italy. Named after the Italian immigrants who flocked to the city in the nineteenth century, to work in the booming woollen industry.

The huge warehouses and mills were being regenerated and many of the imposing buildings had been converted into trendy apartments, like the one I was about to visit.

Jen was right – Leo Fielding's father was no pushover. What I'd hoped would be a call to fob him off had ended with my reluctantly agreeing to meet him in the place where his son had died – or as he preferred to call it: 'The crime scene'.

'Just meet me there,' he'd said, 'then if you don't want to take the case, I won't bother you again.' The inference being that if I *didn't* come, he *would* keep bothering me. On balance, an hour of my time seemed a small price to pay.

I'd read the case file before I left – just to familiarise myself with the details, although I did remember it. Given the prominence of the Fielding family, it made the national as well as local news at the time and Charles Fielding had made sure it had stayed there ever since.

I looked through the windscreen, trying not to superimpose images of my own son, Alex, onto a scene that I knew haunted every waking moment of the Fielding's lives – then taking a deep breath, I locked my car and walked across the street.

Chapter Two

Chapel Mills

Leo Fielding's name was still listed on the polished brass plate beside the door to Chapel Mills. I pressed the intercom for the penthouse apartment that his parents had held onto since their son's death.

'Yes?' A male voice, which I assumed was Charles Fielding.

'Dr McCready.'

There was a 'buzz' and a metallic click as the chrome and glass doors unlocked.

The reception hall was impressive. A wide expanse of caramel-coloured oak floorboards, punctuated by ornate iron stanchions supporting the floor above. The space would have lifted the bleakest of moods had I not come here on such dark business.

But it was the smell that got me. Grabbing me by my olfactory senses and dragging me back to a childhood memory, of my mother's days as a burler and mender in a mill just like this one. The unmistakeable scent of lanolin from the wool. A pungent perfume that over two centuries had soaked into the woodwork – permeating both the fabric of these buildings and the clothes of the people who worked in them.

I took what had once been the goods lift, taking the time to gather my thoughts. The lumbering metal doors opened to reveal the entrance to the penthouse, which occupied the entire top floor of the two-storey building.

The eight-foot-high wooden door with a wrought-iron handle in its centre looked like something from Middle Earth. I pushed the bell – hearing its echoing chime coming from somewhere deep inside the place. The door swung open to reveal a tall, reed-thin man in his late sixties.

Charles Fielding took my hand in a firm grip that for some reason surprised me. 'Thank you for coming, doctor.'

He turned to the small, bird-like woman who was walking across the polished wooden floor towards us. 'This is my wife, Mary.'

Her hand felt cool when she took mine. Her grip delicate – like an imagined touch, half-felt. Her genuine smile conveyed a grim regret that we should be meeting under such circumstances.

I followed them to a pair of deep soft leather sofas, in front of huge windows that overlooked the city, where we sat opposite each other in an awkward silence. Although it wasn't a new experience for me, I was suddenly unsure of the best way to open a conversation about events that had undoubtedly destroyed both their lives.

'This is quite a place,' was the best I could come up with.

'Leo loved it here.' Mary's gaze followed mine. 'He took it because of the northern light – it was perfect for his studio, you see.'

The mill had a traditional slate-and-glass roof which faced north. A feature, I vaguely remembered reading somewhere, which was ideal for artists because it gave a consistent light throughout the day.

'Yes, I understand Leo was an artist,' I said.

Mary's eyes filled with pride. 'A very successful one.' She turned to her husband. 'We were so proud of him, weren't we, dear?'

Charles cleared his throat, obviously unused to voicing emotion, let alone displaying any. 'Yes, he did well for himself.' He waved a hand to indicate the space. 'Well enough to get this place. Didn't rent. Purchased it outright.'

His wife looked down at her fingers, which were twisting in her lap. *Her* pride obviously wasn't index linked. She stood up almost too abruptly. 'Can I get you some tea?'

'The doctor isn't on a social visit, Mary.' He sat forward, leaning over the files laid out neatly on the coffee table.

She shot an uncertain glance in my direction.

I smiled. 'Tea would be lovely, Mrs Fielding. Thank you.'

'Please call me Mary.'

'I'll give you a hand.'

Charles Fielding opened his mouth in protest, but closed it again as I followed his wife to the open-plan kitchen area.

'How long did Leo live here?'

'He bought it the year before he . . . before it . . .'

Her eyes were wet when she looked at me. 'I still can't go up there . . .' Her eyes flickered briefly towards the mezzanine floor. 'To where he . . .'

'I know. It's OK.' I looked into her eyes, forging a connection with her mental anguish. 'There's no manual for this. No rules to follow.'

Her eyes were almost imploring – reaching out to someone she hoped could give her answers. Take the pain away. I wanted to offer her something. But I knew that nothing I could say would end the waking nightmare she had lived since her son's cruel death.

'Just take it one day at a time.' I knew it was a cliché, but it was one way to get through crippling emotional pain. 'Breathe in and breathe out – one minute at a time – one hour at a time – until that day is done. Until one day you realise it isn't the first thing you think about when you wake up in the morning.'

She turned her face from me. Sniffing and wiping her eyes with the crumpled tissue.

'Well, I'm not there yet.'

The raw pain inside this petite, gentle woman was tangible.

How could any parent look at the brutalised, naked body of their child and not lose a part of their soul to the horror of it? It was incomprehensible. Yet it happened, and I walked all too often through the minds of the monsters who did these things and then somehow managed to justify their actions with their own brand of twisted logic.

She glanced over to where her husband was sitting, reading his notes. 'Are you married?'

'Widowed.'

'I'm sorry.'

I shook my head. 'It's OK. It was more than twenty years ago. He was in the SAS. Killed overseas.'

She touched my elbow, her eyes soft with emotion. 'So young. You can't have had much time together. I'm so sorry my dear.'

Such a show of empathy from someone still trapped in the raw torment of her own pain was almost too much.

I always struggled to handle it when people were kind to me. I could take a punch easier than a compliment. Handle a fight better than I could a display of tenderness, which often left me struggling for a response. I knew it was a legacy of my upbringing. A tough Yorkshire-Irish father who valued endurance and strength and an Italian mother who had impossibly high standards neither of us had ever managed to meet.

To the outside world my mother was the epitome of a doting Italian mamma. Behind closed doors, she employed the ceaseless dripping-water torture of negative evaluation and disapproval. A tactic that would have eroded my self-esteem, had it not been shored up by my father's unconditional love. We'd tackled my mother as a team. Coping with her since his death was proving more of a challenge.

My upbringing had forged an emotional armour that proved useful in my career but left me unable to cope when shown gentleness by others. Especially strangers – and always when it was unexpected.

Mary busied herself making the tea. 'You won't have had a chance for children then?'

'Actually, I have a son. Alex. He was just a baby when his father died.'

Her smile trembled as she wiped her eyes again. 'Does he live with you?'

'He went travelling after university. But he's in London now. Starting a new career.'

She poured boiling water into the teapot, risking a glance towards her husband. 'He wanted to sell this place after Leo died. I can't bring myself to let it go. It's all I have left of him. I come here – alone, mostly. To be near him, near the things he loved.'

I followed her gaze to a bunch of white roses in a vase on the counter.

'Were flowers something he loved?'

She went over and adjusted the stems until she was satisfied they were perfect.

'There were roses in the apartment when they found Leo. The police asked me if I knew where they'd come from.' She nodded to the window overlooking the private gardens below. 'He'd picked them from the garden out there. I've been replacing them for him ever since.'

I left Mary in the kitchen and went to join Fielding.

'It's been two years.' Fielding's tone was caustic as he launched straight into it. 'And still no progress because the investigators insisted on seeing this as some gay sex scene that my son was involved in.' His face flushed. 'My son was *not* a homosexual, doctor. The police are taking the path of least resistance and that shuts off any other lines of enquiry.' He strained his corded neck towards me like an aggressive cockerel. '*That's* why whoever killed my son is still out there.'

'I appreciate what you must be going through Mr Fielding—'

'Do you?' Fielding cut across me, his voice rising. 'You've had your son murdered too, have you – and no one giving a damn about finding his killer?'

'I appreciate your *frustration*. Believe me, your son's death has not been forgotten. The case is still open—'

'As a *cold* case file. The clue is in the name – *cold*. And it only *remains* open because I refuse to let it go.'

The tension was broken as Mary brought in the tea tray. 'The police officer who investigated Leo's death was very nice—'

'Nice!' Charles was contemptuous. 'Nice doesn't find my son's killer, Mary!'

My son.

I'd read up on Charles Fielding – high-ranking officer in Naval Intelligence, long retired but still well connected. Trotted out by journalists and news outlets whenever they needed a well-respected military strategist, now out of the game and free to comment.

I studied him. His whole demeanour screamed character traits forged by his background.

Dominance and control are your stock in trade, aren't they Fielding? Born of privilege and nurtured by arrogance and a sense of superiority.

Tinker, Tailor, Soldier, Prick.

'DCI Ferguson,' he was saying. 'They told me he was the best.' He tapped his notes. 'You know him . . . Ferguson.'

It was a statement of fact – not a question.

As if reading my mind, Fielding leaned closer – his eyes glinting. Confident in a knowledge he felt gave him power.

'They say you're in a relationship with him. Is that true?'

I was stunned at the directness of it – but didn't let it show. 'No,' I said honestly.

Ever since I'd been invited to consult on our first case together, almost two years before, Callum and I had danced around the edges of a relationship. The chemistry between us was undeniable. But we'd become distanced by events. By a killer we hunted down together – but at huge personal cost. Those events had changed me – changed both of us.

'Not that it's any of your business . . . or has any bearing on why I'm here.'

'Oh, but it has. Because this was *his* case and it was never solved.' He regarded me through narrowed eyes. 'If it turns out that he missed something . . . I need to know you can be impartial.'

I was at the end of my, already short, rope.

'Whether I can be impartial or not is irrelevant. I agreed to this meeting as a courtesy, but as courtesy seems in short supply, I'll make this simple for you. I'm not taking it on. I stopped consulting on this type of thing last year—'

'I know. I've asked around. Besides, after those murders last autumn, it was in all the papers. You were seriously injured' – he indicated my thigh with a nod of his head – 'and Ferguson got suspended. Nasty business. When you came out of hospital, the papers said you were going to take time out to concentrate on writing your books . . . making TV documentaries.' He tapped the notes on the table. 'Safer than doing it for real I suppose . . . if you've lost your nerve.'

As baiting tactics went, it was pretty blunt. It almost made me smile – almost.

I stood up. 'We're done here.'

'Please.' Mary lightly touched my arm. I'd almost forgotten she was there. 'Don't go . . .' She glanced at her husband. 'Charles didn't mean to offend you, did you, dear?'

He was still looking at me as he spoke. 'I don't need you to speak for me.'

I felt her gentle squeeze on my arm. 'We need you to help us . . . I need you to . . .'

'I'm not the only profiler around, Mary.' I put my hand over hers, returning the touch. 'I can give you the names of half a dozen competent ones who'd be happy to help—'

'Competent isn't good enough.' Fielding's voice drew my attention back to him. 'You're the best. That's why I chose you.'

'*Chose me!*' He made it sound like a done deal – I could feel my hackles rising already. 'And you'd know enough about my field of expertise to be the judge?'

'Not personally,' he conceded. 'But I've spoken to those who do.'

I'd calculated how much it hurt him to be humble. I wanted to hurt him some more.

'That's not enough to convince me.'

He took a long breath, indicating the seat opposite. Reluctantly, but for Mary's sake, I took it.

'In a previous life, I was an Intelligence officer . . .'

'I know . . . I've done *my* research too.'

'Then you'll know that I still have contacts in Government – in the police.' He rested his elbows on his knees, watching me over steepled fingers. 'I know what you did . . . what you've done before. I'm told you have a rare ability. To profile behaviours to the point you can predict an offender's thinking – what he's done . . . will do next. It's been described as "uncanny".' He indicated the files on the table. 'I *know* my son's death isn't as it first appears. For two years I've been trying to prove it – but they tell me that they need new evidence.' His eyes bored into mine. 'I *need* someone who sees beyond the physical evidence they already have . . . sees the things you do. What only *you* can.'

I considered him for a long moment – letting the silence stretch.

'And what if . . . after I've looked at it, I agree with DCI Ferguson's initial conclusion?'

He sat back, his breath leaving him in a long sigh. 'Then I'll accept your findings.'

Mary needed closure – some peace. Even if the result wasn't what she wanted to hear, it was better than the emotional purgatory her husband's relentless quest was putting her through.

She was pouring the tea into china cups, trying to restore normality to a horrifically abnormal situation.

'Leo had girlfriends,' she said, almost to herself. 'All through university. A parade of beautiful girls.' She handed a cup to her husband and then me. 'He wasn't homosexual. He would have told us if he was.'

I couldn't imagine Leo Fielding discussing his sex life with his parents, especially his father, who could barely say the word 'homosexual' without grinding his teeth. I took my cup. 'Did he have a regular girlfriend?'

'He was too busy moving in and then he had an exhibition to get ready for. Edward said he was painting all night sometimes, to get pieces finished before the opening in London.' Her eyes automatically went to the mezzanine, then flickered away again.

'Edward?'

'Morrison. The caretaker,' Fielding explained. 'He looks after the building.'

'The garden as well,' Mary said, sipping her tea. 'He showed me where the roses were. He lets me take them whenever I want.'

'The police suspected Morrison had something to do with it.' Fielding tapped the file with his finger. 'I still do. Not wholesome . . . people like him.'

'People like him?' I asked.

'Homosexual.' He almost spat the word. 'Leo wasn't involved in any of the deviant practices they say he was . . . he wouldn't have consented to . . . what was done. But Morrison – he *was* gay . . . probably *was* into all that. *And* he had access to the apartment. But your "friend" saw fit to let him go.' He glared at me. 'If anyone knows what really happened to Leo, it's Morrison.'

Mary gently cleared her throat, drawing our attention. 'Edward's always been very kind to me.' She somehow made it sound like an apology. 'Especially since Leo passed.'

'Well . . . he *would*, wouldn't he?' Fielding snorted his disgust at her naivety.

'He helped me organise the studio . . . to catalogue everything.' She looked at me over the rim of her cup – eyes shining with pride. 'Would you like to see Leo's paintings my dear?'

'I'd love to.'

'She treats this place like a bloody shrine'. Fielding snorted. 'Won't change a damn thing – keeps everything just as it was the day Leo died. If she could bear to use the upstairs, I think she'd move in permanently and just bugger off and leave me to it!'

'Charles, please don't—'

'I'd love to see Leo's studio, Mary.'

'She can't open the shutters in there – they're too heavy,' Fielding said.

'I'm sure you can open them for us,' My smile was as thin as his patience.

Before he could object, Mary picked up the tray. 'Lovely. I'll join you when I've cleared this away.'